THE SECRETS OF
MABEL EASTLAKE

THE SECRETS OF
MABEL EASTLAKE

DONALD·S·OLSON

 Knights Press

Stamford, Connecticut

Designed by Able Reproductions. Copyright © 1986
Cover art by Gary H. Larson ©

Published by Knights Press, P.O. Box 454, Pound Ridge, NY 10576

Library of Congress Cataloging-In-Publication Data

Olson, Donald.
  The secrets of Mabel Eastlake.

  I. Title.
PS3565.L825S4   1986   813'.54   85-7604
ISBN 0-915175-15-0 (pbk.)

Printed in the United States of America

For
Henry Martin Bair

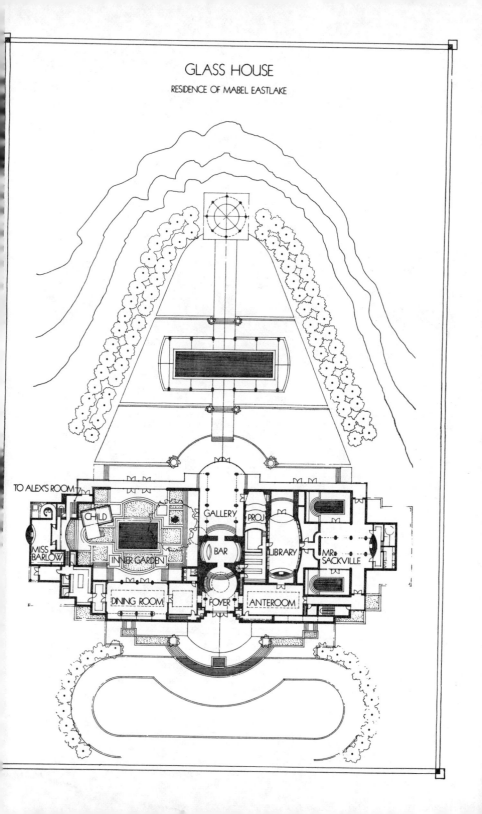

GLASS HOUSE

RESIDENCE OF MABEL EASTLAKE

TO ALEX'S ROOM

CHILD

MISS BARLOW

INNER GARDEN

GALLERY

PROJ.

BAR

LIBRARY

MR. SACKVILLE

DINING ROOM

FOYER

ANTEROOM

1.

If Mabel Eastlake extended her hand to you, people in Hollywood used to say, it was not because she wanted it kissed or shaken. She wanted you to blow her nails dry. Mabel Eastlake had been known for her crimson nails, which showed up black in the movies of the Thirties. Miss Eastlake's nails were daringly long for the period, and someone had once compared them to stilettos.

Alex Klein, parked and fidgeting in front of the enormous Art Deco gates that kept intruders out of Mabel Eastlake's estate, looked at his own nails. Sitting there, in the dark, in his rented Datsun, he had to fight a mounting urge to chew them. He raised one close to his mouth, scrutinized it carefully, and conquered the temptation. Vulgar, he thought, reaching instead for his pastrami sandwich.

As the sweet, slow movement from Gershwin's Concerto in F played over the car stereo, the moon—or perhaps it was the refracted light of Los Angeles—played on the geometric design of the steel gates, giving them a soft, silvery polish. Colors were indiscernible in this half-light. A dense undergrowth of vegetation sucked up the black shadows of overhanging palm trees and flowering shrubs. On this, the highest peak in Beverly Hills, the world tonight was black and silver, not unlike a set for one of Miss Eastlake's movies.

Every day since his arrival in Los Angeles, Alex had

made this pilgrimage high into the hills of Beverly. Every day he parked in this same spot near the gates, hoping to catch a glimpse of Mabel Eastlake. Every day he left disappointed. And now, out of desperation, he had taken to driving up here at night. A naturalist on the lookout for a rare and nearly extinct species of wildlife could not have been more patient or determined.

He tapped a fingernail on the new camera beside him, as though keeping it awake. State of the art, of course. The film speed allowed nighttime shots, and he could use the headlights of his car as an additional source of light. Everything was carefully planned, but the film destined to record Mabel Eastlake's image remained blank. Getting a photograph of her was as difficult as photographing a ghost.

It was more than just a photo that Alex wanted, though. He wanted Mabel Eastlake herself. A biography of the famous star had never been written, and Alex wanted to do it.

There were a number of fascinating facts to consider. When Mabel Eastlake appeared among common mortals, it was in a chauffeured, custom-made, 1934 white Duesenberg . . . the same luxurious automobile in which, at the very height of her fame, she had been found unconscious, not far down the hill from where Alex now sat, smashed into a eucalyptus tree. Beside her in the car, his body mangled by the impact, lay Jimmy Flame, the gangster reputed to have been Mabel Eastlake's lover. On that same bloody night two famous murders took place behind the arched steel gates on the hilltop. Otto Kranzler, the brilliant and eccentric German film director who had discovered Mabel Eastlake and directed all ten of her brilliant and eccentric films, was found dead in Miss Eastlake's black boudoir. He had been shot at close range in his massive chest. Boyd Powers, the actor who had recently become

Mabel Eastlake's husband, was found slumped over in his seat in the projection room. His skull was shattered.

The subsequent inquest received more press coverage than the war in Europe. Behind heavy veils, her voice never more than a hoarse, anguished whisper, Mabel Eastlake testified that Jimmy Flame had murdered Kranzler and Powers. She had attempted to escape, but the crazed and maniacal Flame leapt onto the running board as she, terrified, spun down the driveway. Forcing his way into the Duesenberg, Jimmy Flame grabbed the steering wheel. Mabel Eastlake accelerated in sheer panic. They collided with the eucalyptus tree. Flame was killed instantly.

Those were the facts reported at the time. Mabel Eastlake's movie career ended on that mysterious, violent night in 1939. But of all the legends of Old Hollywood, Miss Eastlake's legend—because it was the most protected— remained most alive, darkly tantalizing.

She had the Duesenberg entirely restored, while her face—so ran the inevitable Hollywood story—she left penitentially disfigured. The heavy veils she wore as a result were allegedly designed by Adrian, who had costumed her in two of her movies. But what was true and what false? Rumors, legends, lies, scandals clung to Mabel Eastlake like the white satin peignoirs she lounged about in on the screen. Alex desperately wanted to be the first to unravel the whole sensational story, but in the course of a month's research all that had unraveled was his confidence. Mabel Eastlake, remained fiercely protective of her privacy.

And yet, right there, just behind those high graceful gates, was Glass House, Mabel Eastlake's legendary home, reputed to be the finest and purest example of domestic Art Deco architecture in the entire United States.

Alex had been parked for nearly an hour already, about as long as he dared to stay. The Beverly Hills police had spotted him once and told him if they found him there again they would take him in for loitering. "If I'd been on foot," he wrote to a friend back in New York, "they would have taken me in for walking." But he enjoyed this element of espionage, of breaking rules, of testing limits. Away from New York and the tight confines of his daily routine and conventional self definition, he could be anyone he wanted, assume any role he wished. Frustrating as this quest for Mabel Eastlake had become, it at least allowed him to indulge his fantasies.

But he was disappointed again tonight. And with only two days left before he was scheduled to return to Manhattan and a life there that had turned, well, not just sour, but positively acidic. Like this sandwich. Swearing under his breath, Alex licked the mustard from his fingers, rewound the Gershwin tape, and reached for the ignition.

It was then that two small concealed lights on either side of the gates suddenly switched on, startling into vivid green the ivy growing around them.

At the same time, a blurred white form, gone before it could be acknowledged, streaked past inside the gates. Alex saw it out of the corner of his eye.

His heart began a sudden, adrenal race. Trying to keep his hands steady, he removed the cap from his camera lens.

With a quiet clank and a low groan the massive front gates of Glass House began slowly to swing open.

"Jesus, she's coming," Alex thought. He started his car, intending to follow the Duesenberg wherever it went that night. First, though, he had to back up an incline and hide around a sharp turn in the road. It would not be wise to be seen parked and waiting for the reclusive, mysterious celebrity.

Before he had the Datsun in gear, however, two low beams of light shot around a curve of the road below the gates and the nose of the Duesenberg appeared. Miss

Eastlake was not coming out—she was going in! Alex had not anticipated this and had less time than he thought to conceal himself.

The worst of drivers at the best of times, he now slammed the shift into reverse, gunned the motor and shot backwards with a wild squeal. Hidden, he grabbed his camera and quickly got out to position himself to take photographs.

But to his astonishment the Duesenberg did not turn into the open gates. Instead, slowly, as in a dream about to turn terrible, it continued up the road in Alex's direction. Why? There was nothing up here, and the road ended in a cul-de-sac behind him. In a mounting panic he snapped two, three, four photos, knowing even as he took them that they would reveal nothing but the insistent glare of headlights.

Nervously aware that the hood of the Duesenberg was moving closer, stately and majestic as some phantasmic ship, Alex hurried back to the protection of his car and hopped in. The vision persisted. A silver panther rose in an arrested leap from the Duesenberg's prow and seemed to be directing the white spirit of motion behind it.

New plans alternated frantically in his mind. If he simply drove downhill now, swinging wide around the Duesenberg, he could get into the driveway of Glass House before Mabel Eastlake did. What could they do to him? He could say that he had gotten lost, or confused. Or he could somehow force an accident—a small, inconsequential one, to be sure—so that at least he'd have to deal with Miss Eastlake's chauffeur. And perhaps then, he thought wildly, he could make some kind of deal with the chauffeur and gain entry to Glass House.

He was trapped and he didn't want to admit it. Before he knew exactly what had happened, the Duesenberg had blocked his downward route entirely.

Alex squirmed and shaded his eyes from the accusing glare of the beams, imagining the worst. He'd gone too far. This was confirmed when he saw the tall blond expressionless chauffeur get out and walk towards him. The headlights from Mabel Eastlake's car gave the man the appearance of someone striding through the brilliance of stage spotlights. He looked immense, unreal and menacing. "I'm no match for him," Alex thought, wondering if he'd have to fight. He'd never been in a situation that called for physical resistance.

He said, "Hey! What the—" as his car door was pulled open and the chauffeur's enormous hand clamped itself around his arm. "Wait a fucking minute, you asshole! What the hell do you think you're doing?" New York street-speak did no good. He was practically lifted from the driver's seat and propelled towards the Duesenberg.

"Let go of my arm, goddamn it." The chauffeur showed no sign of hearing anything Alex said. Alex, several inches shorter and at least seventy-five pounds lighter, tried in vain to twist his arm free from the other's grip. The grip tightened and Alex was wrenched crookedly onto his toes. By this time his head was so light with fear that he felt stoned, floating in a different world entirely. He stopped struggling and was ignominiously carried off, like a broken puppet, one leg hopping for balance and the other trying to paw the ground.

The chauffeur opened the front door of the Duesenberg and, without a word, lifted Alex in. He closed the door, sealing Alex inside, and then took up an Indian-brave stance beside the car, his arms crossed.

Despite the enormous bulk of the automobile, the interior was surprisingly small. The soft leather seat in the front rode high off the ground. Alex was impressed and bewildered by the age and regal luxury of the car. This was a vehicle that had what were called "appointments." The long, beautifully contoured snout of the Duesenberg gleamed through a smallish, two-piece, angled windshield. Positioned in what looked to modern eyes like a very unnatural angle for driving, the large steering wheel was inlaid with mother-of-pearl. Various softly glowing gauges were set behind beveled glass in an instrument panel of richly oiled and very dark mahogany.

The headlights stared out accusingly at Alex's small rented Datsun, humiliating it and its plastic interior. Then they went out and for a moment all was dark silence. The words startled Alex for he could not tell where they came from. It was the famous Eastlake voice that issued into the front of the car—older, yes, and even deeper, throatier, and more theatrical than it was on film. It was an angry and suspicious voice.

"Who are you, and what in God's name do you want from me?"

Alex turned but faced a sheet of black glass that prevented him from seeing who sat behind it. He beheld only his own startled reflection. "My God!" he thought. "Now when you're actually with her, what the hell are you going to do? What are you going to say?" All his elaborate speeches and eloquently worded proposals evaporated in the incandescent glare of reality. He, Alex Klein, was sitting in Mabel Eastlake's Duesenberg! Behind a tinted piece of glass sat Mabel Eastlake herself!

"And don't lie to me," said the voice of Mabel Eastlake. "Don't sit there and pretend you're innocent. I know you've been parked out here in that cheap little car every day for at least a month. How stupid do you think I am? You've been attempting to invade my privacy and I do not allow anyone to do that."

Alex shook his head. "No, really . . ."

"What do you mean, no really? We've seen you. Now tell me what it is you want so desperately to see."

"You, Miss Eastlake." It sounded dramatic and absurd, especially because Alex could not see his audience, only his own excited face in the tinted glass.

After a pause, evidently shaken, the voice said, "That is impossible. I do not allow strangers to look at me."

Alex could not afford to be cowed or defeated. He had waited too long for this opportunity. Ambition gave him the right, even the obligation—or so he felt in the heat of the moment—to be reckless, to force something to happen. The biography of Mabel Eastlake would never be written if he did not do some very fast talking and at least make an attempt to get into Miss Eastlake's good graces and, from there, into Glass House itself. "I'm not exactly a stranger, Miss Eastlake," he said.

"Reporter, aren't you," the voice said with palpable disdain. "I loathe reporters, every single one of them. They say they want the truth, but lies always satisfy them." A bitter laugh came through the intercom. "Lies always appealed to Hilda Hatter; she said that truth never paid the rent."

Hilda Hatter, the famous and much-hated gossip columnist, was a contemporary of Miss Eastlake's. Now in retirement, she had wielded her greatest power—malicious, devastating power—during the Thirties and Forties. With a nationally syndicated column, "The Mad Hatter Reports From Hollywood," she had ruined more careers than Louella and Hedda combined. Alex had written to her, hoping to get Eastlake information, but so far he had received no reply.

"No, I'm not a reporter, Miss Eastlake," Alex said. For after all, he wasn't a vituperative tyrant like Hilda Hatter. It wasn't just cheap Hollywood Babylon gossip that he was after, however fascinating that might be. It was important film history, which elevated his motives for wanting to write the Eastlake story into something above reproach. "I'm a great fan of yours."

"Fans are dangerous," snapped the legendary voice. "Fan is short for fanatic and I've been plagued with those since my career began. The minute you're famous the ones who aren't come sniffing around. Crazies. Lunatics. Wanting some piece of you."

Alex wisely remained silent.

"People still hound me to be in pictures. People still want me. But *I* do not want *them.* That's what you people never understood about me—my need to be alone."

Alone. Alex was reminded of his life back in Manhattan.

"Last month it was some intellectual nitwit from New York," the voice of Mabel Eastlake rampaged on, "writing to ask if he could write a biography of me!" A note of pride could be detected in the exasperated voice.

"That's a fantastic idea—a biography," Alex said quickly. The intellectual nitwit, of course, was none other than himself. Using his pseudonym, A. Liddell, he had written to Mabel Eastlake proposing the idea.

"Fantastic for whom? My life will never be written—never!" shot back the voice of Mabel Eastlake. "The small minds of the world would condemn my life, condemn me."

"Yes, but the people who want to know would finally *know*," Alex said.

"Know what?"

"How you came to be what you were."

"What I was? What I *was?*" The voice was outraged. "I still *am!*"

"I meant," Alex quickly amended, "who you are."

"Who I am and what I am is no one's business but my own," the voice of Mabel Eastlake said abruptly. "Why do you suppose, young man, that I have high walls with electrified fencing at the top of them surrounding my estate? It's not, I assure you, to keep me in. It's to keep people such

as yourself out. Cheap, prying, modern minds. But perhaps you're too stupid to understand subtleties like electric
fences. Perhaps I should take some kind of legal action
. . .Or perhaps *illegal* action?" Outside Alex's window, the
chauffeur shifted his weight.

Alex was disconcerted to realize that he had been
the one spied upon as he sat trying to spy on Mabel
Eastlake. "I'm sorry," he said, trying to sound contrite.
"You mean a lot to me. I was curious."

"The whole world is curious. Why?" the voice of
Mabel Eastlake demanded to know. "Curiosity, in case
you've forgotten, killed the cat. No doubt you've heard the
story of Pandora's Box?"

"No," Alex joked nervously, "but I saw the movie
version with Louise Brooks."

If she heard this, Mabel Eastlake chose to ignore it.
"When Pandora opened her box," the voice explained, "all
kinds of terrible things were revealed to the world. Nothing the shysters in Hollywood didn't know already, of
course, but things it would be better for the rest of us not to
know."

"But it's always better to know," Alex said.

"No, only the young think it is. When you're old,
you'll have a Pandora's Box of your own. Stuffed with
secrets of your own. Secrets," whispered the voice of Mabel
Eastlake. "One has a duty to protect one's secrets from a
vindictive punishing world."

"Punishing?" Alex repeated.

"Pandora had two boxes, you know—her own, and
then Box Office. That's where the world can hurt you the
most if you're a star. That Old Hollywood is mostly in the
grave now, thank God. The grave, young man, is about the
only safe place left these days."

Anything to keep Mabel Eastlake talking and himself in the car. But moments after the voice had spoken, the

car intercom was snapped off and some unseen distur-
bance shook the whole vehicle. Alex's straining ears picked
up what sounded like a pleading moan. Was it possible?
Another voice? The star's angry, muffled voice was faintly
heard, and what sounded like a thud. The gurgle of liquid
being poured could be heard as the intercom was switched
back on.

It was wiser to ignore whatever had happened in
back. "I see every movie of yours when they're on television
or when they play in the revival houses," Alex said, hoping
to gain Mabel Eastlake's attention with flattery.

"Revival houses!" the voice snorted. "It sounds
evangelical. Like raising the dead."

Alex was undeterred. "You should see how
audiences still respond to you, Miss Eastlake. Even men
speak your lines."

"Do they? Well," drawled the voice of Miss Eastlake,
with a slight inflection of intimacy, "a woman's lines are always more interesting, aren't they? It's easier for men to get
what they want, but they lack the feminine style that should
always go along with the getting."

"And it's your style that raises people's spirits when
they see your movies," Alex said.

"That's not all I raise," confided the voice, lowering
itself. With no image attached, it still declared the presence
of carnal, seductive power. "Sam Goldwyn once told me
that he could tell every time an Eastlake picture was showing without even looking up at the marquee. He said the
women came out with their heads held high, but the men
came out with their faces down and their hands in their
pockets. Have *you* ever had that kind of effect on people?"

"In a former life," Alex said. Certainly not in this
one.

The voice said, "It's former lives that can make this
one so piss-miserable at times. Let me see your profile!"

The lights in the front panel grew brighter.

Alex slowly obeyed, apprehensive now that he was under such close scrutiny. Did his hair look all right? Was his nose oily? Had he wiped all traces of mustard from his lips? It was supposed to be just the opposite: he was to be the one carefully studying Mabel Eastlake. When he turned so Miss Eastlake could see him, a sharp intake of breath came through the intercom.

"Abe!" whispered the voice of Mabel Eastlake.

"What?"

The voice sounded shaken. "I said, with a nose job you could be reasonably attractive. Turn back around, I don't want to look at you."

Alex did as he was told and waited.

Again the sound of liquid being poured. "Your hair is interesting," said the voice. "It's modeled after mine, isn't it."

This was not a question but a statement, so he nodded. He had changed his appearance upon arrival in California, allowing his thick, black, wavy hair to be cut and androgynously styled, but it had never occurred to him that the style was similar to Miss Eastlake's.

"Yes, I thought it looked like *Doublecross*. Of course, it was not simply the shock of seeing curly platinum me with short black hair that stunned so many people. That particular style was considered very avant-garde in 1934. Very European. Very masculine. It was the only time Schiaparelli designed a hairstyle for pictures. She wanted me to wear a funny little hat that looked like an ice cream cone, but I had to put my foot down or I would have looked like a clown."

"You were always wonderfully dressed," Alex said.

"Nothing looked foolish on me. I was considered rare because I had a natural talent for wearing clothes, unlike most of the Hollywood cows. Cyggie Sackville helped me. And Kranzler—he helped me. He took me to Europe, to Paris and Berlin. And all of the great couturiers loved to design for my body. Madame Gres, Coco Chanel, Lanvin, Mainbocher, Vionnet, Patou, Scap of course—they all designed specialty outfits for me. And Cyggie dressed me in all of them, just as he still does."

Alex raced on, not knowing how long this encounter would last. "I especially love that dress you wore in *Doublecross*."

"Which, darling? I wore several."

"The incredibly tight white satin one with all the white fur around the neck and collar."

"Oh, the Snake Dress, and you're confusing satin with lamé," said the voice of Mabel Eastlake. "Erté designed it for me, and it cost over three thousand dollars. Kranzler wanted me to look like a walking snake when I wore that gown. The fur was white fox and rose up in the shape of a cobra's hood behind me. I did wear white satin, of course, but in another scene."

"I know the one," Alex said enthusiastically. "You're walking across the room, away from the camera. You walk very slowly, and then suddenly you stop and twist your body around very quickly so your hair flies. And first of all, instead of your face, the audience only sees your mouth—"

"My mouth," said the dark, dreamlike voice of Mabel Eastlake.

"Yes, a pair of large dark lips, drawn back. Your hair covers the rest of your face. Then you shake your head again, and we see it."

"My face," sighed the voice of Mabel Eastlake. "My beautiful, beautiful face."

"And then you walk back directly towards the camera, only we can't figure out what it is you're doing."

"I was doing what Kranzler told me to do."

"You have a kind of secretive smile on your lips,"

Alex continued, seeing the famous scene clearly, "and it turns out, after all this stylized drama, that it's only to get a cigarette.

And you stand there in that incredible dress, all satin and fur, smoking a cigarette."

"That was my first scene."

"No one could do that nowadays," Alex said, meaning it. "No one."

There was a moment of thoughtful silence before the voice of Mabel Eastlake spoke again. "Kranzler had me wear white satin at least once in every picture. It was one of my trademarks. Satin is as merciless as Hollywood. Everything shows, which was the point. But after the new moral code came into effect, Cyggie had to put Band-Aids over my nipples. Will Hays said nipples were immoral. Imagine. Americans weren't supposed to have nipples, or navels." A sharp, derisive laugh. "But Kranzler never showed off my cleavage as much as my derriere. Erté said he'd never seen buttocks as perfect as mine. Why do you think I walked *away* from the camera so often? I never wore underwear, of course."

My God, Alex thought, what fantastic memories of Hollywood in the Thirties does this woman have? It was obvious to him that Miss Eastlake wanted to talk, perhaps even needed to talk. And *would* talk, if Alex were skillful enough to provoke the famous Eastlake tongue into action. The subject mustn't be too personal—clothes. "Another outfit of yours that I've always loved is that white tuxedo you wore in *Desperate Woman*," he said.

But suddenly the tone changed, reverting to its bitter, almost anguished suspicion. "Tell me what it is you really want from me!" the voice demanded. "Why are you haunting me this way? Why can't I get rid of you? Who are you?"

It was easier for Alex to keep cool when Miss Eastlake so obviously was not. He felt now as though he had a slight edge, a slight in. "My name is Alex Klein, Miss Eastlake," he said, not wanting her to make any connection with A. Liddell, who had written from New York. Clearly, Miss Eastlake was suspicious of writers. "And I just thought there might be something—some way I might work for you. I'll do anything, I could help you in a lot of ways."

"Help me?" The voice was incredulous. "*You*—help *me?*" Violent and sarcastic laughter boomed through the intercom.

"Why not?" Alex said, fearing the encounter was about to end. The month long welter of emotions that he had so far successfully suppressed threatened, suddenly, to engulf him. Dismissed by that superior laughter—a failure. The biography would not be written. "Why not?" he repeated. "There's so much I could do for you. You've given so much to me, to moviegoers. You were unique, beautiful, strong, funny, fearless. I want to be able to show you the kind of effect you have on people, what you do for them." There was no response, except that the lights concealed in the dashboard gently dimmed.

Alex waited. Hearing nothing, he assumed that Mabel Eastlake had dismissed him from her presence. "Thank you for being kind enough to talk to me," he said, absurdly polite in his humiliation, groping for the doorhandle, not wanting to find it. The moment he stepped out of the Duesenberg some momentary magic spell—a brief reprieve and sudden fatal beneficence—would be shattered. Life would again become ordinary. He would have to admit defeat, return to New York, and abandon the project that he had come to fantasize about as if it were a kind of salvation. Alex was almost afraid of the realities he had to face once he left Mabel Eastlake's Duesenberg. Finding the doorhandle, he grasped it tight.

"Wait."

Had he heard it, or was he making himself hear it?
"How sly to think you can leave that easily," said the voice of Mabel Eastlake. "Try the door, darling."
Alex did. It was locked.
"Planning to run back to your newspaper office and scribble out a story about meeting Mabel Eastlake tonight?"
"I'm not a reporter," Alex insisted.
"Neither was Hilda Hatter," said the voice. "Hilda was simply a liar. She used circumstances and hearsay to ruin people. She nearly ruined me. But I'm sly too, Mr. Klein."
"You certainly were in your movies," Alex said, surreptitiously trying the door.
"Admit to me that you provoked this interview," insisted the voice. "Admit to me that you have . . . *motives* for wanting to help me."
Alex shook his head. "I have no motives."
"You simply adore me—is that it?" There was an edge in the Eastlake voice. Alex said nothing. "Hilda adored me too," the voice continued, "and that was why she wanted to ruin me. Secretly we hate our gods, we're jealous of them, of their power—isn't that right? Hilda wanted me broken. She wanted me on her level. So a star must be wary of her fans, Mr. Klein. Fans are often out for a star's blood."
"I'm not out for your blood, Miss Eastlake," Alex said. "They always said blood didn't flow in your veins anyway."
To his surprise he heard low, appreciative laughter. "You seem to know so much about me, darling," said the voice of Mabel Eastlake. "You even know that my blood is pure ice water. Wouldn't it frighten you to help someone who tinkles like a cocktail when she walks?"
Alex intuitively sounded a note of mutual conspiracy. "Not at all. I could benefit from an ice cube or two in my own blood."
There was a full, agonizing moment of silence

before the voice of Mabel Eastlake said, "Do you really want to work for me, and will you really do anything I ask?"

Alex nodded solemnly, but a feeling was spreading through him like an intoxicant. Hope—hot, wild, glorious hope. And, at the same time, a certain hidden gloating satisfaction with his own chutzpah made him want to smile. He had put one over on Mabel Eastlake. "Yes," he said at length, when he had found his voice.

"It's difficult and not very pretty, the predicament we're in," said the voice of Mabel Eastlake slowly, hesitantly. "And it hadn't occurred to me until this very moment that you, Mr. Klein, might perhaps be the solution we have been looking for."

2.

So it was ostensibly as the prospective solution to Mabel Eastlake's rather unpretty "predicament" that Alex left—or was allowed to leave—the Duesenberg that night. The great star dismissed her fan and the chauffeur, evidently responding to some command from Miss Eastlake that Alex could not detect, suddenly turned and peered in at Alex through the glass. Blue and intense, his eyes were set in a dark, unreadable face, which a strange poise and almost feline intensity brought into sharp focus. He did not smile, only looked, as an animal in a wildlife park might peer in at a stalled, nervous driver. Alex's legs were rubbery when the chauffeur unlocked the car door and he allowed him to step out. He got an immediate unexpected wiff of the man, a peculiar odor of perspiration and wet animal fur, pungent and powerful. Alex nervously avoided looking at him until he was back in his Datsun.

How the world shrank in a Japanese import!

Before getting into the Duesenberg, the man again looked directly and fixedly in Alex's direction. Alex quickly averted his eyes. Tomorrow, he too would be working for Mabel Eastlake. They would meet again as fellow employees.

In the odd half-light, the enormous vehicle slowly backed up, turned and nosed its way through the steel gates of Glass House. The concealed lights switched off and the car disappeared.

In an exhilarated and half-dazed state, playing the Gershwin Concerto at top volume, Alex wound his way down towards the Beverly Hills Hotel. The price he was paying for a room there reflected his sheer desperation to get out of New York. But what did any of that matter now? It had all been worth it.

If he went back to the hotel he would want to call Frank to tell him the news, and to keep himself from doing that, Alex turned onto Hollywood Boulevard and parked near Mann's Chinese. In Mabel Eastlake's day it had been Grauman's. There, in the garish forecourt, under a green center canopy with pink fluorescent bulbs and Chinese lanterns in red and gold, a slab of cement was covered with uneven, scratched-in printing: "Thanks a heckuva, Sid. Mabel Eastlake, 1939." Beneath this: *Desperate Woman*, the title of her last film and the one they were then promoting. To the left of this inscription were two rather large hand-prints and, to the right, two high-heeled footprints. As her fans screamed and stared wild-eyed, as the news cameras rolled, Mabel Eastlake had been taken in and booked for immortality. What a glorious and ghastly night it must have been—the same night as the murders, the same night that immortal face disappeared forever from the idolatrous gaze of the world.

Alex impulsively stepped into Mabel Eastlake's footprints, wondering how it had felt to be so adored, so publicly touted. Fame, great fame—what was it like? And did Mabel Eastlake have premonitions of the horrors wait-ing for her just hours away?

His feet were small and they fit in Mabel Eastlake's footprints with room to spare. A strange feeling shot up through Alex's legs and lodged in his spine with a prickling shiver. It was like standing on a tombstone and suddenly sensing the presence of a restless spirit below. He quickly headed back toward his car.

Triumph is always less triumphant when there is no one to share it with, and bewildering when the victor is bound to secrecy. Alex was longing to tell someone the strange circumstances that were to take him to Glass House in the morning, but Miss Eastlake had stated the case quite clearly: "If you are to work for me, you must agree to be a willing prisoner."

To get into Glass House Alex would, of course, have agreed to anything. But Mabel Eastlake, in her fanatical quest for privacy, had laid out condition after condition until Alex had to wonder if she was preternaturally shrewd or totally mad. What could possibly be the reason for this intense secrecy? What did she fear would happen if she allowed a stranger to pass through the gates of Glass House?

And Alex had every intention of taking advantage of the situation to learn as much as he could about Mabel Eastlake. He was, in fact, experiencing some moral uneasiness because of it. For if Mabel Eastlake viewed Alex as the solution to her problem, it was also true that Alex regarded Miss Eastlake as the solution to his own; the anticipated biography was a sincere expression of reverence that just happened to have enormous commercial possibilities. But it meant getting her to reveal herself intimately without suspecting that she was doing so. A true invasion of privacy.

The situation was, in fact, not unlike the scenario for one of Mabel Eastlake's movies: a clever and conniving journalist, oppressed by bad luck and circumstances, recklessly decides to "work his way up" by any means available. In the cinematic case of Miss Eastlake this might involve a loveless but advantageous marriage, ruthless golddigging, undermining the competition or even murder. She, the most beautiful of screen images, was called upon again and again to portray women with violently scarred souls.

In Alex's case, the means to his ambitious end were to be completely mundane in nature. He was to go to Glass House to replace the housekeeper Miss Eastlake had retained in her employ for over four decades.

"I'm warning you now," the demanding star had said, "that it may not be easy for you to get along with my housekeeper. She is not only temperamental, she is sometimes dangerous. Fancy Barlow is a liar and a thief and I will take no responsibility for her behavior toward you."

"You mean she's violent?"

"I mean that she is unpredictable. Fancy Barlow was my stand-in at one time, and I keep her on only because one has a responsibility to one's stand-ins. A career that consists of being someone else—me, in this case—doesn't always leave a person well equipped to deal with the outside world."

"And she's been ill, you said?"

A low laugh came through the Duesenberg's intercom. "Did I say ill, Mr. Klein? I meant *sick*."

"What if she doesn't like me?" Alex asked nervously. "If she's been your housekeeper and companion for all these years—"

"Fancy Barlow is not my companion!" snapped the voice of Miss Eastlake. "It is one of her endlessly vulgar delusions that she is somehow a part of me; at times I believe she thinks she *is* me. She may have resembled me once, people did mistake us once or twice, but there was never any real comparison. There can be only one Mabel Eastlake and she knows it."

Surprised by the vehemence of this outburst, Alex kept his own voice as calm as a therapist's. "All I meant was, she might resent me for coming in—"

"Resentment is that bitch's middle name," growled the voice of Mabel Eastlake. "Now, you do know how to scrub toilets, don't you, Mr. Klein? I take it you are one of these lonely modern men who like to clean things until they sparkle? You're not above putting some old-fashioned elbow grease into your work?"

How much intelligence did it take, after all, to clean? It was the implied social stigma far more than the labor itself that Alex found difficult to accept. A Jamaican woman, Hattie, came in once a week to clean his cramped apartment on West 85th Street, and Alex had to remind himself that housekeeping would be a role that allowed him access to his subject. Alex Klein, the domestic servant. He could always pretend he was playing a part in a movie—a comedy, of course.

"You must realize that the work I have in mind for you is not glamorous," warned the voice of Mabel Eastlake. "I am not allowing you into Glass House out of the goodness of my heart, but because you may be able to make our lives easier. Don't mistake my motives, Mr. Klein. They are, and always have been, strictly selfish ones."

If Mabel Eastlake were testing him by making the job sound as unappealing and difficult as possible, Alex was determined not to fail. The old star persisted, however, in making the terms of the offer sound like a form of penal servitude.

"You will not, of course, be allowed visitors. Nor, for the duration of your employment, will you be allowed to come and go as you choose. I am the only one, Mr. Klein, who knows the computer code that operates the front gates and that is the only way a person can enter or leave. So if you truly wish to come to Glass House—if you truly wish to *help* me—you must be prepared to leave the world behind. I do not allow telephone calls or correspondence." The voice paused, as though satisfied that it had been sufficiently forbidding. "These are probably impossible terms for a man who is fairly attractive and still reasonably young—but they are my terms, Mr. Klein, because Glass House is mine to do with as I wish."

Alex's competitive, combative and ambitious spirit was fully aroused by this time. Without sounding overeager, he assured Miss Eastlake that he would like nothing better than to get away from "the outside world." And, in a sense, it was perfectly true. Why not regard this as an unprecedented opportunity to concentrate all of his energies on recording the full particulars of Mabel Eastlake's undoubtedly strange life? The monastic solitude would aid observation and writing, it would be a form of working meditation. And, just as important, a new environment and the work that went along with it would enable him to stop thinking obsessively about Frank and the bitter end of their relationship. Working for Mabel Eastlake would turn his stalled life in other directions.

But in the final analysis it was simply the coup of getting in where others had tried and failed for years that made Alex agree to Miss Eastlake's bizarre and stringent stipulations. Thinking of the book that might result from this experience made him delirious with anticipation.

"*Can* you conveniently disappear?" the voice asked tauntingly. "What of your friends—if you have any—and your family? How will you come to me without telling others where you're going? For I insist on that, Mr. Klein—no one must know that you are coming to Glass House."

"I have no family here," Alex hedged.

"Where is it, exactly, that you come from?"

He did not want Mabel Eastlake to make even the remotest connection between Alex Klein and the intellectual nitwit from New York who had written to suggest a collaborative biography. "I've moved around a great deal," he said.

"On the lam?" the voice asked quickly. "You're not

wanted for anything, are you?"

Alex said he wasn't. And it was true. He wasn't wanted for anything at all.

There was a sigh. "I suppose you're either an actor or a whore."

"An actor."

"Whores of another color," Mabel Eastlake replied. "You don't think I'm going to give you any help with your career, do you? You're hardly star material."

"No, *I'd* like to help *you*," Alex reiterated.

"Yes," said the famous voice, dropping an octave. "So you say. Tell me, are you a little boy blue?"

"I don't know what you mean."

"You know perfectly well what I mean, Mr. Klein. Are you the sort of man who goes in for earrings and that kind of thing?"

Alex hesitated. "What difference would that make?"

"Possibly the difference between allowing you to come to Glass House or keeping you away."

Why should she care? Some part of Alex had come to regard Mabel Eastlake as a sympathetic friend, at least as an ally. That sentiment was based on what her screen image conveyed to him. Now he had to face the unpleasant possibility that she, like so many other very ordinary mortals, was frankly homophobic. In a sudden rage that the question could even arise, that somehow he might be sexually suspect, and fearing that he would be instantly and unfairly typed according to the answer he gave, Alex replied instinctively and indignantly, "No, I'm *not* the sort of man who goes for earrings!" What did it matter what he said if it got him into Glass House?

The silence that followed was broken by the unearthly cry of a peacock hidden somewhere nearby.

"The chauffeur will pick you up at eight sharp tomorrow morning," said the voice of Mabel Eastlake. "Good night, Mr. Klein. Remember, you've given me your word—you won't tell a soul—and I am trusting you as I would trust a gentleman."

Alex did not have much time to prepare himself for this wild and benevolent turn of fate. Just as well, he thought, as he drove back to the hotel. Too much thinking baffles action. As it was, he had only one night to get his affairs in order. Mabel Eastlake would have preferred Alex to disappear into Glass House that very night, as an added guarantee against publicity. "But that would look like kidnapping, wouldn't it, Mr. Klein?" the legendary voice teased. "And I must prepare Fancy and Cygnet for your arrival. They haven't seen a new face in years and there's no telling what their reaction will be to yours. By the way, you do adore cats, don't you?"

Alex didn't, but said that he had two Sealpoints himself.

"Then we have an agreement?"

This was actually a line Mabel Eastlake had used in the movie *Doublecross* when she was subtly and dangerously negotiating the murder of her rich, abusive husband. But the words were sweet to Alex's ears, for they meant that he had scored a major victory—even if it required deception on his part. He gave his verbal agreement to secrecy—on his honor, as a gentleman.

Back at the hotel, he returned the car, picked up his mail and went to his room to pack. The swift, dreamlike rush of events had left him tense and overexcited. He poured himself a Scotch and switched on the television to orient himself in the world while he looked at the mail. There was a brief letter from a friend in New York cataloging all the latest fads and disasters, and another lavender envelope with no return address. A sharp whiff of some heady, exotic perfume escaped from the envelope as he opened it. "Forget Mabel Eastlake," he read. "Be a darling and let her die with her secrets."

A California crackpot. It was exactly the kind of message Alex did not want to deal with just now. To aid in his Eastlake research he had placed ads in several California newspapers, hoping someone who had worked on an Eastlake film would come forth with information. So far, no one had. Records were impossible to check because Paradise Studios, which had retained exclusive rights to Miss Eastlake's services, had been completely destroyed by fire in 1941. This ridiculous message must have come from someone who had seen one of the ads. Alex tore it up.

He opened a third envelope with trembling fingers. The writer's bold monogram was at the top of the page, and her name just below it. It was from none other than Hilda Hatter. The handwriting was nearly indecipherable. "Come tomorrow and I may tell you what Mabel Eastlake never will." He had struck pay dirt at last, but it was too late. Tomorrow he would be with the great star herself. The interview with Hilda Hatter would have to wait, and he quickly wrote her asking for a postponement. Then, smiling and humming, he began to sort through his accumulated notes and research materials, carefully packing them and the copies of his two pseudonymous novels.

Under the pen name A. Liddell, Alex had written two wild, improbable and thoroughly enjoyable tales of romance and mystery. He liked the ambiguity of the name and chose it to give his authorial persona the freedom to assume a female identity. His own name, Klein, meant small or little in German. Frank's typical undermining joke was always, "A. Liddell what?"

Having packed, he was ready to make the necessary telephone calls concerning his apartment and an extension of the unofficial leave of absence he was taking from the publishing house where he overworked. The temptation was overwhelming, but to no one did he reveal where he was going.

On a series of Mabel Eastlake movie–still postcards he kept his messages short. "Staying on. Don't worry. Having a marvelous time." So let them all be a little mystified. Let them know that good old dutiful Alex, ditched after five years and on his own again at thirty-three, still had a few tricks up his sleeve, if not in his bed.

But finally he had to face it, or *him*, rather. Should he or should he not call Frank? Should he break his gentleman's word of honor with Mabel Eastlake? Of all the people he was longing to tell, Frank was the one Alex most wanted to know about his strategems and success. For five years they had shared, on Tuesday and Thursday nights and all day Sunday, their thoughts and plans and hang-ups. What Alex most hated about the aftermath of the breakup was the power Frank continued to have over him in this regard. Even knowing that it was over, Alex still was unable to break the habits they had created together; on the contrary, he hung on tight, pained and full of resentment.

Not only did Alex want and need to succeed on his own, and for himself, to prove that life did not end when love did, he knew in some ridiculous, competitive way that he wanted to succeed to show Frank that he could do it—do anything—without him. Frank's departure seemed to have brought out Alex's latent aggressiveness. With Frank he had always been conciliatory, the one who soothed and gave. And Frank took, all right, because he was a taker.

Frank was a taker. He believed that that was what men were, and he was a man. In every way, except with Alex on Tuesday and Thursday nights and all day Sunday, Frank lived a straight life. His work as an actor, he said, required it. He didn't want to be typed as gay. Once that happened, he said, you might as well throw in the towel as far as future roles were concerned. Alex was caught between sympathy and disgust, but finally came to realize how he had actually encouraged Frank in his soul-destroying duplicity.

Encouraged it by allowing it, by flattering Frank's straight pretensions and thereby enhancing, in his own eyes, Frank's already considerable prestige. Alex chose to overlook the self-hatred this engendered in Frank and nourished in himself. Self-hatred can be a comfortable habit, after all, once you settle into it to keep someone in your bed three nights out of seven.

But there was always a toll. Frank systematically undermined Alex's confidence in order to feel less threatened by him. The small humiliations, the repeated denials of emotional dependence upon Alex, and a rejection of the entire "gay world" were all characteristic of Frank's attitude. . .an attitude that Alex, who had just lied to Mabel Eastlake about his own sexuality, would seem to have absorbed, at least in part.

The strange part of it was, Alex could see in retrospect, that Frank did love him. Loved him in the only way he could, being so cut off from his own emotions. Their sex had been wild, unbridled, almost like a battle at times, with both of them claiming victory when they should have been calling truce. It was precisely what Frank found most repellent in Alex—his capacity for loving another man, his tenderness and acceptance—that drew Frank to him. Every moth finds its flame. But then Frank had dropped the bombshell. On Monday, Wednesday and Friday nights and every Saturday, he had been seeing a woman. He needed a wife and children for business purposes. But this wouldn't change things between them, he told Alex. He'd still come over one night a week, maybe two, for their great sex.

"The hell you will," Alex said, slamming the phone down.

So here he was in Los Angeles, free, eager to cut loose from all the old ties that bound. Dressed in clothes Frank would have derided, with a new style hair cut that Frank would have hated, still in love with Frank. He supposed he would be, in some crazy unhealthy way, until someone else swept him off his feet. But that was hard to imagine. His heart felt small, lonely, encased in glass. At the same time, he told himself, he was ready for anything. Especially for Mabel Eastlake.

Mabel Eastlake, in her films, rarely stood on the romantic ceremonies that Hollywood devised and American audiences cherished. Eastlake was always doing the unexpected and doing it with such surprising style, passion, vivacity, wit and ironic detachment that an audience could only watch her with fascination. Certainly she outraged the morals and attitudes of those who believed that movies should function solely as middle-class propaganda, but she did so with a kind of disarming calculation, as if shocking an audience were also part of her act, her image, her *raison d'etre*. She allowed you to do in fantasy what real life never even offered as a possibility. Mabel Eastlake was certainly a necessary ally in the constant battle for self-esteem that Alex had waged throughout his long affair with Frank.

Was she a brilliant actress? It was difficult to say because there had never really been anyone like her.

She existed in her roles, and out of them, at one and the same time. Her fast, electric manner imbued every swing of her satin-clad hips with intense drama. But she might also appear in trousers and modulate her sexuality in a different key. Always she was a woman out for herself in this world. And from the first moment Alex had set eyes on her in a revival of *Darling Lady*, he had been hooked. It had never really happened to him before. Mabel Eastlake simply answered a call that Alex wasn't aware of having dialed.

He had been so full of instant admiration and excitement about his discovery of Mabel Eastlake that he hunted down all her films and wrote an article, "Mabel Eastlake: Implications of an Image," which had been published in *Film Quarterly*.

"Today [he wrote] we might interpret the Eastlake persona as sadomasochistic. At least Freudians might be inclined to do so. But this is to overlook in a typically sexist way the important feminist, androgynous and sociohistorical implications in the films themselves. If time after time in her movies Mabel Eastlake appears to be emotionally, and perhaps sexually, stimulated by having verbal and even physical battles with archetypically romantic and masculine men—who generally remain the victors—isn't it also true that by taking action, by fighting, kicking, screaming, abusing and sometimes even killing these archetypes, Mabel Eastlake is fighting a bitter battle for moral and psychological autonomy? She lives by her wits, as so many did during the Depression years, and expresses a feminine unwillingness to be left behind in any area of endeavor. By choosing the prerogative of 'acting like a man,' she is, in fact, fulfilling herself as a woman."

Alex gave in and dialed Frank's number in New York. A familiar tension seized him when the phone rang and he steeled himself to hear a woman's voice answer. Hearing Frank's voice, he took a deep breath, only to realize that it was his answering machine. An actor's recorded message. Without waiting for the beep, Alex hung up. He remained a gentleman of honor.

His mouth dripping toothpaste, he came out of the bathroom to watch a news story about a blizzard that had dumped eighteen inches of snow on New York City. There was film footage of poor New Yorkers, bent double against raging winds, walking through Rockefeller Center. Just as he would have been doing two days from today if he hadn't finally met Mabel Eastlake.

He was on his way back into the bathroom when his attention was again distracted by the news. "Police in Beverly Hills tonight are investigating the disappearance of legendary gossip columnist, Hilda Hatter." The report was over in a moment and mentioned only that Miss Hatter had been reported missing by her Puerto Rican maid, who had had the evening off. An old Hollywood photo of Miss Hatter, "reclusive in her later years," wearing a trademark hat and a steel-jawed and somewhat malignant smile, accompanied the story.

Alex looked for a long time at the letter he had just received from her. Coincidence, he thought; don't read too much into it. It would all be settled by the time he returned from Glass House. And it would be wiser, of course, since the police would be involved, not to send Miss Hatter his own request for a postponed interview. That he tore up and sent to the sewers of Beverly Hills.

3.

Miss Eastlake's Duesenberg easily outclassed the various foreign and domestic cars and limousines waiting for other patrons of the Beverly Hills Hotel. To look worthy of the automobile Alex dressed carefully and well. In a moment of flattering delusion he envisioned the chauffeur opening the back door for him. After a brief show of fine French hosiery and paper-thin Italian leather shoes, he would quickly and gracefully disappear inside. They would all wonder who he was. And in the dim, luxurious rear saloon where Miss Eastlake, the star, always sat alone, there would sit Alex, viewing the world from Mabel Eastlake's vantage point, through tinted windows, unseen but seeing.

But the chauffeur again opened the front door, making it very clear that the rear was reserved exclusively for the perfect posterior of Miss Eastlake. The *help* sat in front.

Suddenly, irrevocably, he was on his way to Glass House. Sitting tensely on the high seat beside the chauffeur, Alex was overcome by the weird reality of what was happening. Viewed in the smoggy light of day, the terms and secrecy he had agreed to were not only irrational, they were frightening and even stupid. Who, after all, *would* know where he was . . . just in case. In case of what? he snapped at himself. Worrying, worrying, always certain that something would go wrong, that any new venture was dangerous and to be avoided. The terrible legacy from his family, fear the world because it's a fearful place. Stay where you are. Don't go too far.

It occurred to him that he was sailing off into uncharted waters, like one of the hard-nosed, contemporary heroines in a book by A. Liddell. Fiction, of course, was always safer than real life. He was proud that he actually had the courage to do this, but persistently aware, too, of an emotional undertow that came from knowing just how alone in this strange venture he was.

The Duesenberg turned off Sunset Boulevard and headed toward the higher regions of Beverly Hills. It was like riding in an upholstered cloud, silent and awe inspiring.

Eyes smarting from lack of sleep and exposure to smog, Alex subtly positioned himself to gain a better view of the chauffeur.

With a body that could crush you, he was a true child of California, dwarfing even the giants who grew out here. Underneath his obviously uncomfortable stiff white jacket, this man was the elements—the glowing southern sun and the blue Pacific winds and the golden western earth. There was no self-conscious calculation in the way he looked, only a vital, silent sense of strength.

Alex had a small man's awareness of physical mass, having spent a lifetime gauging himself against those who were larger than he. He was "about the second face up in a totem pole" as Frank once said. He could work out until he was blue in the face—which he did—and could develop a perfectly shaped body—as he had—but he could never grow taller. Size was one of the things he most hated and admired in others.

He wondered now if he should attempt some friendly gesture, try to win the man over to his side. But looking down he saw a heavy half-awake bulge outlined against the chauffeur's loose white trousers and he had to restrain a spontaneous answering call in his own crotch. The physical reality of the man suddenly filled the entire car.

The sound of a loud horn at an intersection startled Alex but the chauffeur did not flinch.

Alex cleared his throat. "I saw on the news that Hilda Hatter disappeared last night," he said.

The chauffeur did not respond.

"What do you suppose happened to the old bitch?"

The chauffeur turned to look sharply and intently at Alex. His dense, sun-scorched hair was brushed back, giving his face a dark prominent thrust and sleekness. Thick golden eyebrows gilded the startling blue flash of his eyes. Alex tried to read them, to extract some emotion, but they yielded nothing.

"What do you think happened to her? Hilda Hatter?" Alex said.

Then something swam up into those eyes. The chauffeur opened his mouth and looked for a moment as though he were about to say something. Instead, his hands tightly clenched the steering wheel and he turned his exclusive attention back to the street.

Leaving Alex stranded. Was the man simply ignoring him? Despising him? *Distrusting* him? This was, after all, a work situation. Alex was a new employee. And, as he knew from his own experience, new employees frequently brought out all the fears and jealousies of the older ones. A fear of role usurpation.

They turned on to Hillcrest Drive and the Duesenberg glided into Beverly Hills. How many times had he made this trip in his rented tin can of a Datsun? Alex's stomach knotted with excitement. If he had not had his fortuitous, late-night encounter with Mabel Eastlake, he would have admitted defeat and gone back to New York.

He thought of the New Yorkers bent double and racing at their usual pace through a blizzard. New York! How far away and unnecessary it seemed now, looking out on these high, undulating palm trees and the riotous, semitropical vegetation. New York was definitely black-and-white. California was early Technicolor.

"By the way, was there someone in the back seat with Miss Eastlake last night?" he asked.

When the Duesenberg rounded the final and sharpest bend in the road, and the chauffeur still had not answered the question, Alex began to realize the extent of his fear. He'd been keeping it at bay, calling it unmanly and prodding it down like a wild animal when it leapt up to seize his thoughts. But now he had to fight a wave of sudden black panic.

The high steel gates were slowly opening in front of them. The chauffeur had done nothing, so Mabel Eastlake must be controlling them from somewhere inside the estate. How did she know they were approaching?

Alex glanced tensely at the driver. Hoping for what? Some kind of reassurance from another human face? This time the driver openly returned Alex's glance. He held Alex's eyes in his own, looking into them searchingly. A strange tightening and turn of the lips—not what you could exactly call a smile, nor a sneer—but some emotionally dislocated message in–between. Alex shuddered in spite of himself.

And then, like a great ship entering port, the Duesenberg turned into the driveway of Glass House and the monogrammed gates locked behind it.

As the car purred along the inner drive, Alex tried to prepare himself for what lay ahead. Reflected in the white curves of the car, the foliage was dense and intensely green. The faint, sour, cat-piss smell of eucalyptus and Russian olive trees hung in the balmy air. Sharp needles of sunlight stitched down through the canopy of leaves, occasionally illuminating the plumage of a startled bird.

And when finally he saw it, Alex's head went light and his uneasiness gave way to awe. For Glass House was beautiful. At least its facade was. Unlike so many garish, overbuilt mansions and undistinguished homes in Beverly Hills, Glass House was a monument to style, a period piece in the same way the movies of Mabel Eastlake were. And, like Mabel Eastlake, its shape and the elegance of its lines transcended its period.

In a rush of enthusiasm, Alex pulled out his camera and began to take photographs through the car window. The chauffeur braked, placed a powerful hand on Alex's knee, and stared at him, appalled. Instantly aware of the transgression, Alex put the Nikon away. Photos would have to wait and he would have to remember that he was Alex Klein, the domestic, not A. Liddell, the biographer of Mabel Eastlake.

The facade of Glass House was perfectly reflected in the still, gleaming waters of a rectangular pool from which rose high retaining walls of white alabaster. The massive expanse of seamless white stone had a starched, hallucinatory glow and was lapped by quivering tongues of sunlight playing off the water.

The house itself sat atop this wall. Three black round towers—the center one taller than the two flanking it and thrust predominately forward—drew the eye to a formal entry. The door into Glass House was recessed in the center tower. From this high front entrance two mirror-image staircases of pale pink marble splayed out like a pincer, bridging the reflecting pool and descending in a grandly curving sweep to the drive.

It was the water in the pool and the shininess of the stone that tricked the eye into a feeling of lightness, for there was no glass to be seen in the front of Glass House. It gave away nothing of itself, made no attempt to welcome. It might have been a skillfully designed fortress or temple.

For a moment, rapt as he was, Alex was unaware that the Duesenberg had stopped and that the chauffeur was retrieving his luggage from the back. He had time for three illicit photos before his door was briskly opened. Later, these photographs always haunted him; the beautiful, lying facade of Glass House as he first saw it, having then no idea of the brutal and bizarre truths behind it.

Stepping out into the dazzle of sunlight on stone, Alex was certain he saw a figure dressed in black looking down at him from the top of the central tower. Functional and severely geometrical railings at its top created a Deco widow's walk, reminding him that Mabel Eastlake was, after all, a widow. But by the time he had shaded his eyes for a better look, the figure was gone. Had it been Mabel Eastlake?

Then, high above him, the recessed entry door was flung open and someone stood staring out with wide but strangely unseeing eyes. Another movement and the person was grasping the marble balustrade in a queerly dramatic pose and looking back over a shoulder as though expecting to be hit from behind.

Jesus Christ, Alex thought, it's Mabel Eastlake.

But if it were, why was she not wearing her legendary veils? From this distance she appeared to have no need of them. Fascinated, Alex stood and watched Mabel Eastlake's fast, tortuous descent down the staircase of pink marble.

She was carrying a sponge mop, used as a cane, an extra limb. Her costume—for what else could you call it?—was beaded silk, but it had burst at one of the side seams. A long scarf of marabou feathers draped around her neck vibrated wildly with every quick, heavy step she took, getting caught in the sponge mop. A shiny little side-cocked hat was perched precariously on her head of platinum, marcel-waved hair. Alex's mother had worn the same kind of pink fluffy mules. An Ace bandage was wrapped around Miss Eastlake's thick ankle.

She kept her eyes riveted on Alex, her bright red mouth puckered with determination. The beautiful string of perfectly matched pearls she wore was too small for her neck and it gave her a straining, strangulated look. Long red gloves the same shade as her lipstick completed her outfit.

Halfway down the stairs she stopped and whispered in the deep voice of Mabel Eastlake, "Darling, do you know who I am?"

"Yes, you're Mabel Eastlake," Alex said, keeping his voice low.

A huge, familiar smile appeared but was instantly replaced by a look of intense concern. "Don't come into this house," she whispered. "No matter what she told you, don't believe her and don't come into this house. Say you're sick, say you changed your mind—anything, but go!" She responded like a whipped animal when a commanding voice from an unseen source issued amplified down the stairs. It, too, was the voice of Mabel Eastlake.

"Who gave the monkey permission to go outside?" it demanded.

The person on the stairs turned back to Alex with a trapped but excited expression. "The voice of my conscience, darling. Do you hear how it tells me what to do? I can never escape it. It's my *leash*, do you understand, that voice."

"Do you want me to send Cocaine out without *her* leash?" the unseen Eastlake voice threatened.

The Eastlake of the stairs raised her chins in an attitude of defiant pride. "She lied to you," she said to Alex.

"Fancy—" the other voice warned.

"*Lied,*" insisted the figure on the stairs. "Withheld information."

"I can hear everything that blind monkeys say," said the amplified Eastlake voice. "So let me hear you introduce yourself to Mr. Klein or I shall be very angry."

To spare the old housekeeper any further indignity, Alex advanced up the stairs with his hand extended. "How do you do, Mrs. Barlow."

"*Miss* Barlow," she sniffed. "It rhymes with Harlow."

"*Miss* Barlow," Alex corrected himself.

"Fancy to you, darling," Fancy said, waving back Alex's hand. "No, I hate to shake. I hate that pressure, it reminds me of my lost humanity." And suddenly, extraordinarily, her face quivering, Fancy Barlow shivered and wrapped her arms about herself, squinting fiercely into the 'sun. "I haven't been outside in years," she cried. "Has it changed?"

"The world? Yes. It changes every day."

"Is it even more loathsome than it used to be?" Fancy asked.

"Difficult," Alex said, "but I wouldn't say loathsome."

Fancy squinted in his direction. "You're not from around these parts, are you," she said, and without waiting for an answer she turned to bawl up the stairs, "Send him back where he came from! I won't have him in this house!"

But Miss Eastlake, this time, was silent.

Seeing a glint near Fancy Barlow's foot, Alex surreptitiously scooped up a square silver earring. A black enameled design was embossed in one corner: HH. He was about to hand it to Fancy—who evidently thought he was bowing to her and dropped a stiff but automatic curtsy—when he saw that the housekeeper's large, red-stoned earrings were intact. Alex pocketed the one he had found and said nothing.

Keeping her voice low and insistent, Fancy was looking at him in great cosmetic earnest. Unfortunately, it was a face difficult to take seriously. "Something terrible is going to happen in this house and it can only get worse if you come in. No! Don't look up at me, darling. I don't want her to know that I'm talking. She doesn't like it when I talk, so I've learned how to do it without moving my lips—well, hardly moving them."

"I'm listening," Alex said, as quiet as an accomplice.

"She said I was her stand-in, didn't she? Well maybe I was. But it was she who looked just like me, not the other way around. And since her face is—well, ruined, darling—I'm the only real replica of Mabel Eastlake left. And that makes me Mabel Eastlake, doesn't it, even if she says otherwise? *You* knew. You recognized me."

Fancy's was a fallen version—evidently, an approximate reproduction—of Mabel Eastlake's screen face. It sent a sympathetic shudder through Alex. The makeup was too thick and white, but not thick enough to hide a shadowy mustache. Looking at her, Alex somehow felt his own integrity threatened.

"You don't believe me, of course, and you will come into Glass House despite my warnings," Fancy said bitterly. "Fool!"

"What are you saying to Mr. Klein?" demanded the voice of Mabel Eastlake.

Alex now saw for the first time, and very clearly, how skilled an actress Fancy Barlow could be. Her face took on an airy, false lightness as she turned up the stairs. "You did tell me that he was a Mabel Eastlake fan, didn't you?" she asked the unseen Mabel Eastlake. "I was just telling him that this is the frock worn in the second scene of *Singing Sinners*, when you dance on the penthouse roof in the moonlight with—"

"George Raft," Alex said. "Just before she pushes him over the railing."

The eyebrows, already plucked and redrawn into high Deco fishhook curves, rose higher in appreciation. "So you *are* a fan." She smiled and took up a dramatic posture. "In the old days, darling, Mabel Eastlake would have glided down these stairs. You would have thought she had oiled ball-bearings in her joints. It's possible she did, of course, given all the body work they did on her. When they finished inventing Mabel Eastlake they could have applied for a patent."

"Fancy, you're being witty at my expense," said the observant but unobserved Mabel Eastlake. "Mr. Klein can already see from your dress and appearance just how witty you are."

"Don't Fancy me, you rotten old robber!"

"Robber!" exclaimed the Eastlake voice tensely. "What have I ever taken from you?"

"That," answered her housekeeper, "which is a woman's most treasured possession."

"Her pearls?" asked Mabel Eastlake.

"Her pride!"

"Both artificial, in your case." The voice now smapped into authority. "Tell the Child to bring Mr. Klein's luggage to his room and then to stable Doozy. Show Mr. Klein only those parts of the house he will be working in, and Cygnet will get him a uniform. And Fancy," the voice said sharply, "watch yourself."

"Why should I bother when *you're* doing it all the time for me?" Fancy said angrily.

Not having known what to expect, this was already more than Alex had bargained for.

Heaving a dramatic sigh, Fancy Barlow motioned for the chauffeur by rapping her fist against her heart. She put a fat, gloved hand on his arm when he came to her. "Watch this, darling," she said to Alex. "I don't have to speak out loud and he understands just by watching my lips. He learned that in school. Life is like a silent movie to him." She exaggeratedly mouthed Mabel Eastlake's directions and watched with a look of half-licentious admiration as the chauffeur bounded up the stairs with Alex's luggage.

"Ah, to be young," she sighed, turning to reclimb the stairs with laborious determination. "It's like getting into heaven, climbing these fucking stairs. I never do anymore, I never come out, but I wanted to warn you. I couldn't believe it when she told me she'd found someone stupid enough to come and work here. Now of all times."

"Is something happening that I should know about?"

Fancy laughed Mabel Eastlake's sardonic, basso laugh. "No, darling, nothing you should know about. Nothing you *could* know about. But for us living here all these years . . ." Concern and resentment alternated in her face as she turned to look down at Alex. "Don't believe for a minute, darling, that I'm as old and tired and foolish as I look today. I do it to fool her! And when I heard you were coming I had to make up so hurriedly. Jimmy always said I was the sort of girl who'd powder her nose before murdering someone. I simply *will not* be seen outside without makeup. Miss Eastlake learned that from me, of course. She must have been juiced to the hair on her chinny-chin-chin to allow you to come here."

"I think it was fate," Alex said. Fancy Barlow's perfume was so overwhelming that he kept a step or two behind her.

"Fate, he says! Fate!" Her laugh shot through Alex, resembling as closely as it did the laugh of Mabel Eastlake. "I wouldn't bargain on it, darling. Fate is never what you bargain for. It's always worse. And Glass House does have a way of bringing out everyone's fate. It's like living in one of those Greek tragedies Kranzler used to tell me about. The scene is set and all you can do is wait for the inevitable to unfold."

"It was kind of her to let me come and help you," Alex said in his most diplomatic tone.

"Politeness is a form of stupidity, darling. She wouldn't have let you come to Glass House unless she had it planned first—very carefully—and wanted something out of *you*. Now what, exactly, did the monstrous Miss Eastlake tell you about me?"

Alex hesitated. "Only that it was more difficult for you to manage the house than it had been."

"If she didn't expect so goddamned much, it wouldn't be," complained Fancy. "Of course *he's* even worse. The Virgin Queen, Keeper of the Keys. Ow!" she cried. "Christ, my ankle. No, don't help me. I don't want you to help me. Jimmy's the only one who knew how to help me—and the Child, now that Jimmy's dead. You know, darling," she said, casting a dark glance back at Alex, "no doctors are ever allowed in Glass House. She wouldn't even let Mary P have a doctor—and how I begged, hearing that poor child's screams. I begged. But no. Our Miss Eastlake is too afraid of what they might find in her dirty underwear."

Alex quickly learned two things: to let Fancy talk without interruption, and to assume that Mabel Eastlake was always monitoring. By remaining quiet and never sounding overtly curious, Alex could not only extract a great deal of valuable information from Fancy, he could also allay Miss Eastlake's suspicions that he was, in fact, scouting such information out. As a domestic in Miss Eastlake's employ, after all, he was not expected to have a personality. *His* personality, as Miss Eastlake had already said, was irrelevant.

"Didn't care if Mary P died," Fancy was muttering under her breath, "and doesn't care if I die either. Neither of them does. I belong in Forest Lawn, darling, with the stars who were my friends, but she'll put me out with the garbage. I had to beg her—*beg* her—to let the Child buy this elastic bandage for me. She said I might use it to strangle her . . . and don't think for a moment the thought hadn't occurred to me before she suggested it. I'm very suggestible, you know."

"Who is the Child?" Alex asked. And who, he wondered, was Mary P?

"The Child," Fancy said impatiently. "You know, the Child. He drove you here."

"Doesn't he have a name?"

"Of course he has a name, darling, but since he's deaf we never use it."

"Completely deaf?"

"The deaf always hear something," Fancy said. "Buzzings and cracklings. They have horrible noises in their head, just like the rest of us. And he can always hear the high frequency of Miss Eastlake's whistle. That's how she gets him to come to her, you know. Whistles. It's unnatural. I said, a dog comes to a whistle, a man shouldn't. But she said, the Child *is* our pet. He's our watchdog and takes care of us and the gardens and Cocaine."

Alex fingered the earring in his pocket. The design had reminded him of something and he couldn't place what it was.

"I suppose she told you stories about me. They always tell stories about me. Of course, darling," Fancy shot a coy, sidelong glance at Alex, "there *are* stories to tell. That's why she makes it so impossible for people to get in. She's afraid of the stories that will get out. But it wasn't always this way, not when Jimmy was alive. Ah, if these walls could talk, darling."

"I thought they did," Alex said. "Where *was* Miss Eastlake when she was talking earlier?"

"Up in her Throne Room with Cygnet," Fancy said, distracted by the appearance of the Child at the top of the stairs. She paused coquettishly and waited for him to come down to her. "Such a good boy," she purred, taking his arm. "So kind and considerate. And so handsome. Ah, why am I always such a sucker for beauty? Can't you see his beauty, darling?" She stepped back to give Alex an un-obstructed view. "Don't you find him desirable?" She evidently played this kind of game with the Child often, for he responded with the half-smile of a shy boy who loves to be teased. "Show him your arms, Child—"

Underneath the jacket of his chauffeur's uniform, which he now removed, the Child was wearing a sleeveless white silk jersey. His bare arms, momentarily engaged in folding the jacket, bunched like twisted rope, then relaxed into smooth, sculptural compositions.

To Alex, who stood dumbfounded as this operation took place and the sun glinted off those gleaming white teeth, Fancy said under her breath, "I can see you'd be putty in his arms. Just don't let Miss Eastlake catch you."

"Catch me?" Alex said, for her voice had dropped to an intimate seriousness.

"Ah!" she laughed, loud again. "Our Child of na-ture, our sunlit Apollo, who makes sweet our numbered days. I don't know *what* we'd do without him—and don't think, darling, that I haven't thought often of what I'd like to do *with* him." Again she let out her superb imitation of the Eastlake laugh. "Of course, it would be practically in-cestuous, wouldn't it—since I am almost old enough to be his mother."

At last they reached the top of the staircase. Fancy stood panting, the marabou feathers around her neck ris-ing and falling with each breath. "Look around you, dar-ling, for one last time, before you enter Glass House."

The porch looked out over and into the northern-most section of Beverly Hills; further still, Alex could see the hazy outlines of the Santa Monica mountains. "I had no idea we were so high up," he said, amazed at the vista, his excitement expanding with the view.

"Any higher, darling, and you'd be in a coma," Fancy said. But her comic voice trailed off. She took a step forward and stared out into the distance. Life within the normal range of vision was a smeared blur to Fancy, but when she stared out into the vast distances that could be seen from any part of Glass House, she seemed to be acutely watching for or actually seeing something beyond sight.

"Why is it that the past always seems more beautiful than it actually was?" she asked.

"Inflation," Alex said drily.

"The old days are so much on my mind lately. They sweep over me like a dream, so I hardly know who I am and what I'm doing. Everyone from the past is coming back in my dreams. Only Jimmy stays away. But I see him in the distance, standing dark and quiet, and I know he's waiting for me too. I feel him, I know he's there."

Alex was suddenly aware of the Child's blue eyes on him, and he shifted uneasily.

Fancy turned back to him, almost gay. "Let's have a drink, darling, shall we? I need to freshen my mood a little, and it will still be hours before one of my terrible lunches."

Dismissed by her gentle, abstracted gesture, the Child went to stand beside the Duesenberg. His eyes did not leave Alex. Alex turned away from them.

"And now, darling, let us enter," Fancy said formally, shuffling towards the front door. "She said you liked cats. Personally, I despise and detest them—except as ornaments, of course. I find it's the same way with people—so long as they're accessories and match your table setting, they're fine. But Miss Eastlake, now, always had to have large, dangerous-looking animals at her side. Only in white, you know." She laughed. "I'll bet she never told you that people used to call this Cat House behind her back."

She pushed open the glossy black door and Alex, with some trepidation, followed her into Glass House.

4.

The interior was black.

Floor, walls, ceiling, a sea of shining, reflective black. Alex, who could cover the entire length of his apartment in ten to twelve steps, realized after a few moments that the sheer size of this seamless, gleaming room had actually taken his breath away. At first he was repelled by the chill, mirroring surfaces, by the dizzying confusion of solids and voids, but then, slowly, he began to admire its high Deco drama.

Lines played off curves, reflections off reflections. Square against the curvature of the rear foyer wall, impossible not to see when you entered, was the large, famous painting by Vargas. Painted entirely in whites and pale flesh tones, it showed a silk-clad Mabel Eastlake, her famous buttocks raised high under a tight backless gown, reclining playfully with half-closed eyes and lips open in laughter or mockery beside a large, aroused white panther. An optical trick of the painter could catch you unawares into confusing the two: it wasn't easy to tell where the woman ended and the beast began.

Like a twisted spine, each of its vertebra a slab of polished black glass separately set in the mirrored wall, the staircase followed the spinning vortex of the room up to a high recessed doorway. There was no handrail, nothing to guide the eye or to protect one from missing a beat and falling into the dark, waiting air.

Fancy, shuffling ahead, stopped and turned around. "What? Oh, you're stunned. They're always stunned. If you live here awhile, darling, you get used to it."

"It's overwhelming," Alex said. And sinister, he thought, as the personality of Glass House slowly introduced itself to his dazed senses. Whatever profound psychic dislocation the place had induced in him, and despite his sense of it as a world folded darkly in upon itself, Alex was also aware that Glass House evoked in him a strange covetous longing.

"Darling," Fancy said, "you should never let anyone see you're from a small town. The people in these parts take advantage. You still have twenty-two rooms left to see . . . and clean."

"Is that the original?" Alex asked of the painting.

"Everything in Glass House is an original. I call it 'Miss Eastlake's Ass,' and oh, how are the mighty fallen."

"You should know about that," the Eastlake intercom-voice said, startling Alex into the awareness that, somehow, somewhere, Mabel Eastlake was watching everything.

"Miss Eastlake," Fancy said, raising her voice, "was always terribly vain about her ass, you know. It was because she didn't have any tits."

A new voice—high, controlled, British—was now heard from above. "Tits?" A pale, fluting laugh. "Miss Eastlake is much too moderne to be bothered with such archaic encumbrances."

A slim, attenuated figure dressed in a black jumpsuit was standing in the recessed doorway at the top of the stairs. "You were a very smart monkey to sneak outside like that when the door was open," it said, starting down the stairs, "but the new boy doesn't wish to be subjected to your endless vulgarity on the subject of bodily appendages and functions."

The whiteness of Cygnet Sackville's neck and face, glowing ectoplasmically against the blackness of the foyer and his own black clothing, including gloves, was macabre in its effect. Unlike Fancy, who was slower and more over-blown in her physicality, Mr. Sackville moved with the tight, rigid precision of a nun in an old order, accustomed to unvarying laws and inflexible routines. Even the sharp, scalloped waves of his purplish-blue hair looked implacably controlled and unalterable. The keys of Glass House hung on a silver lanyard affixed to his tightly cinched belt.

He noiselessly made his way down the treacherous staircase in a manner that would have done credit to any Hollywood star. Which made sense, Alex thought, since Sackville had at one time been a popular actor in silent movies. But when Talkies came, the crude recording apparatus of the early Thirties pitched his already thin voice much higher than it was in actual life. And there was no arguing with sound, as there is with the camera, for visual camouflage is easier. Still a young man, Cygnet was a has-been overnight, along with the rest of the exotic silent stars who failed because of thick, incomprehensible accents or otherwise unacceptable voices.

Mr. Sackville did not so much carry a beautifully arranged silver tray as compliment it with his presence. On a piece of fine ciel-bleu linen sat a silver nickel Bauhaus teapot and a mauve teacup of eggshell china. A small tea rose, the same color as the linen, nodded in a crystal bud vase. A dainty spoon rested on a folded napkin, and beside it, arranged with the same fussy precision, lay a slim silver hypodermic syringe.

"Miss E said you looked like Abe West," he said accusingly, coming close to examine Alex.

"Like Abe?" The housekeeper sounded alarmed.

"But I'd say you look more like Mary P."

"Mary P?" There was a catch in Fancy's breath. She

hurried over to squint closely in Alex's face, drawing back suddenly once she had done so.

"Lift your head and draw your lips back," Cygnet ordered, touching Alex's chin.

Alex restrained an angry impulse to protest and did as Sackville asked.

"Yes, now you look like Mary P," Cygnet said impassively. "Angry and wild and full of hate." As he spoke these words, staring full into Alex's face, the china teacup began to chatter on its saucer. Cygnet looked down at it with veiled alarm, as though finding it incomprehensible that any part of his body might not be subject to his perfect, conscious control. He furtively moved the tray to his other hand and watched despisingly as a spasm shot down the arm and made his hand shake.

"Mary P, my poor baby," Fancy was moaning. "Are you Mary P come back like all the rest of the dead?"

"Get back in your cage if you're going to slobber," Cygnet hissed, thrusting the tray into Fancy's hands. "What ridiculous lies have you been telling him?"

Fancy, her face smeared with emotion, slammed the tray down on a black, almost invisible ledge that protruded slightly from one wall. The tray looked as though it were balanced in space. "You let her die here," she said. "Hating us. Cursing us."

"She did things she shouldn't have done and she paid the price," Cygnet replied. Folding his arms, he now walked around Alex, openly appraising him and shaking his head disapprovingly. "Not only are those shoes of yours inappropriate for morning wear, boy, they are damaging to my floors. Anyone who wears shoes in my house must have felt backing attached to the soles."

"*Your* house," Fancy mocked. "Glass House isn't yours."

"I designed it. I had it built."

"And then lost it," taunted the housekeeper. "When they heard your voice, you lost it. Hilda destroyed you when she wrote that you sounded like a capon in heat. Destroyed you. And you had no choice but to sell to Mabel Eastlake, who *could* talk, and whose voice became a legend."

"You may soon be a legend yourself," Cygnet said, stiffening. Again the spasm shot down his arm, but this time he clamped his right hand with his left and held it. "I hope you brought some more practical shoes to wear while you're helping the monkey," he said to Alex.

Alex said he had his Nikes.

"What are those? Are they black?"

"No, blue and yellow."

Cygnet shook his head with prim disgust. "I couldn't bear to see them on my floors. They would match nothing. Don't you have anything in white? The help always used to dress in white. Miss E and I had Travis Banton design special outfits for them."

"Tennis shorts and a white shirt?" Alex suggested.

"This isn't Wimbledon, boy, and you won't be playing much tennis."

"What's the difference what I wear? No one's going to see me."

"*I* am going to see you," said the voice of Mabel Eastlake.

Alex turned to locate the voice. Fancy pointed the end of her mop to a corner of the ceiling. Mounted there was a small rotating security camera.

"Mind your angles, darling, because you're being filmed," Fancy said. "You may as well get used to being in the pictures because she's going to be watching everything you do. And as a director, she's even more dictatorial than Otto Kranzler used to be."

"Because I insist on a certain style around me," said the voice of Mabel Eastlake, "as Cyggie well knows."

"Style," Cygnet agreed, "is the only thing that separates us from the apes—and even then," he said, looking meaningfully at Fancy, "it's sometimes difficult to tell one from the other."

"You're the monkey gland expert, darling," Fancy countered. "I never touch the stuff."

"No need to," Cygnet said. "Your Simian soul shines through without it." He turned with a slight bow to the camera. "I will see that the new boy is properly outfitted, Miss E."

"You need a drink, poor darling," Fancy said, pushing open a black door Alex hadn't seen and leading him down into the next room. "We *all* need a drink after what we've been through these last couple of days."

"You mean to tell me," Alex whispered, "that Miss Eastlake sees and hears everything?"

"Boring, isn't it?" Fancy said, motioning him over to a smoothly curved chrome bar. "It's enough to drive a person to drink. What will you have, darling?"

The entire room, along with the three of them contained within it, was weirdly reflected in an etched deep blue mirror that stretched the length of the bar. Another darkly odd spatial effect that made Alex almost dizzy. Except for the mirror itself, and the chrome beneath it, every visible surface, as in the foyer, was black and reflective.

"This, darling, is called the Black and Blue Room," Fancy explained, "because people tend to stumble out of it. The Bar, you might call it. Which Mr. Sackville planned as a reflection of his overall personality. No windows because when you're drinking it's too difficult to face the reality of the outside world. The outside world, after all, is why you're drinking."

"Beautiful piano." Alex touched F.

"Take your finger off that key!" Cygnet commanded. "You may touch things, boy, when you're cleaning them, and then only if you are wearing gloves."

"Join me in a Tequila Mockingbird, darling," Fancy said. "It will take your mind off any woes you may have now that you're stuck here with all of us. Now my Mockingbirds are perfectly deadly and I made them up myself. Three parts good Mexican tequila to one part Pernod, for a dark licorice taste, and then a few drops of Moxie to blacken it all and make it match your heart." She turned to Cygnet with malicious courtesy.

"Hemlock for you, Mr. Sackville? Or something to put a little hair on those itty bitty titties?"

Cygnet ignored her and turned to Alex. "You have yet to meet Cocaine," he said.

"Cocaine?"

"Our puddy tat, our great big puddy," Fancy lisped.

What passed for a frozen grin appeared on Cygnet's face. "Just walk into the next room, boy, and look into the inner garden, and there you'll see her."

"And here—take a Mockingbird with you," Fancy said, handing Alex a drink.

Alex pushed open the blue-mirrored door they indicated and entered the next room. A sudden change. An immediate, startling difference. The room was flooded with light from within and without. The far exterior wall, curved and amazing, was glass from floor to ceiling. The view beyond was so vast that Alex knew he could not take it all in now and at once. He turned instead to the inner source of light.

Through more glass walls, but to his left, an enormous inner courtyard in the style of a Roman villa could be viewed. It was slightly artificial, like the planned habitat for tropical animals in a zoo. Open to the sky, wildly overgrown with tropical vegetation, the area enclosed a hothouse jungle. A small, curved balcony protruded from one wall. A grass hut, roped with vines, stood in a grove of tall bird-of-paradise and trumpeting lilies. There was a large pool and the green jungle air was thick with the trapped cries, whistles, rattlings, chatterings and laments of exotic birds.

What Alex first assumed to be a primitive sculpture turned out to be a colossal statue of Mabel Eastlake, eyeless, its stone face partially destroyed. Like the Venus de Milo, Miss Eastlake was armless. She was posed with one leg thrust forward, toe pointed down. And what had been intended as a bright alluring smile now looked, amid the destruction of the face, like the agonized jeer of a captive monster.

Beside the statue grew a banyon tree, and on one of its twisted, muscular branches Cocaine lay, taking the sun.

Alex dropped his glass, shattering it, and stood frozen among the shards.

"You're here to clean up messes, boy, not make them," said the irate voice of Cygnet.

Alex was unable to take his eyes off the white panther, which leapt off the branch and slowly approached the glass partition. "Sorry," he wheezed, "surprised—didn't expect—"

"What didn't you expect, darling?" Fancy asked, appearing in the doorway with her drink.

"That," Alex said, nodding his head in Cocaine's direction.

The cat moved with deliberate, lascivious grace, staring at Alex with hostile blue eyes.

"But she said you liked cats," Fancy said, grunting as she bent over to pick up the broken glass Cygnet was pointing to. "I'm the one who hates 'em. Don't I? Don't I?" She tapped on the glass wall. Cocaine, in response, cocked her head and opened her mouth to snarl, banging on the glass with a paw as Fancy continued to tease her. "If anyone ever got in and tried to hurt Miss Eastlake, her giant white pussy would take care of him fast enough—wouldn't you?

Wouldn't you, darling?" Jingling the pieces of glass in her hand, she turned back to Alex. "The things they do to pets around here! She had to be declawed because her toenails were worse than high heels on Mr. Sackville's floors. But of course, darling, a cat without her nails is no different from a woman without hers, and she never forgave them for that. Then she went into heat. Have you ever heard a panther on the make, darling? They scream. They scream like terrified women. So they had her sex removed. But she yowled and growled and screamed anyway, so finally they had her vocal cords snipped. Can you imagine a worse fate for a woman, darling? Not being able to scratch, scream or screw?"

It may have been Fancy planting the suggestion, it may have been a sound in his own blood or the outraged primal spirit of the animal itself, but Alex at that moment was certain that he did, in fact, hear or *sense* a scream. A faint, buried sound of pain or terror rose in a gathering spurt somewhere within the field of his awareness.

Fancy stopped talking. Cygnet betrayed no emotion. Perhaps they hadn't heard it. But if they had, Alex thought, they know that I heard it too. He spoke quickly, wanting to erase the sound, the sensation. "Do you let her out?" he asked.

"Of course, darling," said Fancy. "Coop up a frustrated woman too long and she's likely to turn on you."

"Miss Eastlake allows the animal to retain its hunting instinct by feeding it live prey," Cygnet added. "Small imported mammals."

"Cats only hunt when they're hungry," Fancy said reassuringly.

"And she's starving right now," Cygnet added in an undertone.

A tap on the shoulder sent Alex reeling around. The Child, flushed and breathless, his loose silk jersey fallen to expose one burnished shoulder, was carrying a basket of fruits and freshly picked flowers. He stood without saying anything, clearly intending the basket to be for Alex.

"How very extraordinary," Cygnet said, narrowing his eyes in Alex's direction. "Vulgar looking things," he sniffed, examining the poppies and marguerites heaped in with the glistening fruits. "I've told him over and over that nothing but orchids, lilies and roses are allowed in here."

"I adore vulgar flowers, don't you?" Fancy said, limping over to console the Child, who had tensed and was scowling bitterly at Cygnet. "They look so real. The Child grows all of our favorite flowers down in his own special garden by the gazebo, don't you? Well, don't be rude, darling," she said abruptly to Alex. "Tell him thank you. He won't hear you but he'll know what you mean."

Alex reached for the basket and thanked the Child, who smiled sheepishly at him.

"And now to clean up that spill, boy. In the old days, Miss Eastlake would have made you lick it up."

"Wait, darling," Fancy said. "I have the utterly perfect cleaning solution." After a brief silent consultation, she sent the Child into the inner garden through a door that was barely visible in the glass wall. Once inside, he coaxed the panther to his side.

When Cygnet wasn't looking, Fancy quickly deposited the broken glass in a wide-mouthed vase and then turned with a nervous smile—catching Alex's observant eye—to the inner garden. "They're like brother and sister," she said, looking in. "Cocaine grew up with the Child, you know. He raised her for Miss Eastlake. We needed a pet in the house after Kilimanjaro died. It was the only thing that would console the Child and I won't tell you all the lies and all the dreadful things Miss Eastlake had to do to get him that cat. It's such a rare animal that if anyone knew we had it they'd arrest us and take her to a zoo somewhere. Cocaine, I mean, not Miss Eastlake."

"Miss Eastlake," the drowsy, amplified voice of the star reminded them, "was in a zoo for her entire career. People staring, staring, staring at her."

"Miss Eastlake was as rare as Cocaine is," Cygnet said reverently.

"Yes, darling, she was," Fancy whispered, and then pointed a chipped red nail and said to Alex, "That statue was part of Paradise Studio's Star Sculpture series. It was exhibited by the front gates, and fans traveled for thousands of miles to touch Mabel Eastlake's stone toe. They thought it would give them luck, poor fools. Her arms were held out like so, hands extended so she looked as if she were blessing them. When the studio burned down, everything pertaining to our revered Miss Eastlake was destroyed except that statue."

The Child now had Cocaine by nothing more than the scruff of her neck and was leading her toward the door. The cat was resisting and looked tense and unpredictable, her ears flattened, her lips raised from her front teeth. Alex wanted to run from the room. He closed his eyes and took a deep breath.

"Another male in the house—she may be jealous," Cygnet said. "Let her smell the new boy, Child, to get used to him—as I suppose we all must."

"Oh Christ—no—that's all right . . ."

"Don't ever let her know that you're afraid of her!" barked Fancy. "Animals smell fear and use it to their advantage. After all, darling, she's afraid of you, too."

"Yeah, but she has teeth," Alex stammered, holding his breath again as the animal's wet snout gingerly sniffed at his crotch. An eternity passed before the Child led Cocaine over to the spilled drink. The cat slowly, savoringly, licked up the puddle.

"She wants her elevenses too, doesn't her," Fancy

cooed, keeping a distance.

Kneeling beside the cat, stroking it, wrestling with it, the Child reminded Alex of a boy who wants to hear his favorite pet praised. When he smiled up at Alex, as if to show him that the animal meant no harm, Alex nodded woodenly back. He did not want to give the keeper of Cocaine any reason to dislike him. Heated from his exertions, the Child led the animal back into the inner garden and let her go, then stripped off his clothes and dove naked, exultantly, into the pool. Both Cygnet and Fancy were at the glass wall, watching.

"Tarzan, and he doesn't even know it," Fancy said. "Sometimes I think it's good that he can't hear the world. That's his world, in there. Miss Eastlake gave that to him."

"You mean he lives out there?" Alex said.

"In his *hut*," Cygnet replied, emphasizing his disapproval with a sniff. "The one thing in Glass House I did not *design*. The Child made it all by himself; just took over in there once Miss Eastlake said he might."

"I'm sorry. If you don't mind, I think I need to lie down for a couple of minutes," Alex said, cradling his basket of fruit.

The somnolent voice of Mabel Eastlake came over the intercom. "Fancy, take Mr. Klein to his room. He can *rest* until lunch, even though he's done absolutely nothing. And Cygnet, you come to me at once. There's something pressing that I must discuss with you before slumber."

5.

Alex paced and repaced the length of his room. "You can be a coward," he said to himself, without much conviction. Plans kept forming in his head, plans he did not want to act on, but which, because they were based on good intentions, and he had been raised to be a good boy, would not let him go.

A very strange story was gradually unfolding before him, a story hidden for decades and revealed now, through the weight of time, by looks, gestures, tones of voice. For all its outward purity of design, the spiritual atmosphere of Glass House was dense and disturbed, full of hostilities barely held in check by the daily rituals of the place.

Alex had a frustratingly incomplete sense of something urgent and awful going on just outside the range of his own knowledge—and participation. He questioned himself now as to whether or not he really wanted to know more, to learn things that might then lead to necessary action. "You can be a coward," he told himself again.

But if he left, what of the biography? And what of Hilda Hatter? For he was convinced that the missing columnist was hidden somewhere in Glass House. He even thought he knew where.

Enough was enough. Someone had to know about this and advise him what to do. His habitually communicative New Yorker tongue positively ached to tell Frank, one of his friends or even his therapist, exactly what had so far happened. To gain some perspective on recent events he had, he felt, to hear himself describe what was going on. But there was, of course, no telephone—just as Miss Eastlake had promised.

His nervous sense of unprotectedness was increased tenfold by the absence of a lock on his door.

"These were all servants' rooms, back when we had houseboys," Fancy had told him, "and since Boyd always hired ambitious young Mexicans, Miss Eastlake always assumed they were ambitious young thieves. She would periodically have Cygnet burst in to inspect the rooms for her, surprise inspections, anytime, day or night. She didn't want them to be warned by the sound of a key in the lock."

Alex's room was somewhere under the east wing of the house, the backside of Glass House, as it were, where the social hierarchy was made particularly manifest by the small size and sparseness of the room as well as by its proximity to the kitchen and housekeeping cupboards. A collector would have paid an astronomical price for its original Deco fittings, but in Alex's eyes it remained a servant's room. It was, or seemed to be, slightly below ground level, and chilly as a result. It was impossible to be certain just *where* it was, for the windows were glass brick and the room's inhabitant received only an indistinct impression of the world outside.

It was access to the view, as Alex would eventually discover, that contributed to one's sense of power in Glass House. Here, just as in New York, your importance was measured by what and how much you saw from your window.

And yet this room was probably a deluxe suite compared to Hilda Hatter's quarters.

Much of the afternoon Alex had spent trying to get

his bearings. The size of Glass House, however, and the intricacy of its design, baffled immediate comprehension. He roughly understood that the house was divided into two rectangular wings, one on either side of the central axis that led from the foyer into the Black and Blue Room, extended into the next enormous gallery, where the Child's inner garden could be viewed or entered to the left, and ended at the great curved wall of glass with its extraordinary view south and west. Mabel Eastlake's private quarters were atop a second story built along the line of this center axis.

The wings were designed with long vistas from one room to the next, then to the one beyond and the one beyond that, creating an almost hallucinatory perspective, especially since each room was stepped and graded and peculiar in the materials used to create it.

From the central axis, doors leading from the foyer in front or opening onto the connecting glass corridors in the rear took one into the east or west wings. Glass corridors formed the southern face of the house and the view from them was casually stupendous. A high terrace just outside overlooked the rest of the terraced and landscaped gardens.

To be as far removed from one another as possible, and perhaps from the demanding Miss Eastlake as well, Cygnet and Fancy occupied opposite ends of the west and east wings, respectively. Where, exactly, their rooms were located was a matter of some mystery to Alex, for at its furthest reaches the formal logic of Glass House dissolved into abstract speculation. Fancy was close to the kitchens. Some rooms in "her" east wing looked into the Child's inner garden. Others had no windows at all.

Cygnet's private domain was beyond a projection room located beside the central gallery of the house. Below the projection room, reached by endless corridors and stairs, there was another level of the house. Here, close to the protective Mr. Sackville, the wardrobe rooms were located. Earlier in the afternoon, to be outfitted, Alex had followed Miss Eastlake's dresser down into this part of Glass House.

They entered a long, softly lit vault with walls of dark cedar, the pungent smell muffled by sharp, coldly dry air. On either side of the narrow corridor were recessed doors. As he led Alex deeper into the corridor Cygnet became something of a tour guide.

"The wardrobe of Mabel Eastlake is kept in darkness. Temperature and humidity are carefully controlled. We had this storage vault built after consulting with experts in the Metropolitan Museum's wardrobe collection. We wanted Miss Eastlake's clothes to be preserved for all time, just like her films. And I like to think," he said, turning his tight white face to Alex, "that on the Day of Judgment, all of Mabel Eastlake's clothes will rise from Glass House and accompany her to the judgment seat. God would have to let her in, just on the bias of her gowns. Don't you agree?" His smile was as dry and sharp as the air.

"I didn't know clothes could be refrigerated," Alex said.

"Oh yes." Since their descent, Cygnet's voice had become mysterious, almost reverent. Its curiously high pitch, however, was acoustically heightened by the wood and set Alex's teeth on edge. "Clothes on ice. Just like careers, boy." Sentiment crept into his voice as he stopped and took a deep breath. "It's like coming down to an old family burial vault, this place, where one's ancestors rest and wait for one to join them." He pointed a gloved finger to the silver plates on the doors. "Every costume from every picture Miss Eastlake made. We made Paradise Studios agree to give her everything she wore. *I* made them put it in her contract. They're all here: *Moonstruck, Daring Lady, Fast and Loose, Two-Faced Woman, Hearts Aflame, Silent Fury*. Do you hear how still it is?" he asked. "Stiller even than the rest of the house. When one hears nothing day after day, boy, one begins to detect the different qualities of silence. One becomes a connoisseur of quiet."

"I've always been used to noise," Alex said, thinking of far-away New York and its endless whooping sirens, roaring subways, ranting lunatics and reverberating streets.

"Everyone is until they come to Glass House. Sound! Noise! There's too much of it in the world. It's only in silence that one can really hear anything. Hear oneself. And when I had Glass House built, when I supervised every detail of its construction, I saw to it that there would be as little *noise* as possible. I wanted sound to be absorbed, as it's absorbed in some great cathedral. This house and its silence are mine, boy!" he said vehemently, fixing Alex with a sharp gray eye. "I know Glass House better than anyone. I *appreciate* it. No person can ever give one the silent submission and total pleasure that an object can. And, in any case, the world outside these gates never had much meaning for me. How I despised it, despised all the false and bloated emotions of Hollywood. Glass House for me was the attainment of everything I needed. Can you understand that, boy? It is satisfying in ways that mere love never is."

"Glass House was yours before Mabel Eastlake bought it?"

"And it was mine after she and Fancy Barlow moved in," Cygnet said. "I made them submit to its will, which is my will. But for the longest time Miss Eastlake resisted. Glass House back then was always filled with coarse people and their cheap noise. Animals in a zoo. Gibberish. One hated them and their disrespect of one's home. Pigs at a banqueting table, hardly tasting the food they shoved into their greedy mouths—ach!" he exclaimed, disgust weighting his face. "To see them eat was enough to make a grown man vomit. Idiot organisms that never stopped moving or ingesting. It was like a movie that never stopped running.

Until finally there would come a lull, and all the people would be gone or dead drunk or drugged and sleeping. That was when one could walk around Glass House again, the only one awake, and gather it back up into one's possession, listening to its immense quiet." He gave his keys a faint, meditative jangle and continued down the corridor.

Desperate Woman, possibly the most unusual of Mabel Eastlake's films, happened to be Alex's personal favorite. Seeing the title engraved on one of the silver plates, he reached for the door, freezing when Sackville's tense and suddenly furious voice screamed down the corridor.

"That door is locked, boy! All of these doors are locked! Don't ever presume to touch anything or open anything in this house without first consulting Miss Eastlake or myself."

The reprimand, which may have been just another example of Cygnet's neurotic fussiness, was cut short when the steel door at the end of the hallway suddenly opened and the Child, evidently expected, entered carrying a tray. Seeing him, Cygnet quickly pushed in front of Alex and hurried down the corridor, but not before Alex had noticed the glimmer of another silver hypodermic on the tray.

"What are you doing down here?" Cygnet shouted at the Child, pushing him out the door.

Before he disappeared, the Child's eyes found Alex's and seemed to convey some message that Alex could not read.

The instant they were outside, Alex tried the door of *Desperate Woman*. It was, as Cygnet had said, locked. But a small, square object on the floor next to it caught his attention. An earring, identical to the one he had found on the front steps, with the same design, or monogram. *HH*. And suddenly Alex saw that the design *was* a monogram. The very same he had seen at the top of Hilda Hatter's notepaper.

As quietly as he could he rattled the knob and slapped the door with the palm of his hand. "Can you hear me? Is someone in there?" The stifled cry he had heard, or imagined, earlier now came back to haunt him.

Cygnet re-entered the corridor and Alex quickly pocketed the earring.

"The Child is evidently confused by your presence in the house," Cygnet said, moving rigidly back down the corridor. "He's no better than a dumb beast at times. Now I believe the houseboy's uniforms are stored in the back of *Silent Fury.*

He unlocked the door and Alex slowly followed him inside. Here, on a posturing bevy of Mabel Eastlake mannequins, the superlative gowns created for her in *Silent Fury* gleamed and sparkled. Even in the dim light the fabrics and tailoring conveyed a vision of sleek Thirties extravagance.

It was the sight of all the staring Mabel Eastlake eyes that gave the small room its queer, entranced intensity, eyes that silently and unseeingly watched and searched and stared.

"If I didn't approve of these clothes," Cygnet said, lifting a piece of gossamer and letting it flow through his fingers like water, "Mabel Eastlake would not wear them. Because I knew that body better than anyone, better even than Abe West or her lover, Flame, knew it. And I knew exactly how to clothe it. Kranzler didn't need to tell *me* that Mabel Eastlake could never be anything less than perfect. I knew that. Never a hair out of place or a false eyelash missing. A goddess at all times. And she came to depend on me utterly. She wouldn't go to sleep at night until I had arranged her in bed, and in the morning no one saw her until I made her perfect and presentable."

He has Hilda Hatter locked and drugged down here, Alex thought.

"What size, boy?" Cygnet asked, looking Alex up and down, his lips pursed. "We always had lots of boys working for us—Boyd insisted on that, of course—and some of them were small and overweight, like you."

Alex, who had painfully acquired a washboard stomach, who did five hundred sit-ups every morning before breakfast, ignored the taunt. "I could get into a twenty-eight waist."

"By squeezing, you mean." To emphasize its size, Cygnet momentarily clenched his hands around his own tiny waist, and then turned to flip through a rack of garments, pulling out a black uniform. "Here. Take off your clothes and try this one."

"Try it on here?"

"Do you want a dressing room?" Cygnet cried, exasperated. "If you were a star of Miss Eastlake's caliber, boy, you'd have a dressing room—the biggest on the lot—and your own dresser. Mabel Eastlake had the kind of body that deserves great respect and artistry. You, so far as I can see, do not." And before Alex could say anything, before he even knew how to react, Sackville's long, spidery fingers were unbuttoning Alex's shirt.

Alex's arm protectively shot up and he stepped back.

"Haven't you ever known the luxury of being undressed by a man?" Sackville laughed sarcastically, removing his hand. His face was suddenly close and his voice serious. "Don't think for a moment, boy, that you can move in and take over and make Miss Eastlake trust and depend on you. She is mine, boy. She belongs to me." He took Alex's chin between two very strong gloved fingers and pushed his head back. "But I never really thought for a moment that you came to Glass House to help Miss Eastlake. You're here for some other reason."

It was catch himself or be caught. Regaining his control and his temper was difficult. "I'll undress myself, thanks," he said, stepping behind several of the Eastlake mannequins.

"Everything looks so cheap today," Cygnet sniffed, fingering the material as Alex hung his shirt on one of Miss Eastlake's arms.

Alex hunched his shoulders against the cold and the disquieting discovery he had made about Hilda Hatter. "That was not cheap, Mr. Sackville, believe me."

"One didn't say it was cheap—nothing is cheap these days—one said it *looked* cheap. That's one thing Mabel Eastlake and I could never tolerate. Joan Crawford may have done her shopping at Bullock's, but never Miss Eastlake. She was custom-made by the greatest couturiers in the world."

"She always looked terribly elegant in her movies," Alex agreed, slipping into the trousers Cygnet held out for him. "Even when she was supposed to be poor."

"Poverty demands a certain style to make it bearable," Cygnet said. "That was the secret of her success, for even the poorest of women can dream, can't they? Mabel Eastlake was a by-product, a *buy-product*, of the Depression. All over the country, all over the world, people were desperately poor. But the fools saved their quarters and went to the Bijou Dream to see my Mabel Eastlake. They needed to see her rise from the gutter to the heights of glamor and success. The all-American dream. They didn't know that you never leave your gutter behind."

Alex put on the white shirt and coat of the uniform and stepped out. "It fits pretty well."

"Except for your body shape you could almost pass for a woman," Cygnet said. Again the narrowed, clinical eyes. "Tell me, boy, have you ever had a homosexual experience?"

Alex, startled, anxious about the consequences of saying yes, shook his head.

"Never even danced with a man?" Cygnet persisted.

Not liking this sudden curiosity, Alex said, "No, never."

Cygnet regarded him with contemptuous scorn. "You should have seen Mabel Eastlake and Hilda Hatter on the dance floor, boy. That was a sight no one ever forgot and no one dared to laugh at. Two of the richest, most powerful women in Hollywood, dancing close in a slow tango. Hilda in black voided velvet and Miss Eastlake, dressed by me, in a tight gown of white silk marquisette. Dancing together at Jimmy's club, The Black Orchis, right under his nose so that he had to see them."

Why was he suddenly talking about Hilda Hatter? A bluff? Alex told himself not to react. "Was Miss Eastlake having an affair with Hilda Hatter?" he asked casually.

Cygnet let out his thin, sharp laugh. "Miss Hatter was madly in love with Mabel Eastlake, boy. Does that shock you? But Miss Eastlake was perverse enough to stay in love with Jimmy Flame, even after Flame sold her to Kranzler."

"Sold her?" Alex was shocked now.

"Sold the rights to her. She had been Jimmy's exclusive property before Kranzler got her. You know, boy, they always whispered that your adored Mabel Eastlake worked in Jimmy's brothel before she became a star. That was one of those rumors that would never go away."

"They say that about every star. Either they made a pornographic movie or they worked as prostitutes."

"Mabel Eastlake did both," Cygnet said, watching for a reaction from Alex. "Flame had a strange hold on her, and for a while she used Hilda to make him jealous. No one dared to say no to the Mad Hatter! And then there was Kranzler with all of his insane demands, and Boyd Powers, an idiot running his race towards hell. Fools! All of them fools! They all got exactly what they deserved, except Hilda. The Mad Hatter didn't get what was coming to her. She escaped."

"Escaped what?"

"The fate that should have struck her down and ripped her filthy tongue out of her mouth," Cygnet cried savagely, a spasm shooting his arm out. "Miss Hatter, you know, thought she was in charge of the Fate Department in Hollywood. She doled out favors to those she liked, and destroyed the ones she didn't." The veins on the side of his head were distended with rage.

Knowledge of his vulnerability in this subterranean place, in the company of this strange, unpredictable man, reduced Alex's resolve to outright panic. He moved instinctively towards the door.

"Wait, boy. We must find you a pair of felt-soled shoes." Sackville's mocking tone quickly returned. "I suppose we've been in Miss Eastlake's sepulchre too long, and you're getting nervous. Well, lifting a shroud to gaze at the secrets death likes to keep for his own amusement is never wise for the uninitiated." He fixed Alex with a chilling gaze. "And of course we wouldn't want to run into Abe West, would we?"

"Abe West?"

"You didn't know Glass House was haunted?"

It was impossible to tell whether Cygnet was being serious or not, and Alex wasn't certain that he wanted to know.

"I have myself, with my own eyes, boy, seen Abe West. Down here, in fact."

That name again. "Who is Abe West?" he asked.

"Glass House is strange that way," Cygnet said, ignoring Alex's question. "When you're alone, you may see, for just the space of a moment, out of a corner of your eye, the reflection of something—or someone—not yourself."

Alex could hardly find his own voice. "This Abe West. He's dead?"

"I didn't say that, boy." And Cygnet smiled.

Later, when Alex asked Fancy if Mabel Eastlake or

anyone in Glass House was diabetic, hoping that this might logically explain the hypodermic syringes, Fancy let out a gruff, snorting laugh. "Diabetic? Yes, darling, in the sense of not having an ounce of natural sweetness in her, Mabel Eastlake is diabetic."

"I meant," Alex whispered, "does she have to give herself insulin?"

Fancy fished a pink, handrolled cigarette out of her pocket, offered one to Alex, and screwed her own into a red ebony holder. "Well, darling, if that's insulin she's shooting up, it must give her the very sweetest of dreams." Holding the cigarette out from her body, Fancy laughed at her own joke. This was a typical Mabel Eastlake screen gesture, and Alex was surprised to see it so well done. When she smoked, Fancy had an extravagant habit of flicking out the tip of her tongue and picking real or imagined tobacco from it. "That's her sleep-a-bye, darling, that Miss Eastlake is shooting up. Her forty winks juice. When Cygnet brings Miss Eastlake her tea on a tray, he's removing her consciousness."

By now Alex was almost certain they were keeping Hilda Hatter heavily sedated down in the wardrobe vault. But what was Fancy's part in all of this? How much did she know, to what degree was she participating? He had a sudden impulse to ask her, but did not know whether he could afford to trust Fancy or not.

"Sometimes I take a shot myself," Fancy continued, opening a small refrigerator. Inside, stacked neatly, coldly, precisely, were dozens of the silver syringes. "Cygnet may be a royal pain in the ass in every other respect, darling, but he is a wizard when it comes to concocting herbal cocktails. This one is really quite marvelous, but very strong and definitely not recommended for newcomers to the game." She ticked off the ingredients. "Glands from virgin monkeys and sperm from fertile elephants and every vitamin in the alphabet and minerals up the old wazoo. Puts you out instantly, and when you wake up you don't care *what* sex you are, you feel so much stronger and better. It takes years off your mental life, believe me, and keeps you young forever. Or so they think." She slammed the refrigerator door with her left buttock and motioned for Alex to follow her.

"But it's *their* whole diet, you know," she said in a low, confiding voice. "Another one of Cygnet's recent obsessions."

"What do you mean?"

"He's weaned her away from all solid foods," said Fancy, shaking her head as she led Alex through the food storage pantries. The shelves were stacked and packed with everything from soup to nuts, and enough of it to feed a conquering army. They passed into a boxlike room beyond, where three enormous freezers hummed their icy hymns. "And you know people without good solid food in their bellies tend to be a little . . . crazy. Fanatic." She now raised one of the massive freezer doors to reveal, among cold, swirling mists, an enormous array of stone-hard meats, and stood back with a gloved finger to her mouth as she deliberated on her choice. "I've been on starvation diets, darling, and believe me, I know. You start to see things. You begin to hallucinate. If you aren't careful, you stop believing that you have a body at all—which is what our darling Virgin Queen with his tiny scented farts would like to believe, of course. He can't bear anything so vulgar as an ordinary human body."

She stubbed out her cigarette in a pillbox ashtray covered with shagreen and set with a fiery red stone. "Untanned sharkskin," she said, handing it to Alex to admire. "The ruby is real, of course. I'm completely allergic to artificial gems. A gift from Miss Hatter, who said it matched my true personality. She knew how I loved accessories. I've always felt a profound need for them, props, things to hold onto, little hankies to twist, *men*." She cast a flirtatious glance at Alex, who returned what he hoped was an ambiguous smile. "My little fetishes, Kranzler called them. Well," she said, looking down at them, "I never knew what to do with my hands. Now what shall we have for supper?" And she turned her attention back to the freezer. "Those two can starve themselves into stick figures, but not me. When I got the drift of what was happening to the food supply around here, I made the Child stock up for those of us who *do* eat. I ordered tons of candy and whole sides of beef, freshly killed, and cut them up myself, just like Abe West taught me years ago. Abe was always looking for any excuse to have a knife in his hand, you know. So we have enough here for the rest of our lives, and it doesn't matter if Cygnet refuses to give us money for shopping. Every night the Child and I fry up a couple of big steaks for ourselves and have fresh canned vegetables or something from one of his gardens. It makes Cygnet furious, but he can't come close to the kitchen because the smell of fried meat makes him sick."

"I wanted to ask you," Alex said, "just when does Miss Eastlake take her sleep-a-bye? Is it at some regular hour every day?"

"No, it changes," Fancy said, prying loose various cuts of meat and tossing them to one side. "Whenever life becomes too horrible for her, when she can't bear the guilt, out she goes. But generally it's towards morning that she asks Cygnet to come and kill her. We call it Miss Eastlake's Profound Slumber." She lifted a finger and an eyebrow and whispered, "She's sleeping now, can't you tell? The whole house changes when she's out. She wouldn't let me stand here talking to you, darling, if she was upstairs monitoring. And I may be going blind, but I've lived here long enough to know by sense alone just when she's watching. I know how to avoid every camera in this place, too, which absolutely infuriates her." She laughed heartily.

"It's unpleasant, that sense of being watched," Alex admitted. "Makes everything you do feel suspect."

"Why do you think she watches?" Fancy said. "It's only the guilty who try to make others feel guilty."

"It makes everything seem so—important," Alex said.

"When it's all so fucking trivial," Fancy agreed. "Well, I'm used to being watched, darling, so it doesn't bother me in the same way. I've always been on camera. It's just that *she's* my director now, or so the bitch thinks. Half the time I'm acting for her. And she doesn't know it, of course, but half the time I'm watching her, too. Brrrrr!" She stepped back from the freezer with a shiver. "Alex, darling, you look strong for your size. Can you pry out those three fillets for us? They're down near the bottom."

Alex, smaller than she, reached with difficulty into the freezing depths and tried to pull loose the cuts she indicated.

"She always wanted to be me, you know," the house-keeper said.

Fancy's *idée fixe*, Alex thought; it's compulsively mentioned every chance she has. "I can't get these loose," he said.

"Well climb in, darling, and then you'll have better leverage."

He hesitated. No, ridiculous. But the thought had occurred to him that if she slammed the door down on his head he'd be dead from hypothermia within minutes. He braced his hands on the side of the freezer and vaulted in.

"Everything she knows she learned from me," Fancy went on. "I was the ambitious one back then. I'm the one who did the hard work and paved the way. She just took over at that point. There was no comparison between us, of course, and she hated me for it. I was always prettier. Funnier. Had far more class. And, darling, before I gave it up for Lent one year, I had style. Jimmy and Kranzler brought out my *true*, *original* style. That, my dear, which cannot be faked. That which is given only to a rare handful of true artists."

"You have a real style about you now, Fancy," Alex said, kicking at the frozen fillets, his breath appearing in the frosty air.

"Of course I do, darling. I know how to act like a woman. She learned that from me, too. Jimmy would say, 'Act like a woman who wants to be a man. Let them know you have the balls.' And I would. Because he beat it into me."

Alex asked if it were true that Mabel Eastlake had worked in Flame's brothel.

"Who told you that?" Fancy asked in surprise, coming over to peer into the freezer.

"Mr. Sackville."

Up shot an eyebrow. "The Virgin Queen told you that? Well, darling, if that old capon thinks his cock-a-doodle-do is going to grow back by telling you dirty stories about Miss Eastlake, I don't see why I shouldn't have the same privilege." A voluptuously malicious twinkle shone in her myopic eyes.

And Alex suddenly saw the potential benefits of playing one person off against the other. A way to gain more biographical information. Be loyal to no one, not even Miss Eastlake. He watched Fancy over the top of the freezer as he said, "Mr. Sackville told me that she had worked in Jimmy Flame's brothel and made pornographic movies."

For a moment Fancy's thoughts seemed to stumble visibly in her face. She looked uncertain, nervous. "Did he tell you that Hilda Hatter was in possession of some film footage and has been blackmailing Miss Eastlake with it for over forty years?" And then she let out an unexpectedly bitter charge. "I hate this place, darling, and what it makes you. Hollywood *eats* you and not where it feels good. Blackmail! That's a venial sin in these parts. The footage that Hilda has, that she *stole* the night of Miss Eastlake's instant retirement, that footage, darling, has kept all of us like scared rabbits all these years. Hilda's mattress has been stuffed with our fortune for a very long time because with that film Hilda was the only one alive outside of Glass House who *knew*. . ." She stopped short.

Alex gave a last mighty wrench to the frozen steaks. "Knew what?" As the ice-bound packages came loose, he fell backwards and the force of his fall caused the freezer door to slam down on top of him. It took him a fraction of a moment to realize what had happened, but by then, just as he was about to panic there in the frozen black depths, Fancy had opened the door again and was peering down at him.

"Darling, you're turning blue! Hop out of there at once!"

He needed no coaxing. But as he was clambering out, slipping on the frozen packages of meat, he was certain that he saw out of a corner of his eye, wrapped in cellophane, frozen solid, a human face. He leapt out with a pounding heart. Instantly, without knowing why, he had connected the glimpse of face to Hilda Hatter. Perhaps she wasn't downstairs, but had been carved up and frozen like a side of beef, which made another question inevitable. Who had done it, and why?

Later, when Fancy was not in the kitchen, he sneaked back to look into the deep freeze again. There was no face. "Jesus, Alex, calm down!" he said to himself.

He received no further information from Cygnet or Fancy for the rest of the afternoon. Alex Klein, the domestic, clumsily performed the household tasks Fancy assigned to him. Fancy's orders came from Cygnet, and Cygnet's, presumably, from Miss Eastlake herself.

Together, he and Fancy mopped the marble floors of the glass corridors. There was something poignant and unbearable in the sight of the old housekeeper, with her bandaged leg and odd dress clothes, silently huffing away with a mop, and Alex, forever the good boy, the ex-Boy

Scout, told her to rest while he did most of the work.

"Darling, you'll spoil me," she said gratefully, easing herself down with one of her Mockingbirds. "Can you handle a floor polisher?"

"I don't see why not."

"It's awfully large," she said.

But whenever size was mentioned in connection with his ability to do or not to do something, Alex would do it just to prove that he could. So, mopping of the corridor completed, he stood behind an enormous floor polisher, his mouth dry, and switched on the power. The machine instantly bolted away from him towards the wall of glass.

"Catch it! Darling, catch it or it'll smash everything!" Fancy cried.

Alex caught firm hold of the polisher's handles and tried to turn it away from the glass panes. The heavy machine, like something possessed, shot off in the other direction. Fancy screamed as it careened towards her. "Turn it off! Darling, turn it off!" But Alex could not let go of the handles without losing complete control of the machine. "Pull the plug!" he shouted, but by then it was unnecessary. His feet had become tangled in the cord, tightened snake-like around his ankles, and he fell over, wrenching the power plug from the wall socket.

"Darling," Fancy panted, "I thought you told Miss Eastlake that you were experienced!"

"I am," Alex insisted, untangling himself from the power cord, "but just not with floor polishers."

"We'd better leave that for the Child. I've got a million other things to do," Fancy said, yawning, "so why don't you, darling, start on the glass. You *do* know how to clean glass, don't you?"

"Of course I do."

Now the glass had to be cleaned. Everywhere. All of

it. Perfectly. Cygnet could not bear to see streaks.

As he ineptly maneuvered the elaborate glass-cleaning apparatus, terrified that he'd shatter one of the fragile, enormous panes, wincing from the sharp smell of the vinegar solution he had to use, dwarfed by the immensity of the view he was sharpening and the hopeless sensation that cleaning the glass of Glass House was like shoveling sand in the Sahara, Alex was dreading the prospect of his first night in Glass House. The front door was kept automatically locked. No one could get out of the house that way, unless Mabel Eastlake opened the door by means of a computer code. Once outside, there was no escape. The estate was surrounded by high stone walls capped with electrified fencing.

And when, after a steak dinner which he was too nervous to eat, he'd been allowed to go to his room, Alex had been unnerved to discover in one corner yet another of Miss Eastlake's surveillance cameras. His exhausted sense of privacy could tolerate just so many outrages, and he draped a pair of black underwear over the lens. So far Miss Eastlake had said nothing about this.

Now he was stalling himself, putting off the moment when he would have to go back down into the wardrobe vaults without being seen. He had to find out if Hilda Hatter *was* down there. "You can be a coward," he told himself for the last time. He had no excuses left. It didn't matter that the prisoner was a malicious and scheming old blackmailer. What mattered was that she had evidently been brought to Glass House against her will. Alex wished his sense of justice and compassion would fire him with more courage.

When he finally made his move, it was prompted by the prickling certainty that he had seen a low white indistinct outline creeping slowly along outside his windows. Jesus Christ, what *was* going on here?

*   *   *

The old woman lay on her side, her closed eyelids twitching frantically, her breath stertorous. Moaning, she rolled onto her back. Her eyelids suddenly flicked open from one darkness to another. Before consciousness claimed her one hand flew to her throat. The diamond choker was still around her neck. She felt safer.

"Mabel?" she said, her voice faint, her tongue thick in her mouth. The name and the image had pursued her throughout her drugged sleep. But she was no longer asleep and she sat up, alarmed. Mabel Eastlake mannequins surrounded her, staring with a radiant and ghastly impassivity. She knocked one over as she slowly got to her feet. When she stood up a terrible pain rippled from her skull to her toes and she groped for the solidity of a wall. She put her arms up against the wall and leaned her head against them, like a child counting for Blind Man's Bluff.

I'll work myself up for a scream, she thought, although even the idea of exertion was painful. And then she thought, Why scream? What good would it do?

She shook from her thoughts a sudden terrifying vision of herself as a rat in a trap. *Their* trap. Finally she had been caught. After all these years of accepting their terrified homage, of enjoying her undisputed power, she was now in their hands. They had waited patiently and at last they had recovered both her and the film.

She heard the sound of a key in the lock and watched, her heart pounding, as the door opened ever so slightly. "Mabel?" She waited several moments before pushing open the door. Nothing. But they were cunning.

Even the dim light in the corridor hurt her eyes. How strange to her was the renewed experience of vision! And, suddenly, how frightening. Slowly she advanced down the corridor. The steel door at the end was open. She stood with her ear to it, listening. Faint, receding footsteps.

She knew Glass House. She hadn't set foot in the

place since 1939, but it came back to her with the vividness of a recurrent dream.

The past was instantly upon her and she could not shake it off. A December night in 1939. She ran from Glass House that night, terrified at the extent of her own daring and resourcefulness. She ran from the projection room just beyond that door through that great room with the curved glass at the end, up four stairs and through the bar, up four more stairs and into the foyer, and then outside, racing like the wind down the marble staircase. She could do it then. Being younger, she could run and she had to run because she was being pursued. The wordless terror and exhilaration of that night! For the words which were her business and which had always flowed so easily and maliciously from her pen had lost their ordering power; her brain was an incoherent jungle of sounds. She could not so much as cry out. She could not describe, even to herself, what she had run from, what she had seen in the projection room—that image, that hellish, frightful, stunning reverse-image that she now carried under her arm, knowing that at last it was hers, and that if it was hers, so was Mabel Eastlake hers, and all the rest of them in Glass House. She ran from Glass House that night, leapt into her small Stutz roadster and tore off down the drive.

The potency of the past! Like a bulb storing its later growth and blossom. The inescapable design on the verge of revealing its pattern at last.

The past. Hilda tried to shake it from her as she reversed her escape route of that night in 1939. Now she crossed the foyer and descended the tier of steps leading into the Black and Blue Room. From there, another flight of steps down into the gallery where, suddenly at a loss, she stood on the great expanse of shining black floor like an entranced, solitary dancer waiting for her partner.

"So you've returned to us after all these years."

With a startled cry, Hilda tried to locate the voice.
"We've been waiting patiently for you."
"Where are you?"
There was a moment of silence. "Everywhere." Low
gloating laughter filled the room.
"You have the film back, Mabel, so you can let me go."
"Let you go?" The laughter was voluble and incredulous. "Why, were you counting on a comfortable
death at home? In your deep and dreamless sleep?"
At the word death, Hilda's hand again went to her
throat. She pressed the diamonds there as if they offered
her magical protection.
"It's true, darling, we do have the film back, but
what are we to do with you? You still have a tongue and you
can still hold a pen. My secret wouldn't be safe."
A buzzing vibration could be heard, the sound of a
hidden mechanism starting its work. And then, as Hilda
watched amazed, a wall of glass separating this room from
the inner garden slowly, with quiet finesse, like a fragile
eyelid, gave a delicate shiver and began to move. It rose
into the ceiling and the pent-up rankness of the inner jungle, suddenly freed, shaken loose, invaded the room where
Hilda stood.
"I swear I won't tell," she cried nervously. A brightly
colored bird swooped past her with a scream. "I haven't
told anyone yet, have I?"
"I don't know, have you?"
"Not a soul. Truly, darling, not a soul. And I won't.
And I'm sorry for what I've done." A large white shape began slowly to emerge from the vine-draped darkness of the
inner garden. "So very very sorry."
"How easy it is to repent when death is close at hand."
Hilda did not scream. She couldn't. A scream would
set the true gibbering terror of it all into motion. With each
quiet step the panther took towards her, she took one step

back, until she was flattened against a section of the curved glass wall at the end of the room, her heart aching with its frantic engorgement.

"Where are you?" she whispered, mindless with fear. "Show me your face, bitch, show me where you are!"

"Here, darling, here I am." A figure appeared on the small balcony overlooking the inner garden.

"I kept your secret," Hilda said, one word at a time, unable to breathe for the length of a sentence. "But I swear, I swear, I'll ruin you yet. I'll make you pay for this."

"We've paid quite enough already, Hilda, darling. And now that we have the film back, it's time to close our account with you."

Hilda turned quickly towards the glass wall. She did scream then. Standing just outside, staring in at her, was another Mabel Eastlake. This one, with a face smiling as rigidly as one of the mannequins, was holding aloft a small knife.

There could be no thought now, no planning, no calculation. The panther, dropping its weight, its eyes fixed and targeted, was slowly creeping towards her. The room filled with laughter. Hilda found the handle and burst open the door to the terrace. The Mabel Eastlake there, terrifying in the moonlight, glided swiftly towards her with the knife raised and the smile on her face. Hilda cried out as the knife came down and slit her arm. The smell of her blood was now released to the dark night air. She began to run.

Her feet remembered the layout of the gardens. She had no goal but to escape this nightmare. To escape she must run. She managed to reach the lowest level of the gardens and was gasping towards the gazebo there when the panther finally caught her. A leap. She screamed again, the sound picked up by an echoing peacock. The panther bit into her leg and pulled her down. Wounded prey, sobbing with terror, she somehow managed to drag herself on a step or two. She felt the panther's weight on her back and fell with a clumsy grunt. In her last moment of vision she saw the cat's shining, enraged, merciless eyes, the stain of her blood on its teeth. Then it was upon her, moving in for the kill. Her head was caught and pulled back in the vice of its jaw, her skull was pierced by its incisors. She was violently shaken, nothing more than a dead rabbit. The panther lifted its head and gave a silent bellow. It snuffled around her, took her diamonded neck in its mouth, and began to drag her carcass someplace where other predators would not find and demand a share of its private feast.

It was very dark in the domestics' wing. High, cantilevered windows cast down cagelike bars of shadow. Alex carefully pressed his way down the corridor until his eyes had become fully adjusted to the dimness. Soft as a cat, his bare feet chilled by ceramic floor tiles, he turned into the hallway that led, after further turnings and twistings, into Fancy's "suite." The sounds of some old Thirties dance music hovered faintly in the air.

In the kitchen he grabbed the flashlight Fancy had pointed out earlier. Hand-made for Miss Eastlake by Tiffany's, it was a memento from Otto Kranzler to celebrate the completion of *Daring Lady*, in which Eastlake played a tough female detective who falls in love with the missing man she's tracing.

He stood in front of the door that led down into the nether regions of Glass House.

And then he dared himself to do it, and did it, watching himself with amazement as he opened the door and moved stiffly down the stairs into darkness.

The silence at the bottom was intense, absolute, mixed with that mysterious and half-sorrowful smell of a generic past always given off by damp cellars. Here and there in the vague gloom were indistinct outlines of furniture and what appeared to be old stage props.

A sudden scurry and the dirty black eye of an enormous rat stared at him. Chased by his light, it whipped its long naked tail and scuttled into a darker corner.

"For Christ's sake," he whispered to himself, walking deeper into the darkness, "what the fuck are you doing?" By the time he reached the steel outer door of the wardrobe vault he was wet with fear. For he could see that it was open, and now more than ever he was compelled to see if Hilda Hatter was inside. There was no locked door as an excuse.

He shined the light down the quiet, woody corridor.

The door of the closet for *Desperate Woman* was wide open.

What would death look like when he saw it fresh, raw, undisguised? Not like death in Mabel Eastlake's movies, always done so stylishly, even bloodlessly.

Again he commanded himself to perform. He ordered his legs to walk down the corridor. At the open door, pausing, preparing himself, he took a deep breath before bombarding the closet with light.

A surprised coven of Mabel Eastlakes stared at him with refracted fury in their blind, painted eyes. It took him a moment to defuse the weird power exerted by the mannequins. His heart racing, Alex shined his light down to see what had fallen into their midst. A body. He waited a moment to catch his breath and then looked closely. It was another mannequin, bald, lying on its back, arms raised like an exultant saint or waiting lover.

Relieved, he flicked his light across the clothing. The gowns and tailored suits were sinfully voluptuous for this, the last of Mabel Eastlake's films. They represented the apotheosis of her style, which seemed to culminate at the tremulous moment when the Thirties drew to a close, Deco became Late Moderne and then extinct, and the masculine military lines of the Forties began to appear. In *Desperate Woman* Mabel Eastlake was the final fulfillment of Kranzler's vision: a sleek Deco automaton, utterly beautiful and utterly soulless. Mabel Eastlake, molded into a final Deco icon by these very clothes.

Alex turned to leave, and let out a startled gasp. Someone he had never seen before, with a face wide-eyed and outraged, was standing in the doorway, watching him. Before he could think of anything to say, fully register who or what or even what sex he'd seen, the figure had disappeared.

"Wait!" Gone to tell *them*, Alex thought. To turn me in. He shot out of the corridor after the figure, but it was gone. Now what? He switched off the flashlight and stood in the dark, considering. And then he heard a scream from somewhere upstairs. Alex raced up the stairs two at a time.

Fear confused him. Standing at the top of the stairs, his heart pounding, he had no idea where he should go or what he should look for. The Child? The mysterious figure? The source of the scream? His own escape route? And then it seemed as though Glass House itself were laughing at him and his disorientation. He could hear its echoing dark laughter.

His route was decided for him when he heard a faint clicking sound and sought to elude it. He remembered Cygnet telling him that Glass House was haunted, that he had seen Abe West down in the wardrobe rooms. Was it Abe West that Alex had seen? Who was he and what had happened to him? Alex did not want to believe, on top of everything else, in spirit manifestations. The living were frightening enough. But the terrible realization that some threatening unknown was loose in Glass House, was awake and stalking with murderous intent, unleashed the full Pandora's Box of his imagination. Every terror he could think of crowded into his head.

Retreating from any hint of movement behind him,

he got himself, somehow, back into the foyer. The Vargas portrait of Mabel Eastlake glowed from the wall with a malevolent sensuality.

Then, suddenly, in the shiny reflection of a wall, he caught sight of an approaching figure. With heart-pumping terror he concealed himself in the shadows so he wouldn't be seen. Who was it? The same figure he had seen in the wardrobe rooms? Its reflection was distorted by the mirrored concavity of the foyer wall. It could not be Fancy because there was no sign of a limp. Not Cygnet: too large. Not the Child: the Child was Alex's age, and this, whoever, whatever, it was, seemed to carry a full burden of years. The black mirrored surface of the foyer weirdly allowed Alex to follow the disembodied progress of the blurred reflection as it made its way from the Black and Blue Room through the foyer and into the first room of the east wing. Alex squeezed his eyes, bit his lip, and looked again. The image was gone.

The other sound, the faint clicking. Silence. Alex stole into the Black and Blue Room, crouching behind the bar. The door into the room beyond, the one that looked into the inner garden and terminated in the great curving wall of glass, was closed. From that room now came a steady hum, as of stage machinery being moved behind curtains.

He caught a flash of white moving past the foyer door and into the library, the first room of the west wing. A creak. The clicking sound again. It was approaching the bar. It was moving toward him.

Alex lunged for the doorhandle of the next room expecting it to resist him, but it opened easily and he almost fell in. Before he could close it there was a heavy feathery swoop of wings and an enormous parrot flew past him. It landed, cocked its head and regarded him with one mocking eye. After letting out a strange whistling cry, it began to amble down the room, its nails clicking on the floor. Alex laughed with embarrassed relief.

But better to be outside, drawing a free breath, than closed up in the confusing unknowableness of Glass House, where even birds could terrify an overly imaginative mind. If he wanted to, he could stay awake and outside until dawn. Set into the great curving wall of glass at the end of the gallery there was a door that opened onto the highest terrace. Alex stepped outside.

There was moonlight over Beverly Hills. The luxurious cars had been stabled. The pools were empty. Doors everywhere had been locked, double-locked, relocked. Vicious animals prowled the grounds of the estates, trained to kill, trained to protect.

It was historical fact that when Mabel Eastlake first moved to Beverly Hills, the police barred the masses of jobless and hungry from entering the city limits. But in their dreams, Alex thought, the Depression-weary souls must have entered anyway. For it was here that their favorite stars lived, hidden away in these green groves, amid sweeping lawns the color of money. Beverly Hills, fabled city of greed and waste and extravagance, locking itself away and allowing no one to judge it.

Keeping its dark secrets locked within, Glass House presented a perfect facade for the silent adulation of the heavens, gazing down at the place that had inspired and spawned it. Its great division of sweeping horizontal lines and curves, the reflectiveness of its glassy surfaces, gave it continuous visual motion and a buzz of low black energy. As perfectly lit as the face of an aging star, Glass House looked particularly beautiful in the moonlight.

"How kind you look in the moonlight," Alex murmured, looking at Glass House. A line from *Lady With A Past*, spoken by Mabel Eastlake to the man who is about to rape her.

The views from everywhere in Glass House were

staggering, especially to someone whose adult life had been spent in a cramped Manhattan apartment on a cramped Manhattan street. "After fifty years of it," Fancy had said of the view, "your sense of reality evaporates entirely." And it was this view that now opened up fully to Alex as he stood on the highest of the three terraces. The unimpeded expanse of space and vista provided relief from the inner disorientation of the place.

In the daylight, and looking south, the entire Los Angeles basin was sometimes visible through its perennial haze of smog. Century City, where once Fox and Paradise Studios were located, appeared to the west, with Santa Monica further in the distance. Beyond that the continent ended, its demise marked on the horizon by the thin, glowing bar of the Pacific.

All Alex could see of this now was a soft, throbbing blue net of light that stretched along the horizon, the bright moon poised serenely overhead. Calmed by degrees, he stepped further into the chill sweetness of the evening. Scents from the Child's flower gardens and the fragrance of watered lawns drifted up to the terrace. He breathed gratefully, his chest still swollen with tension. Set around him in enormous tubs, Gethsemane cacti cast down their chesslike doubles in shadow.

Then he heard a cry further down in the gardens. This time there was no mistaking its human reality. However stifled, it was the sound of a terrified woman and it beat its way into his unwilling consciousness with a terrific jolt. Fear instantly shrank the world close around him. The thorns of the cacti, cruelly outlined by the light of the moon, suddenly reminded him of the eyelashes of Mabel Eastlake in her glamour portraits.

He ran to the balustrade and peered down into the next, lower level of the grounds. Classically framed by tall white columns, the pool glowed as mysteriously as the eye of a cat. Cygnet's rigidly parterred and very formal gardens were set on either side of the pool. Groves of old trees at the perimeter faded into the darkness hiding the walls of the estate. Had the cry come from there?

Something, someone, was moving in the distance.

Wide steps descended to the third and lowest level of the estate. It was darkest and wildest here. Old cypress trees lined a grassy walk. The earth was carpeted with wildflowers allowed to seed themselves and grow freely. In the far distance was a domed gazebo, pure Deco in its symmetry, whitish-gray in the moonlight.

The dark bladelike outlines of the cypress trees stabbed themselves into his unwilling vision as he ran. Running was a luxury. Panting, his mouth gulping in air, he gave himself over to physical motion, with no thought of what he would do or see when he got there, only that he must be prepared to help.

"Oh no. Jesus Christ."

On the marble floor of the gazebo the mauled body of the famous columnist lay on its side, legs partially drawn up . . . dress shredded, flesh lacerated, a diamond choker glittering crazily around her neck. Hilda Hatter's death-startled face rested in a pool of shadow and blood, her mouth hideously and unnaturally wide, as though a final scream of agony had cracked free her jaw. And beside her mouth, neatly severed, her eyes staring at it with a bulge of surprise, lay Miss Hatter's famous and much-hated tongue.

Alex put a hand to his stomach.

A sound. Rustling. A shadow.

Above him, on the ledge of one of the open, rounded arches, the bristle of an animal's presence.

The panther jumped quietly to the floor. Only a few feet away, it crouched and stared malevolently at Alex. Slowly it inched over to regain its jealous possession of the corpse.

Frozen, Alex watched it sniffing Hilda Hatter's face. In the shadow-drenched moonlight the cat appeared to be kissing Miss Hatter lightly on her very red lips.

Inhaling the scent of a fresh kill, fresh blood. The animal began to lap up a congealing puddle, keeping its suspicious eyes on Alex. Suddenly it lunged in earnest, tearing into Miss Hatter's soft stomach.

Alex was inching backwards when another shadow appeared in the doorway. He dared not turn around. He could only watch, unable to move, as the shadow grew larger, engulfing and ingesting his own. He saw it slowly raising one arm to strike. He fell into his own darkness.

6.

Pursued down endless inescapable corridors, through impeccable, magnificently perverse rooms. But by what? For what reason? Forced to run nimbly along tightrope-wide ledges hundreds of feet above the ground and to climb vertiginous staircases without faltering. Why? What had he done? What unknowable law had he broken?

And who was he?

There was Hilda Hatter, her mouth a silent cry. There was Mabel Eastlake, a tiny distant figure advancing towards him, growing larger, springing like a panther. Fancy Barlow, waving desperately from a high window. Cygnet Sackville, naked, embracing the Child. The Child catching Alex in a forbidden place and moving inexorably towards him with what intent? Alex, in the Child's arms . . .

A dream of outwitting menace, a dream slurred with impending inevitable violence. Nothing was clearly articulated, but he sensed the approach, at some crucial moment, of a transformation.

"Alex!"

He heard his name being called and sat straight up. "Who said my name?"

Consciousness altered nothing. And yet everything had changed. He was naked, sitting now on satin sheets slick with his sweat.

The Child's face was hovering close to his in what

looked like tender concern. Alex wanted to swim in the blue innocence of those eyes.

But were they innocent? Was anything in Glass House innocent?

"Who said my name?" he asked with an urgency inherited from the lingering dream. "Someone said my name. Someone called me."

The Child narrowed his eyes and shook his head.

Alex could not move as fast as he wanted to, as fast as he had moved in the dream. Placing a broad hand across the width of Alex's chest, the Child pushed him back down on the bed, slapping the back of his own head to mimic a fall.

"I know," Alex said, touching a swollen lump behind his ear. "I fell. In the gazebo." Suddenly he remembered clearly everything that had happened . . . what he had seen. A sickening pain shot through his head and he fell back into the slippery pile of pillows.

Upset, uncertain, the Child took one of Alex's hands in his own. Alex pulled it away. "Where are my clothes? I have to leave here."

Now the Child looked alarmed. No, he kept shaking his head. No. No.

Careful, Alex said to himself. Move slowly. You're not strong enough yet to fight back. The very thought of having to fight was unreal, of fighting the Child, downright insane. Yet they must all know that he had seen Hilda Hatter's body.

Why, then, hadn't they killed Alex as well? Who had decided, he wondered now, that he was to live? The Child? This strange mute creature beside him? And whose had been the shadow sliding along the gazebo floor, sliding like a snake, raising an arm . . .

"How did I get here?" he asked the Child. "Who brought me here?"

The Child shyly indicated himself.

"From the gazebo?"

The Child's large dark face was in sudden turmoil. No. He had not been understood. No. There was something he must say. But he couldn't. Mustn't. And his inability or unwillingness to communicate the knowledge he had was at first painful and then infuriating to watch.

Alex himself was afraid of hearing the answers he felt compelled to seek.

For a moment the peripheries of vision widened and he was able to comprehend the full soft silver splendor of his surroundings. He sat up again and asked the Child where he was.

The Child cautioned him once more against moving too quickly and kept glancing towards the door as if he feared someone might enter. Alex had seen the same cringing, furtive look on Fancy's face when they had first met. The fear and resentment that came from having to obey a threatening unseen. An unseen that held power and punished mercilessly when it was not obeyed.

Alex jumped naked from the bed, ran to what he thought was a closet door and flung it open. Behind it, a giant cat sprang forward in a snarling leap. With an amazed cry Alex fell backward onto the floor. The animal remained poised hugely above him. The Child slammed the door shut and then spoke for the first time. His voice was painfully distorted and it obviously took great effort for him to produce even these barely comprehensible sounds.

He slowly enunciated the name of the wild beast who, before Cocaine, had been his companion, his beloved pet, whose wild animal consciousness had gone so awry in Glass House that it had to be destroyed "Kil-i-man-jar-o." The taxidermist had done a superb job.

Alex suddenly grasped the Child's hand and held it tight. "Please. Give me my clothes. Help me to leave this place. Help me to get out."

The Child stood deliberating. His eyes were as serious as Alex's. Now he moved quickly.

Alex pulled on the clothes he was handed, his aching body resisting every movement. Where was the speed and agility he had in the dream? As he dressed, excited by a sudden hunch that the Child was actually going to help him, going to get him out and away, he gradually became aware that the Child was staring at him with intense interest.

When Alex was dressed, the Child again extended a large hand to him. Alex watched it reaching out toward him while a chorus of voices in his head warned him to be careful, careful, careful. Strong hands could strangle, could twist, could maim.

He looked into the vast ambiguous innocence of the Child's eyes. I have no choice, he thought. I have to trust him. He took the Child's hand.

Guided by the Child, Glass House lost some of its frigidity and terror. The sense of violence and violation that weighted the air was if not dispelled at least laid to temporary rest.

How long had it been since he had touched another person? Held a man's hand? Alex gave himself up to the Child's warm, rough pressure.

The Child moved through the large, perfectly ordered rooms with the familiar grace of one who has desanctified a place through familiarity. This place is his home, Alex thought; he knows no other. For him this is daily reality.

And the truth of it was that except for his natural grace, itself a kind of beauty, the Child with his wrinkled white trousers and bare feet looked entirely incongruous in the beautifully executed aesthetic achievement that was Glass House. Wandering with him through the silent rooms, many of which Alex had never seen before, was like being pulled through a dangerous dream by one who had already dreamed and conquered it.

It was still very early and a steamy glare of morning light shone through the windows and walls of Glass House. Several successive days of hot windless weather had set up an inversion over the Los Angeles basin. The great city below was almost entirely cut off from view by a brown dirty haze. Standing on the top terrace, Alex and the Child looked down on the phantasmagoric scene of the city, shimmering, out of focus. The view was alienating; it made Alex's eyes sore.

When the Child led him down the stairs towards the gazebo, Alex pulled back, the memory of terror rising painfully in his throat. "No, I can't go back there—"

The Child's eyes coaxed him. He touched Alex's arm, unfroze him.

A fuzzy white light blurred the perspective, wrapping the lush vegetation in gauzy film. Even the birds were muffled. As they walked down the cypress-lined avenue towards the gazebo, Alex heard only one thin drool of birdsong, faint and bewildered. He found this undefined hum in his ears more ominous than the constant barrage of alarming noises he had learned to live with in New York. But the Child knew this kind of silence always, he thought pityingly.

And despite a curiously oppressive heat, a dirty stinging heat that was imprisoning all of Los Angeles, shivers flashed down Alex's spine when they finally stood in front of the gazebo. This was where Hilda Hatter had been killed. This, the place of final struggle and surrender. Alex knew his fear had to be confronted. He waited for the Child to go first, then, cautiously, he stepped inside.

It was bare within, but hotly reverberating with its own recent history. Built originally of the cleanest alabaster, the gazebo had suffered over the years from acid rain. A spreading rusty discoloration gave the otherwise calm interior an unsettling, crucified appearance.

The Child pointed to something on the floor.

Even knowing that the body was gone, Alex still dreaded to look at the spot. "Yes—blood. *Her* blood."

The Child gently touched the back of Alex's head where it had been cut in his fall.

"So you did find me here," Alex said.

No. Again the confused half-wild look, the impulse to deny. Pained, frustrated noises hung in the Child's throat.

"You found me here," Alex said, "but you don't want them to know?"

Then relief, relief that Alex had understood him, flooded into the Child's eyes.

Alex touched him gratefully, without shyness, believing at last that the Child had been his protector. "Will you help me?" he asked.

Without replying the Child led him away.

As they were climbing the stairs from the pool to the highest terrace, Alex looked up and saw a veiled figure standing behind the glass wall of the second story. Mabel Eastlake's floor. For a few intense seconds Alex stared at the figure and was stared at in return. He watched transfixed as the figure's hands moved ever so slowly towards the veil, grasped it, raised it.

There, standing above him behind the glass wall, staring down with the unfathomable eyes of a goddess come suddenly to life, was the youthful beautiful screen face of Mabel Eastlake. Making no sign of recognition, Mabel Eastlake slowly turned and left the place where she had been standing.

The Child had evidently seen her as well, for the sight of her withdrawing deeper into the luminous recesses of her room acted upon him like a visual narcotic. Alex could feel the Child's attention slipping away from him, moving elsewhere. The Child's grasp weakened.

"Wait," Alex pleaded. He did not want to re-enter the house before some specific plan had been fixed between them. The Child must help him to leave. "Wait!"

But the Child's emotional focus was gone. He dropped Alex's hand and started for the house. Alex ran after him, desperate at finding himself abandoned. He did not dare to be alone in the house, haunted as he now was by the sight of Mabel Eastlake watching from the upstairs window. *Was* it Mabel Eastlake? How could she not have aged over the years? This startling vision of youth, which gave Alex the unsettling feeling that he was dealing after all with a woman of his own age, made him doubt its reality.

Then was someone impersonating her? Who? That possibility, coming so soon after Hilda Hatter's death, was particularly horrifying. And with a jolt he remembered the figure in the wardrobe rooms and the flitting reflection of it—or someone else—in the foyer. How many unimagined inhabitants were there secreted away in Glass House, hidden and waiting?

Alex followed the Child, now deep in his trance, into the long gallery and from there into the projection room. The Child disappeared into the darkness and Alex was left alone. He hung close to the door. Someone was running a projector from the back of the room.

The projection room was dark gray and very soft. A viewer felt strangely cushioned within it, like a fetus riding comfortably in a mother's belly. In this room the Child sat every day, watching the movies of Mabel Eastlake over and over again. They had become a kind of personal mythology for him, a daily mass or lesson that Miss Eastlake forced him to attend. He had grown up watching her movies in this room. The prints in Miss Eastlake's collection were far better than any to be seen in a public theatre.

Mabel Eastlake had never been filmed in Technicolor. She existed for her fans in shades of white, black and silvery gray. The ten films she had starred in from 1931 to 1939, all directed by Otto Kranzler, visually sealed her for all time in a world of stylish fantasy. It was here in the projection room, her image mummified with protective chemicals, that the potent spirit of the old movie goddess roamed from scene to scene. Here it was that she could watch herself, watch her life, watch her work and brood incessantly on the past, her past, with all its terrors and wonders.

Alex was mesmerized by what he saw, as though he'd walked into a place of enchantment, a waiting spell. The hypnotic sound of the projector accompanied the images, intensifying them. He was watching film that had never been publicly released, that no one knew existed. Outtake footage that allowed a viewer the strange sensation of watching people act in character and then suddenly break from their roles and become "real," human.

A large, breathtaking close-up of Mabel Eastlake appeared on the screen. "If you'd angle your goddamned camera right, the way I told you to, you wouldn't need another fucking retake!" she said angrily.

A voice offscreen said, "Put some ice on it, Mabel. You were slightly off from direction."

The eyes flared. "The hell I was!" she shouted. "I was perfect in that scene. *You* were the one who was off. *I* can tell when the goddamned camera isn't staying with me. That's one fucking thing I do know." She stormed off camera and then paced back with a furious, bitter look on her face. End of clip.

The next one began as a passionate love scene between Mabel Eastlake and Boyd Powers. Alex remembered it from *Two-Faced Woman*. Eastlake and Powers sparred with great verbal wit until Eastlake was required by the script to grab her co-star and kiss him. As soon as she had, the scene was to cut elsewhere. But a cameraman on the set had kept his camera rolling.

"Cut."

Mabel Eastlake shoved Boyd Powers away from her with a gesture of impatient disgust. "Christ, can't someone teach this fish how to kiss a woman?" she breathed.

Off camera a voice said, "He's your husband, sweetheart. If you can't teach him how, nobody can."

Boyd Powers, smiling but tense, nervously patted his sleek hair. "If she'd let me into her bedroom I'd show her more than a kiss."

"No thank you, darling," Mabel Eastlake said, a hand on her slim hip. "I don't like the taste of Mexican food on anyone's lips." End of clip.

In the footage following this, the cameraman started to film before the scene actually began. There stood Mabel Eastlake in the Snake Dress from *Doublecross*, a truly Ertéan and unbelievable sight. The giant cobra's head of white fox rising behind her head shimmered with every move she made. She was surrounded by makeup men, wardrobe mistresses, hairdressers, sound and lighting men.

"I tell you I can't walk in this goddamned dress!" she shouted, waving away the professional entourage around her. "Kranzler!" she bawled, looking over her shoulder, past the camera. "Kranzler! When the fucking hell are you going to tell that goddamned French fairy that in order to *walk*, I have to be able to *move my legs*! I'm numb, I have no feeling left in my body!"

"You look divine, just as you should look, Mabel darling," a heavy and heavily accented voice replied.

"Like a corpse?" Mabel Eastlake snorted. "That's how I'm supposed to look? This dress, Kranzler, is a fucking shroud. A winding-sheet. It makes me feel crazy, like it's bad luck, like it's a straitjacket."

Another voice. "Get that sidelock of her hair a little looser."

Mabel Eastlake pushed away the makeup man who appeared with a comb raised in one hand, a brush in the other. "No!" she said. "No, let me fix it the way you want. I hate the way this one fusses with my hair. I can't stand all these people touching me all the time. Everyone wants to touch me. Where's Cyggie?" She stepped back with a cornered, suspicious look on her face. "They all want to look at me and touch me."

"Christ, the dame's goin' off her rocker again," complained a low voice.

"Mabel darling." The voice of Otto Kranzler. "You are holding up production with these tantrums of yours. If you will not continue, I will send Miss Barlow to wardrobe immediately. I am certain she can do the scene if you cannot."

"Don't fucking threaten me with that bitch!" screamed Mabel Eastlake. "The way she's always hanging around the set, waiting, hoping she can be me. She'd never get away with it. They'd know in their souls that it wasn't me. Vampire!" she shrieked.

"You are going to be perfect in this take, Mabel darling," Kranzler said evenly, threateningly. "You are going to be perfect because I am not going to shoot it again. We have shot it eighteen times already. You are making us lose a great deal of money."

"Don't be angry with me, Otto," pleaded Mabel Eastlake, suddenly contrite, approaching the camera with her hands outstretched in an attitude of supplication. "I can't act when you're angry with me. I can't do it the way I used to. You have to help me."

"I am helping you. You are refusing my help."

"Where's Cyggie? Oh God, give me something to help!" Mabel cried, clutching at a startled stagehand for support, bending over, disappearing under the cobra head of fur. "I'm having problems, Otto. I can't be perfect."

"Places everybody!" a voice shouted. The set was cleared.

Mabel Eastlake stumbled back to her place. She looked dazed and terrified. "Where am I supposed to be?" she wailed. "Someone tell me exactly where I'm supposed to be!" Her voice was booming and scared. "I don't know exactly where I'm supposed to be." End of clip.

On the same reel there were home movies, shot on location in Glass House. The participants pretended to be making a feature film. Someone held up a placard that read THE ALLIGATOR HUNT. Alex recognized the faces of Hilda Hatter, Boyd Powers and Otto Kranzler from photographs in old movie magazines. They and several other elegantly dressed men and women were standing around the pool of the inner garden, armed with long spears. The space that was now luxuriantly overgrown, reclaimed and defaced by nature, had then been a classical atrium.

From one end of the pool a servant tipped up an enormous crate, and three alligators splashed heavily into the pool. Amid great excitement, the assembled guests began to hurl their spears at the confused animals.

The camera tracked to one side, away from the pool. There stood Mabel Eastlake and Jimmy Flame. They quickly stepped apart and Mabel Eastlake waved the camera away with an annoyed gesture. She was wearing smoked glasses and a tailored white linen suit with spectator shoes. In the crook of one arm she held a small white dog. Flame, pulling deeply on a cigarette, turned to avoid the camera entirely.

The two of them looked furtive, guilty, caught doing something they shouldn't have or that was not supposed to be seen.

And then Fancy Barlow appeared wearing an outfit identical to Mabel Eastlake's. No one would have confused the two of them, but the resemblance was weird, uncanny.

Both of their faces remained inscrutable behind the old-fashioned and rather unbecoming dark glasses.

Turning away from Fancy, cradling the dog tightly under her arm as though it were a purse, Mabel Eastlake clearly did not relish participating in this home movie. Fancy, however, continually looked back at the camera, mugging, laughing, coaxing the eye to her. But, strangely enough, it was Mabel Eastlake that one instinctively wanted to look at. It was as simple and miraculous as screen chemistry.

Suddenly Fancy Barlow grabbed the dog from Mabel's arms and triumphantly ran with it to the pool, standing for a moment like a priestess holding aloft the sacrifice. She hurled it into the water. The clip ended with an image of Mabel Eastlake staring, stunned, at the churning water.

Whoever was running the projector rewound the film and replayed this segment a second time.

His eyes having adjusted to the darkness, Alex now looked over and saw the Child hanging back in a corner of the projection room, staring at the screen with a troubled look on his face.

The remaining footage was puzzling, suggestive but enigmatic. Coming immediately after the vision of Mabel Eastlake transfixed with horror, its wild effervescence was unnerving. The film was older, coarser, and seemed to be slightly speeded up, making the figures look fast and frantic. A dance floor in a dark nightclub. Formally attired men and women dancing and drinking and talking. The camera tracked around the outskirts of this dance floor, startling and amusing the people on the periphery. And it was the people themselves that made this footage so odd and fascinating. Caught in the light, they looked like exotic creatures from another world, aquatic, artificial, unready to be disclosed. Yet at home in this place, happy to be here.

And the sights became odder. Men or women, one could not tell which exactly, wearing tall plumed headdresses stepped past. Some of the people wore masks. There was a woman visibly naked beneath a transparent dress.

One young man was filmed for some time before he realized that the camera was on him. When he slowly turned to face it, Alex's heart stumbled. The face was so familiar . . .

But the image vanished an instant later and in its place appeared, professionally titled, as though for a feature film, THE SECRETS OF MABEL EASTLAKE.

The projector stopped. The room was dark again. From the back came sounds of deep, painful sobbing. Standing beside the projector, her face hidden, was Fancy Barlow.

She warded Alex off with a gloved hand and said finally, with a catch of breath, "Renewing some memories, darling. Did you enjoy Miss Eastlake's home movies? I didn't show you the best one." She laughed and sniffed. "We were still friends then, of a sort. It's difficult to forget past adorations, you know. Ah! But seeing Jimmy! Seeing all of us so young. I wanted to die when I was young and still beautiful, darling. I can't bear to think of what I've become."

The room was suddenly awakened by the amplified and terrible rage of Mabel Eastlake's voice. "Thief!" she bellowed. "When did you sneak up like a monkey to steal my film?"

"It's mine!" Fancy growled. "It's my footage. Me."

"I warned you about coming up here. I told you what would happen to you if you ever showed it. I'll—"

"You'll what, darling?" Fancy scoffed. "Take my dog away? Murder me?" She turned to the video scanner, a hostile and triumphant look on her thickly made-up face. "Don't forget, darling, just how lost you'd be without me. I don't need you, but you darling, certainly need me. Seeing this again just reminds me just how *much*."

"We keep monkeys here only out of pity," said the voice of Mabel Eastlake. "Would you rather be turned loose in a world that would laugh at you? Ridicule you into small pieces?"

"Piss on your version of pity, darling," Fancy replied. "Darling," she said, turning to Alex, "do you know what it's like to be so beautiful that someone else steals your identity out of sheer jealousy?"

"But your jealousy isn't sheer, darling," countered the voice of Mabel Eastlake, "it has a great big ugly run in it."

"To be so beautiful, Alex darling, that you *almost* look like someone else who is even more beautiful still. And you are consumed with a passion to steal that beauty, that image, steal everything that belongs to it, and make it your own, knowing somehow that it will always remain counterfeit and untrue, an image without a soul. Ah, to be beautiful," Fancy said, walking over to stare malignantly into the video scanner, "and then to have your beauty recalled, completely destroyed. To have your image totally annihilated. Can you imagine a worse fate for a woman?"

"Yes," said the voice of Mabel Eastlake. "Yours."

"Mine?"

"A thing, a nothing who never had what it takes to become the real thing, the genuine article, who never had the proper ambition or courage to take over its own life. Someone who could never be more than a cheap copy of a woman."

"At least I, darling, didn't have my face smashed into mush for the love of a man who didn't love me. I, darling, at least have a face to show for my life."

"And look at that face, monkey! Look what your face has become!"

"Without my face around here you wouldn't know what you were supposed to look like," Fancy shouted.

"Cygnet wouldn't know what to do with you. You'd have your virgin glands, darling, and your elephant sperm, but no identity. You'd be even more of a ghost than you are now. You don't exist!"

There was a pause. The videoscanner turned quietly from side to side. Then Mabel Eastlake said, "Jimmy did love me. That's what you can't forgive."

Fancy gave a vicious laugh. "Those champagne enemas Cygnet's been giving you over the years have destroyed your bowels *and* your brain. Jimmy was mine, completely mine, from the first moment I saw him. You never stood a chance."

"If Jimmy loved you, why was he running away with me? We were going, going away from here, leaving crazy monkeys behind. You were nothing more than a freak to Jimmy—he told me so—a freak he could use to make money, and an excellent whore."

"Your ambition should have stopped between your legs," Fancy said, her voice shaken. She looked up, eyes narrowed. "I was the star of The Black Orchis. It was *I* who had what they all wanted. You! You were too easy for Jimmy. A dumb cow with calluses on your knees and in your cunt."

"And where were your calluses?" asked Mabel Eastlake venomously. "Around your hemorrhoids?"

Fancy presented her malicious face to the scanner. "At least, darling, my face doesn't *look* like an asshole with piles. How does Cygnet do it, I wonder? There's really nothing to put makeup on. No nose, hardly any mouth—at least I still have my face."

"Stop talking about your hideous face, you thieving foul-mouthed lying bitch monkey!" screamed Mabel Eastlake.

Fancy dropped her affected theatricality. "Don't you think I know that it was Jimmy who destroyed your face, darling?" Her voice gleamed now like steel. "Don't you think I *know* that he did it for me?"

But Mabel Eastlake broke in, having regained the masterful and authoritative lunge of her voice. "Of course Jimmy did it for you. That's why I told the D.A. that Jimmy murdered Boyd and Otto. That's why I said nothing about *you* that night. That's why I saved you. So you see, darling, you may have your face, if that's what you insist on calling that thing on your neck, but *you're* the one responsible for Jimmy's death. You. *Someone* had to pay for your sins." Low quiet laughter came through the intercom. "And without your Jimmy, just what are you? Less than nothing. Without your Kranzler and your Hilda and your Boyd, you are nothing. You have no life, except that which I give you. I am Mabel Eastlake, darling, remember that no matter what else you may conveniently choose to forget. I have Glass House. I have Cygnet. And I have the Child."

"He's not yours! You will not possess him!"

"Mine, darling. Mine, Mr. Klein. Shall I show you just how much he belongs to me?"

There was a moment of silence in the projection room. The Child tensed suddenly, inexplicably, and was gone before Alex knew what was happening.

"Yes, blow your fucking whistle!" Fancy cried, pounding her hand on a seat back. "Blow, because it won't help you in the end, believe me!"

Fury had been mounting steadily in Fancy's face. Alex was amazed and frightened to watch it; the kind of physical transformation that only extreme emotional stress, or extraordinary acting ability, makes possible. From the vague state she seemed normally to exist in, Fancy now concentrated herself, focused intensely within her own body. The high cheekbones, Mabel Eastlake cheekbones, pushed through the enraged and tightened flesh. Her eyes flashed violet sparks. She seemed to grow to a dazzling height, back rigid and broad, thin shoulders straightening in preparation for combat.

"The soul of a woman, darling, lies in her face," she whispered in a low voice to Alex. "If you want to see the real face of Mabel Eastlake come to my suite tonight. There are plenty of secrets of be told, lots of cats to be let out of Miss Eastlake's bag, and I, not she, will be the one to reveal them." With one last tempestuously bitter glance at the scanner, her rival and her mistress, she swept from the room.

Alex was alone. He eyed the reel of film on the projector.

"Now that you're up again, Mr. Klein," the voice of Mabel Eastlake said, "you may get back down on your knees. The floors haven't been dusted or polished for three days. Cygnet is waiting for you in the kitchen."

7.

Dust on her soles sometimes left the old movie queen's imprint as she made her nocturnal inspections of Glass House. Erasing this faint trail, along with any other smudges or spots, was to be one of Alex's jobs. The enormous rotary polisher, suitable for the lighter-colored marble in the southern corridors, was deemed too coarse for the other floors, which were thick polished slabs of black cast glass. And so, armed with a small brush, a flannel cloth, a spray mister of ammonia and a dustpan, Alex was to creep absurdly through the front rooms, sweeping up or rubbing away any visible outrage to the black mirrored sheen of Miss Eastlake's impeccable floors.

"We can't bear to see tracks, even our own, in this house," Cygnet had explained, handing Alex large pads of chamois to strap to his knees. "This may seem odd to anyone from the outside, boy, but please remember that Glass House is more than a mere home. It is a monument. A set for our lives. And when the camera films it, when Miss Eastlake views the rooms, they must be as perfect as a set waiting for its star. *Perfect*, boy, do you understand? The camera sees everything, as Kranzler used to say. It's the audience that's blind."

This obsession with time and order—the external structure—was insane, Alex thought, when their internal worlds were so blasted with evil. With murder.

As he moved over the floors, Alex pondered what Cygnet had said. Did they think they could erase all traces of Hilda Hatter's death so easily? Swallow her life and digest it in darkness?

If killing was so matter-of-fact to them, Alex had to be very careful about everything he did and said. Until he understood more clearly what their plans might be for him, and who, exactly, he was dealing with, he must do nothing to awaken suspicion. Once he got out he could destroy their conscienceless way of life forever.

Knowing this was the only thing that gave Alex enough strength of purpose to keep from begging Miss Eastlake to let him go.

Cygnet said nothing about Alex's "accident"; he was preoccupied with his clipboard on which he was making an inventory of the contents of the house. He treated Alex with his usual overseeing scorn, as though Alex were nothing more than an anonymous object created for the purpose of functioning silently and without complaint.

"But where's Miss Eastlake's flashlight?" he asked suddenly, turning to look fiercely at Alex. "It's gone. It always rests exactly here, on this counter. Have you seen it boy?"

Alex shook his head, his heart thumping. He had left the flashlight somewhere in the house.

"Probably the thieving Miss Barlow brought it to her room for illicit purposes." He seemed to be looking right through Alex, forcing him to participate in this conjecture, testing him to find out how much he knew. But what Mr. Sackville was actually doing, Alex realized, was studying his face, minutely, as one studies a painting or *objet d'art*.

The man reached out suddenly and took Alex's cheek between his fingers, quickly moving on to sample the quality of flesh on other parts of his body. Alex, this time, did not resist.

"How I'd love to work again on someone young," Cygnet murmured. "How old are you, boy?"

"Old enough not to be called a boy," Alex said. "Thirty-three."

"Mary P's age when she died," Sackville said. "You don't really look like her, you know, even though Miss Barlow thinks you do. But little Mary resembled her father, Abe West, and I can see Abe in you. Amazing." He stared down at the unarguable certainty of his clipboard with its neat list of objects and locations and values. "Abe West. That's why Miss Eastlake had so much trouble with little Mary. Why she sometimes hated little Mary so. Mary reminded her of too many things, haunted her, just as the thought of having a double haunted her." He looked up to see if Alex was listening. "Miss Eastlake was superstitious and it scared her to death to think not only that her double existed, but that her double had *found* her. Do you know the Doppelgänger theory of twin souls?"

Alex shook his head.

"You spend your life searching for your secret double and fearing to find it."

"Why fearing?"

"Tsk, boy, because when you do find it, one of you has to die. And when one image dies, so dies the other. Miss Eastlake would have had Fancy put to sleep long ago were it not for that."

Alex asked Cygnet if he believed in this dubious theory.

"Believe it? I live by it," he said, evidently amazed other people did not. "It's not simply a *theory*," he insisted, "no more than Glass House is a theory. It's a world complete, our beliefs about what we are, who we are. Our fate, Glass House. *Your* fate too." His voice rose with the enthusiasm of a fanatic expatiating on his favorite topic. "I designed Glass House to be perfect, you know. Draw a line through any piece of Art Deco and the design on either side will be exactly the same. Balance. Perfect symmetry. Thus I planned Glass House, which came to me like a vision." He raised his arms and he looked like a dancer about to begin. "Everything doubled and perfectly counterbalanced, smoothly finished and made equal. Imagine my surprise when Miss Eastlake and Miss Barlow came to look at it. They suited the place perfectly, as though they'd been created for it, looking so alike and acting so differently. Miss Eastlake loud, vulgar, a delicious joke. Fancy silent, purposeful, always waiting her turn. Twin sides of the same soul. I stayed on to direct them, knowing they'd ultimately destroy one another. Strange loves, boy, can turn into stranger hates."

Alex agreed the two ladies could be very cruel to one another. But Cygnet seemed to treat this emotional brutality as a kind of perverse joke served up for the delectation of the spectator.

"I want to work on *your* face," he said suddenly, drawing close again and studying Alex with a clinical interest. "I want to make you as beautiful as I ultimately made her." Alex drew back, saying nothing. "I *could*, you know. You have the perfectly ambiguous face for it."

"I feel ambiguous enough already, thanks."

"Don't be a fool, boy. Don't be common. Don't be afraid. And don't make me force you."

"I wouldn't let you," Alex said.

"Let me work wonders on you," Sackville said. He paused and lowered his voice. "In exchange, perhaps I could tell you a few shocking things about your revered Miss Eastlake . . . "

"I'm here to help Miss Eastlake," Alex said, trying not to blush as he always did when he lied, "not to pry into her secrets."

"What would it take to make you agree?" asked Cygnet.

"I want to meet her. I want to see her."

"Miss Eastlake?"

"Face-to-face."

Cygnet grew excited. "Ah, but that's prying of the worst sort, boy, because Miss Eastlake's face *is* her secret."

"She appears to be very beautiful," Alex said cautiously.

"Beautiful?" Cygnet dismissed the statement with a scoffing laugh. "Mabel Eastlake is more than beautiful. Her face is perfect. Perfect. And every perfect face conceals its own agony, did you know that? To be beautiful is to be as lonely as a monster. To be isolated in the awareness of your own perfection. Do you know what it's like to be so perfectly beautiful, boy, that you are terrified to walk out on the street among other people? Everyone will stare at you. Or worse, someone may *not*. That is why Miss Eastlake cannot allow strangers to see her." He stopped to consider. "But . . . I might get her to agree to meet you. And if she does, you'll allow me to work on your face? Transform you?"

Backed into a corner, Alex had to agree.

Now, armed with brush, cloth and dustpan, Alex was alone in the foyer. What was it that made these rooms so sinister and so beautiful at the same time? Perhaps it was the absence of any small, ordinary, human touches; the taste was perfect and relentlessly unvarying. Nothing spoke or suggested human emotions, or human magnanimity. There was no sentiment, no concession to imperfection. The floors were icy black lakes to be skated across at your own risk. Knowing that Hilda Hatter's body floated somewhere under the surface made Alex fearfully aware of the frigid, treacherous currents below the polished crust.

Floors that today were inscribed with a frantic riddle of footprints, all sizes and shapes, his own among them, made Glass House appear to buzz with invisible motion, coming alive around him.

In this place of endless dark reflections, even his own pale shadow glimpsed unexpectedly in some shiny surface could slap his heart into a terrified panic. What if he were to encounter again the unknown thing—the image skimming along the foyer wall—the reflection he had come to believe was Abe West? Alex had never truly been afraid for his own life—no, not even in New York—and the realization that he was frightened, and had to be, sharpened his senses to an almost unbearable degree. Knowing that he was watched made him, in turn, more watchful, listening and looking for clues that might help to interpret *his* fate in Glass House.

The panther! Alex raced in to see if it was safely locked in the Child's inner garden. Lying taut and intensely observant, Cocaine was stretched out on one of the higher branches of the banyan tree, her tail hanging over the side, slowly twisting and stirring the air.

"Mr. Klein."

Alex whirled around as Mabel Eastlake's voice pierced the silence.

"Come up the front stairs to my room."

Alex all but bowed. As he climbed the stairs he kept his eyes on the hypnotic Vargas portrait until it was lost below him by the curve of the wall. He moved slowly, feeling his way along the wall. There was nothing to hold onto. A fall on the glassy steps would be simple and fatal. The unarticulated black surfaces made it difficult for the eyes to adjust and grasp perspective.

From the landing he cast a timid glance into the unbarricaded depths below, then turned to face the monumental entrance to Mabel Eastlake's bedroom. In the recessed doorway there was a heavy black and silver door, flanked on either side by heraldic panthers carved in relief.

"You may enter, Mr. Klein."

Alex was expecting to see the greatest room in Glass

House, throne room of the star, with the star turning to face him. His view as he entered was blocked, however, by a tall screen of stretched, watered silk. His nose was instantly pinched by much sharper and colder air.

A vague silhouette, like a shadow seeking a body, flitted back and forth on the other side of the screen. Was this Mabel Eastlake, the youthful beauty Alex had glimpsed in the window? He no longer could be sure that this *was* Mabel Eastlake. If her face, as Fancy claimed, was disfigured beyond recognition, how could Cygnet maintain that Miss Eastlake's face was perfect? Alex had seen such a face, but from that distance any trick was possible.

When Mabel Eastlake spoke, it was the first time Alex heard her voice without electronic amplification. It remained sharp and deep, but with the microphoned edge missing it was almost possible to imagine a human being behind it.

"After what has happened, Mr. Klein, you can understand what a sick woman Fancy Barlow is and why we are compelled somehow to get rid of her. I warned you about her but you would not listen. You did insist on coming to help me."

Alex, with feigned innocence, asked Miss Eastlake to tell him just what *had* happened and what Fancy's part in it had been.

"You were foolish enough to be wandering through Glass House late at night. Whatever happened was your own fault. I warned you not to trust her. She's cunning and dangerous."

Alex did not want to believe her. If anyone was dangerous it was Mabel Eastlake herself or Cygnet. Or, more frightening because even more unknowable, Abe West.

"Fancy makes us fear for our lives, Mr. Klein. She is an expert at setting clever traps and waiting patiently until her victims fall into them."

"I don't intend to fall into any traps," Alex said.

"A person never walks *intentionally* into a trap, Mr. Klein. Traps catch you by surprise, when you least expect them. Experience has evidently not taught you that."

"I'm learning," Alex said tensely.

"Life is a trap, Mr. Klein, and you should always be cautious and look out only for yourself. 'Trust no one and nothing in Lotus Land,' as I said in *Doublecross*."

" 'There are scorpions in the palm trees.' "

"There's danger in being sentimental," said Mabel Eastlake. "It's hardness and endurance that makes you win this game. That's why I never had children, they take the hard edges off life and you have to talk about them instead of yourself. What could be more boring than that? Having a heart in Hollywood, Mr. Klein, means having someone else's—preferably on a platter, with garnishes."

The sudden sound of a telephone, odd and jarring in the perennially still atmosphere, was sweet to Alex's ears. So there *was* a connection to the outside world. He might have expected it would be in Mabel Eastlake's room, from which all access to Glass House was controlled. A lifeline. A telephone. But how could he get in to use it without Miss Eastlake's knowledge? And he needed to know where, exactly, it was . . . for when the time came, not a second could be lost.

His heart beating fast, Alex went to a join in the silk panels and put his eye to it. Before he had time to register the little he could actually see, the door from the landing opened and the Child, carrying one of Miss Eastlake's hypodermic tea trays, stood staring at him through dark glasses.

Alex clumsily stepped away from the screen. Behind it he could hear Mabel Eastlake hanging up the telephone. More than hearing her, Alex could feel her approaching.

He turned, silently pleading with the Child not to expose his attempted spying. The Child's face in response was cold, distant, unreadable. He nodded once towards the ceiling. A small camera was mounted there.

Miss Eastlake transferred her attention to the tray and Alex quickly left the room and hurried down the stairs, hugging the wall. He was as far as the reception gallery beyond the Black and Blue Room when Mabel Eastlake's voice, drowsier now, caught up with him.

"I meant to ask you, Mr. Klein, were you aware that two men had been murdered in Glass House before you arrived?"

Alex stopped, scrutinizing the high-heeled footprints of Mabel Eastlake and those of Cocaine beside them. There was another track of prints that led to the wall of curved glass. He got down on all fours and started polishing.

"There is absolutely no sense in lying to me, Mr. Klein. You may as well admit that you knew. You knew so much else about me, after all."

"Yes, I knew."

"Murder keeps a person box office. Don't you think I know that? And Glass House has a lovely aura of murder about it. I'm sure Fancy's told you all about it by now, hasn't she?"

Alex shook his head.

"She's an expert at letting people know the worst about her. I suppose protecting a murderess does implicate one in the crimes, but if you could have seen her state you would have been merciful too. Poor Fancy. So sloppy. She is that most appalling of God's creatures, Mr. Klein, a woman who looks *older* than she actually is. And completely artificial as you've probably seen by now for yourself; one of those freaks you hear about, 'the born actress.' Actresses aren't generally born, Mr. Klein," said Mabel Eastlake's voice, dropping, "they're *made*."

If Miss Eastlake's sedative made her inclined to talk, Alex would let her.

"And she's a born thief, too. Steals all the time and

thinks we don't know. I always hated to take her along with me. She was good for a laugh when she did her Mabel Eastlake impersonation, but obviously she'd stolen that from me. She fingered a sterling silver compact from Carole Lombard once. Carole used it for her hop and she was hopping mad when it disappeared, believe me." Suddenly, surprisingly, Mabel Eastlake laughed. Alex wondered if this pleasantly altered state of hers had anything to do with her sudden offer of confidences.

"Seeing you down on your hands and knees, Mr. Klein, reminds me of the time Jimmy arranged a hop race here in Glass House. Each participating guest was presented with a silver nose straw we had specially made for the event. When the signal was given, they all got down on their hands and knees—in full evening dress, mind—and snorted their way across the floor, following the lines of hop that Jimmy had arranged from the foyer to the bar." Again the laughter.

"Who won?"

"In a hop race, Mr. Klein, there are no losers. But what I started to say was that our monkey-fingered Miss Barlow stole Carole's hop compact. And then she stole Anna May Wong's emerald-studded tweezers. Dear Hilda once presented me with a small pocket ashtray covered with shark's skin and set with a ruby. It was a treasured possession and I'm certain Fancy also has that. I've also lost a pair of silver earrings lately and wondered if you'd come across them somewhere and not bothered to tell me."

"I haven't found them."

"If you can help me to recover any of my property, Mr. Klein, and if you can help us to hasten Miss Barlow's departure, I may see fit to reward you generously."

Alex looked out the great wall of glass. The city, shimmering through its dirty haze, spread out beyond him, impossibly beautiful, impossibly distant, something one could covet from afar.

"That view is mine, Mr. Klein," said Mabel Eastlake, as if reading his thoughts. "It belongs to me. I own it. I will not give anyone that view. Do you understand?"

Mulling over Miss Eastlake's request that he "hasten Miss Barlow's departure"—whatever that meant—Alex said nothing and continued his work. In the east wing drawing room, the faint, ghostly prints of woman and beast disappeared at the border of a pale violet carpet inset with contrasting rectangles of black and yellow. There were lacquered screens and tables carrying a stylized, stream-lined jungle motif. This was set off by the civilized frostiness of high-art Lalique crystal. Steel and black leather chairs were Breuer originals. A very slight indentation in the gray wool of the sofa indicated that either Miss Eastlake, or her cat, had rested here sometime recently.

Feeling the silent but continued weight of Miss Eastlake's electronic observation, Alex slid into the dining room on his chamois kneepads. He was being tracked from room to room.

"Brush the hairs off the top of the banqueting table, will you?" Mabel Eastlake said. "Cocaine loves to leap up on the furniture and I haven't the heart to say no to her."

The massive tiger-maple tabletop rested on black lacquered supports, each support terminating in a silver claw. A vanished way of life! Eighteen chairs, each with high back and sidewing, were arranged around it. Against another wall stood an enormous sideboard of the same wood, and behind it a mural depicting stalking panthers. The ceiling of patterned gold leaf took the maple coloring and flung it from corner to corner.

"Cygnet used to say that a house should be like a basic black dress," Mabel Eastlake dreamily intoned as the cameras scanned her domain. "The smart woman knows how to attract attention by the accessories she chooses for it."

And murder, thought Alex, is one of the accessories adorning Glass House. The golden stillness and the persistent suggestions of violence in the decor bore in upon him with an ominous effect.

"I am prettier than she, Mr. Klein. Hers is a common face, by any standards." Miss Eastlake's yawn anticipated a long, voluptuous sleep. She was evidently on the verge of a Profound Slumber. "Wouldn't you agree that I am the more beautiful?" she asked. "Time hasn't touched me, but it's flattened her, stretched her out of all proportion. While I look today exactly as I did when I was the highest-paid star on the Paradise lot. The highest-paid star in Hollywood! You look as though you don't believe me, Mr. Klein."

"It's just that . . . time has to change the way we look," Alex said.

"Time! What do you know of time?" spat Miss Eastlake. "What do you know of the effects of time? There is no time in Glass House."

"Miss Eastlake," he blurted out, trying to disguise the urgency in his voice, humiliated by his need to ask, "I want to leave Glass House."

There was a long silence. Alex felt nailed to the floor.

"Mr. Klein," Mabel Eastlake finally said, her voice frigid, "your wanting to leave and our letting you go are two entirely unrelated affairs. One does not follow from the other."

Having tested her, Alex now had to bite down hard on a rush of fear. "Are you telling me that I'm your prisoner?" That, anyway, was the question he wanted to ask and dared not, for fear of Miss Eastlake's answer.

Until he knew more, it would be wiser to continue the game of cat-and-mouse. Wiser for the mouse, anyway.

8.

"A re you positive she's asleep and not watching us?"

"Darling," Fancy laughed, lounging on her enormous feather pillows, "when you live with someone for fifty years you become finely attuned to her presence. I should know by now when Miss Eastlake is off in her Profound Slumber. And haven't you noticed?"

Alex looked around. "What?"

"There are no cameras in my suite. I made a deal with Miss Eastlake many years ago when she turned Glass House into a set with all her ridiculous cameras. I said no cameras were to be allowed to penetrate my boudoir. I said, 'You've taken everything else, darling, at *least* leave me my dreams.' "

She paused to dip into a large box of candy, her fingers wandering over to read them by touch, like chocolate braille. "You know, darling, it's possible to feel sorry for those we hate." Finding the right chocolate, she popped it into her mouth. "But sometimes we're doing them a favor by wishing them in eternity."

Alex was on the alert. "You want Miss Eastlake dead?"

"Heavens, I can't possibly answer that on an empty stomach. Champagne, darling?" Fancy wriggled into her large Cuban-heeled satin mules, each with a puff of feather over the open toes, before flowing dramatically across her "suite" to a mirrored, glowing alcove filled with bottles. "I discovered long ago that a bar and a make-up room are one and the same thing, darling: *both* help you put on a new face."

Fancy's face this evening was a bizarre sight. Using surgeon's tape to draw back her fallen neckline, she was giving herself a homemade facelift. Except for this bonnet-like strap under her chin, the tape was hidden under a strange beaded cap which crowned the rest of her extraordinary outfit: a Pierrot-styled lounging suit of pearly charmeuse, the pegged bottoms stitched with tiny beads along the side seams. Her loose overcoat with its outsized sleeves was garnished around the neck with a luxurious collar of white fur. Enormous geometric rings of jade, onyx and silver were worn over her tightly gloved fingers. The hair that Fancy was *not* wearing—"Miss Eastlake's scalp, darling"— a blonde wig sideclipped with matching jewelled combs, sat on a queer, stylized head of Mabel Eastlake. It took Alex a moment to realize that the head had been sculpted by Brancusi. "Homage to Mabel," it was called.

Again that unsettling unsettledness in Fancy Barlow: that fleeting suggestion of doubleness, of one image resting over another.

"That houseboy's uniform they make you wear is a humiliation," she said to Alex from the mirrored alcove. "I stole a delicious costume from *Daring Lady* from the vaults today, just for you."

"For me?"

She kept her eyes fixed on Alex as she returned. "Darling," she said, putting down the tray of drinks and approaching him. One of her hands cautiously moved to rest on his head and then gingerly stroked his hair. "You can tell me."

"Tell you what?"

"Alex, darling—I can tell. I know."

"Know what?"

"You'd like to be Mabel Eastlake, wouldn't you?"

He was suddenly flushed and uncomfortable. "What do you mean?"

"You can be, you know," Fancy persisted. "You can be whatever you want."

"I'm fine just as I am, thanks," Alex said stiffly.

Fancy laughed and brought over the outfit. In *Daring Lady*, Miss Eastlake's wardrobe had been designed for rigorous spying. Her costumes were those of a fast-moving, sexy and unsentimental detective. Molyneux had designed these navy blue trousers and the pale fuchsia jacket. The lines and colors were no different from what fashionable women and more daring men of today were wearing. The difference was that Mabel Eastlake had worn these. Mabel Eastlake was a woman. Alex was a man. And he had never been in drag.

. . . Except in the novels of A. Liddell, where with pleasure he attempted to impersonate as accurately as he could the woman he might wish to be. Except in the safety of a movie theatre, watching Mabel Eastlake. But those were private fantasies, spun out for a short time in a private, unseen place.

"Alex, darling." Fancy's voice was serious and low. "You are gay, aren't you?"

It didn't sound like much of a question. He nodded.

"Oh darling! I knew it! I knew the instant I saw you." She tousled his hair again and kissed his ear. "It makes me so happy!" she whispered, holding out the sleuthing outfit from *Daring Lady*. "And darling, not that the two things are connected, but it would fulfill a fantasy of mine to see you wear this," she said. "Are you afraid?"

"Of course not—"

"Well, then—?"

Alex took the outfit and looked around for a screen.

"Don't be modest, darling. Undress here right in front of me. I won't hurt you." When he was down to his underwear she came closer and squinted. "Darling, you have an exquisite body for someone so little. Is it all real?"

"Of course it's real," Alex snapped, prudishly turning away.

"This is Beverly Hills, darling. A person has the right to ask. Reconstruction isn't what happened after the Civil War, you know, to people of the Hills." She stepped back. "Now don't forget the hat and gloves."

The hat was a modified Tyrolean, very jaunty, in black felt with a grosgrain band. The gloves were blue antelope.

"Now when you walk," instructed Fancy, "sway back and forth rather broadly and you'll feel the *flow* and *meaning* of the design, as Cygnet would say. And he should know, since he loves Miss Eastlake's clothes more than he loves Miss Eastlake." She made Alex perform an exaggerated walk, correcting his deportment. "Beautiful, darling. You were made for clothes like that."

It was certainly true that they were and felt wonderful. Alex went to one of several full-length mirrors and regarded his image. There he was, Alex Klein . . . but with his new haircut, and wearing clothes that had been filmed in a Thirties movie, he was someone else besides. The image he saw was not one he could ever persuade himself to carry beyond the confines of this room. But as a glimpse of other possibilities, other personalities, it was intriguing. My God, he thought, what would Frank say if he saw me like this? And he suddenly laughed.

Fancy's suite had a cooling psychological effect on him—the undefinable atmosphere of friendliness, comradeship—and he longed, even for a few minutes, to sink into its deceptively reassuring tranquility. It was in this room that he had awakened after his "accident".

Fancy had described the room's theme as "silver, darling, as in screen and sterling." And it was indeed silver—silver and white—and flagrantly voluptuous.

She had the lights dimmed. Silver half-moons concealed the bulbs, which cast a whisper of illumination
across the white satin wallcovering. A miniature wood fire
was burning, its flames leaping up in the mirror of a
sinuous silver-surfaced fireplace. "I always turn on the air
conditioning and then light a fire," she explained.

Fancy's was a room of reflections reflecting reflections; a room soft, luxurious, extravagantly feminine in the
elegance of its proportions and design. It had, however, no
view. The space was completely contained within itself; a
seductive lair where Venus might have lived, perfecting
the accouterment of seduction.

Impossible to imagine the eccentric, nearsighted
woman who inhabited this room carrying out diabolical
schemes of murder. Still, Alex was cautious; he had to be.
Mabel Eastlake had warned him about Fancy Barlow, and
there was no reason to disbelieve or take lightly what Miss
Eastlake said.

Except for a hunch, an irresistible intuition that told
him Fancy was or could be his ally. The perpetually unseen
Mabel Eastlake was far more ominous than Fancy could
ever be.

"I remember the scene in *Daring Lady* when she
wears this outfit," Alex said. "She's investigating an apartment in New York—"

"—the apartment of the mysterious millionaire she's
tracking," Fancy eagerly put in. "Boyd played the role. He
was good in mysterious parts because he didn't know beans
about acting."

"—and she hears footsteps and has to get through a
window, out onto a fire escape."

"No, darling, a high ledge. She was in a penthouse,
remember? And there was quite a show of leg as she pulled
her skirt up to get out." Fancy mimicked the scene, her

joints popping. "Kranzler had a genius for figuring out logical ways to show off Miss Eastlake's ass and legs without getting into trouble with Will Hays and his dirty-minded censors." She laughed. "If Will had only known!"

Odd to think that the hardest of economic times had produced the greatest extravagance in Hollywood. While the jobless starved and froze, Vionnet invented the bias cut, requiring three times the normal yardage for a dress, "and Miss Eastlake, darling, was definitely cut on the bias." The texture of the luxurious fabrics and the sensuous effect of the tailoring made the seductive appeal of Hollywood operate more powerfully on Alex than it ever had before. For the first time, he really understood what those movies could mean to poor people, people worried about paying electricity bills and buying enough food for their families. While on the screen, Mabel Eastlake stalked millionaires in *Daring Lady*. Outwitted danger in haute couture . . .

"To celebrate," Fancy said, handing him champagne in a paper-thin goblet.

"Celebrate what, for Christ's sake?"

"Life, darling, what else? Coming out of your spell."

"Fancy, I wasn't in a spell," Alex said, irritated.

But she became visibly nervous when her version of things was questioned, and before Alex could go on she said quickly, "I watched over you, darling. I and the Child. They wouldn't have minded if you'd died, out with the garbage you'd go. But we rallied. I haven't seen the Child so upset since Kilimanjaro went berserk and had to be shot. It was agony, darling, to watch him watching you. He stayed inches away the whole time, just staring and sniffing."

"Sniffing?"

"I told you, darling, the Child is our watchdog. *Her* watchdog, I should say, since she's the one who trained him for that. And watchdogs have very highly developed noses. They can smell a hot asshole from miles off." She laughed at Alex's offended exclamation. "Well, darling, if you lived with three old vampires for years and years and all of a sudden some attractive and somewhat younger blood showed up . . . but *now* he's terrified that you'll go away again. Just like a man. He must think that Miss Eastlake brought you here as a kind of toy for him to play with." She laughed again. "And our Miss E is absolutely terrified that her little scheme will backfire."

"What little scheme is that?"

"Well, darling, Mabel Eastlake has programmed the Child to adore her. I mean it. Quite literally. She is a goddess to him. And a goddess must be obeyed. The Child would kill, if she told him to. Now usually he sits in the projection room for hours on end watching all of Mabel Eastlake's pictures. But the whole time you were in your spell, darling, he didn't go once. *Her* image didn't interest him nearly so much as *your* reality. And that made our Miss E so very angry, so furious, that I locked you in here with me, for your own safety. Since you're the help, there's no lock on your door, you know."

"I know."

"Even so," Fancy went on, "I came in here once and found Cygnet hanging over you."

The hairs on Alex's arms rose. "Why? What was he doing?"

"Taking a likeness, he said. I was afraid he might have given you the needle. But don't worry, darling, I got him out of here fast enough. This is my *private* padded cell, and only my *guests* are allowed in. Feel the walls, darling. They truly are padded. This was the room where they'd have to throw your exquisite Miss Eastlake when she was in one of her states. The room was much different then, of course. I've fixed it up with some old things, to make it feel like home. I don't believe anyone should suffer without beautiful things around them, do you?"

"No, of course not," Alex said. He remembered the voice that had awakened him, called out his name firmly and gently. "Fancy, thank you. Thank you very much."

"For what, darling?"

"Watching over me."

"It was mostly the Child. Miss Eastlake trusts him so he's never monitored. She tries to have *me* on camera every moment, of course."

"What is this control she has over him?" Alex asked, remembering how the Child left him the moment Miss Eastlake appeared in the upper window. "How does she communicate with him?"

"They never speak, Mabel Eastlake and the Child," Fancy whispered in her hoarse, dark voice, "but he knows exactly what she wants and is compelled to do it. It's unnatural, darling—but, then, what here isn't? She imposes her will on him. It's only her *will* that keeps her Mabel Eastlake. And she knows the Child truly *feels nothing* for her. She cannot force his heart to love her—and that's the greatest agony for any woman or man, isn't it? When the heart you want for your own goes off in its own direction, away from you."

Alex nodded ruefully.

"The Child acts for her, he does what she commands, but no matter how hard she blows that whistle he will never love her." She glanced significantly in Alex's direction, narrowing her eyes for focus. "You know, darling, I used to admire that cold-heartedness of hers. But after a while it's like sucking a dry tit." A heavy sigh. "Not that the milk of human kindness flows in my bosom all the time, but I'm still the feeling one—here in my suite, away from them and what they do to me."

"They do torment you, don't they," Alex sympathized.

"*Torment!*" Fancy exclaimed. "Torment, he says. Darling, you don't know what torment is until you've had those two vultures picking at your bones. Feeding like rats off my carcass. They frighten me, darling, with their heartlessness. They don't respect people, only things, objects, money, this house . . . which they've made me a slave to for all these lonely years."

"You don't have to stay."

Fancy nervously looked away. "At my age there's no point in going anywhere else. My fate is here; this is my home. My *life*," she croaked, "which they took away from me that night . . . that awful night . . ."

Alex, heart thrumming with expectation, waited for more revelations.

Fancy looked up with sudden intensity. "Well, I am sick of sharing the Child with them. He needs to be taken from her. And I am sick of having to steal what is rightfully mine. It's time that bitch learned how to deal with her jealousy of me. Ha!" she laughed, downing her champagne in a gulp, "Mabel Eastlake with her silver whistle. She's no match for me. I'm strong as a bull, always have been. She knows I can blow the whistle on *her* any old time I choose. And that's why she's so nervous these days, why she'll strike now with the least provocation. She knows that I can tell the secrets that make Glass House hers—*theirs*."

"What are these . . . secrets?" Alex asked, as innocently as he could.

"Miss Eastlake's secrets are mine, darling," Fancy said, stretching her lips in a frightening, joyless facsimile of the enormous Mabel Eastlake smile, and went to get more champagne. "She wants to bury me with them, like those fucking Egyptian pharaohs with their slaves. Glass House—Miss Eastlake's pyramid! And all of us mummified here forever. God, I hope death is different from life, don't you darling?" she asked. "I hope it's less boring. And those two would prefer me to be a corpse. I'm an encumbrance to their plans, I know that. But they have a secret fear of me too." She toasted Alex. "And I, darling, have decided that I simply will not die. I can't. Not yet. Not until I make that bitch and her eunuch consort pay for every last insult and humiliation of the last—God, how many years *has* it been?"

Never one to perch for long, emotionally or physically, she now shimmered her way over to a large silver radio and switched it on. "They play music from the Thirties every night at this hour. Oh listen, darling, Gershwin." Fancy turned up the volume and listened dreamily, her fallen bottom swaying back and forth. "He sat at the piano one night in the Black and Blue Room and played all of his tunes for me. 'Your theme song,' he said, and played 'Oh, Lady Be Good,' So I said, 'George, darling, I couldn't be good *or* a lady for all the hop in Hollywood.' "

Her memories and the telling of them brought out a steady series of low, self-appreciative chuckles. "Tell me, darling, don't you think Cygnet is like the perfect lady? The kind who always keeps her legs crossed like this, even when she's being screwed?"

"Frankly, he gives me the creeps."

"It's such a joke to think he tried to make Mabel into a perfect lady, like himself. And Kranzler, on the other hand, wanted the man in her to show. Otto said there was a great man in every great woman. Well, darling, look at *me*."

Alex did. Fancy took up a strange, theatrical pose, a Mabel Eastlake of the Thirties pose. With softened light behind her and the white padded satin of the room acting like gauze to diffuse the harsh betrayals of daylight, Fancy was able to appear uncannily like Mabel Eastlake. Alex stared, fascinated and a little drunk, remembering Miss Eastlake's description of her former stand-in as "a born actress."

"The fire never goes out in a genuine diamond," Fancy said. "And though a woman is only as good as her camera angles, even a flawed stone looks good in an exquisite setting."

Alex picked up a small photograph and asked who it was.

"The Child as a child," Fancy said, holding it at arm's length and squinting.

"Did he go to school? Did you tell me that's where he learned to read lips?"

"Well, darling, also by watching all of Mabel Eastlake's movies from the time he was born. She or Cygnet would lock him up in the projection room and play one picture after another. He had to watch. So he knew language before his ears got hot inside and burned out his hearing. And he's smart, very very smart. I made them send him to the finest school money could buy. But he wasn't happy there and he got in trouble—"

"What kind?"

"With the other boys. You know. An intimate moment with one of them turned into an unfortunate tragedy. He simply does not know his own strength at times. So we brought him home and it was Glass House he wanted all along anyway. This is his home and where he belongs and what he'll ultimately get."

"You mean the child will inherit Glass House?" Alex was dumbfounded.

"Of course, darling, so long as they don't cheat him out of it. Despite what they may think, none of us is going to live forever. And Miss Eastlake's entire fortune will one day be his . . . unless Cygnet's figured out some way to get it for himself." This was a source of agitation and she began to pace back and forth. "I can't help but wonder what will happen to him when I'm gone. He'll have no one to guide him. No friend to share Glass House with. And with such an immense fortune, darling, how easy for him to fall into the hands of some predator who'd come to take over Glass House and him. That's what I'm afraid of. The Child does not need another Mabel Eastlake in his life."

"He might meet someone who loved him," Alex said.

"Bah!" spat Fancy. "Money has a way of bringing out the stars in anyone's eyes. Who wouldn't murder for a fortune? Ask Miss Eastlake, she'll tell you. And for someone as emotionally naive as the Child, someone so completely natural and guileless, it would be as simple as ABC for some fortune-hunting seducer to ruin him. Oh, they'll smell the money, darling, and come running."

Alex sat meditatively fingering a ruby-colored bottle of heavy cut crystal, the original *Forbidden!*, concocted and designed in a rare limited edition by Schiaparelli back in 1936. When he lifted the sharp crystal stopper, the overwhelmingly ripe scent of Fancy Barlow rose into the air. The perfume was heavily laden with the oils of gardenia, lavender, patchouli and roses, and it had a musky edge. Was this the hypnotic scent he found lingering in faint pockets around Glass House? If so, the aroma changed subtly over time, the musk base becoming dominant. It had some other association as well, but Alex could not place it.

"Hope for the best," he said to Fancy. "Don't you think the Child is strong enough to determine his own fate?"

"Hope for the best—here?" Fancy snorted. "Darling, I know the folks in Hollywood and the Hills. I used to *be* one of them. Fate is something no young innocent should be left to determine around these parts. Especially a young handsome innocent worth a fortune." She eyed Alex. "That's why he needs a strong man, a companion of sorts, a tutor . . ."

"Does the child know how much he'll inherit?"

"Miss Eastlake is afraid to tell him, not wishing to hasten her own departure. She's afraid if he knew, her watchdog might turn on her."

"I thought her will was stronger than his."

"Speaking of wills, darling, I can see that you have absolutely no idea just how *much* money we're talking about. Mabel Eastlake is worth millions. Back when land on Wilshire was selling for ten cents a foot, Miss Eastlake purchased what is now over two city blocks. And those city blocks are what Cygnet would call prime real estate, generating more money in a week than Miss Eastlake made in a year. It was a very smart move, of course. Cygnet handled all of her financial transactions. He still does. That's why she's so ridiculously dependent upon him. He holds the purse strings."

"How did the Child come to be here?" Alex asked, warming to questioning.

Fancy was surprised. "Darling, he was born here. Mary P died giving birth to him."

"And Mary P was a maid?"

"A maid?" Fancy sputtered. "Darling, Mary P was Mabel Eastlake's daughter!"

Another photograph was shoved into Alex's hand.

"Mary P. Current address: Happy Gardens Lane, Forest Lawn Cemetery. They've never even let me visit her there."

In the photograph, Mary P was a young, rather homely girl with a full face and lanky disinterested hair fixed in a Forties style that did not become her. And this was the person whom he was supposed to resemble? Alex looked deeper, his vanity wounded. There was some quality that rose almost psychically from the photograph and repulsed him. Mary P looked distant and disoriented—"not there"—as if some strong, vital part of her had fled, as if the camera picked up and focused on whatever was not there.

"I thought Miss Eastlake was childless," he said, putting the photograph down and stepping away from it.

"It was all very hush-hush," Fancy said. "So hush-hush that even the all-knowing Miss Hatter was unaware of it. Mary P was something Miss Eastlake's fans weren't supposed to know about. It would have detracted from her image. And she was such a confused young thing when the stork flew into her cabbage patch, didn't know beans about the world."

"What does the P stand for?"

"Pickford, darling, what else? Mary was named after America's Sweetheart, *aging* sweetheart by that time, but no matter . . . it was supposed to be a name for luck." She sighed. "But good luck was something that poor kid never had—not growing up the way she did, first in The Black Orchis and then here. Mary P had no sense of reality, no sense of right or wrong. Life was a movie she never got a part in. And once she became famous, Miss Eastlake denied being Mary P's mother, even to herself. Fancy Barlow became the substitute." Emotion was gathering like a distant storm cloud in her voice. "I will never forgive them for letting her die. Ah, her screams that night—her screams of agony!" She looked at Alex, a terrifying glow in her eyes. "Have you ever heard a real scream?"

Alex stared at her, suddenly frightened, remembering the screams he had heard in Glass House, the tortured cry of Hilda Hatter.

Fancy screamed. She put her hands to her ears, crouched down like a primitive woman in agony and let out a horrible, soul-piercing cry.

"Miss Eastlake refused to call a doctor," she continued. "She was incensed that Mary P had found a way to sneak out—'like a dog, to copulate on the sidewalk,' she said—and she was even angrier when Mary P refused to tell her who the father was. As if *she* hadn't been lifting her skirts in alleyways since she was twelve. And Mary P died . . . cursing us, cursing Glass House, in her pain, cursing her child. *I will never forgive her for that*," she said, giving full emphasis to every word. "One of the many injustices of the past that I must live to set right."

"Someone named Abe West, according to Mr. Sack-ville, was Mary P's father," Alex said, wanting to draw out more information while Fancy was, so to speak, hot. He wanted to tell her that he had seen someone or something in the wardrobe vaults, ask if it might have been Abe West, but hesitated. To ask would be to reveal that he had been where he shouldn't have been, had seen what he shouldn't have seen.

"My *Forbidden!* is evaporating as you play with the stopper," Fancy hissed, abruptly snatching it from Alex's hand. "That's *my* scent. That's how they could always tell when I was around. Jimmy always loved for me to wear it—he said my smell should linger. It always did smother *hers*, of course. Ah," she purred darkly, putting the stopper to her nose and sniffing deeply, "believe me, darling, I've often looked at this piece of crystal and thought what a good dagger it would make. How easy to come down like so—puncture the heart, or a lung—"

Alex sat frozen at Fancy's toilette table. Its mirrored glass surface was overwhelmed by small, potent-looking jars, atomizers, bottles. A hinged three-piece mirror reflected the image of Fancy's enormous satin-covered bed . . . and Fancy herself, three images of her, standing with the crystal icicle raised aloft.

He suddenly remembered the scent. It was the same one that rose from the envelope he had received at the hotel. "Forget Mabel Eastlake," it had read. "Be a darling and let her die with her secrets."

"No!" he cried, drawing back in fright.

"What? A dab on your pulse points, that's all I'm of-fering you. This scent is as rare as good whiskey during Prohibition." She touched the cold point of the stopper to Alex's neck. "Did you know it's the pulse that sets off a person's scent? How fast the heart is beating determines how strongly you smell." She sniffed Alex's neck, planting the soft touch of a kiss on it. "Mmm, you were made for *Forbidden!*, darling."

He had noticed her flirting before and had never paid much attention to it. But a stray thought now occurred to A. Liddell, the biographer. Was it possible that Mabel Eastlake, the most erotic and emancipated sex symbol of the Thirties, created to lure men into the Bijou Dream, was really a lesbian? And had Fancy Barlow once been Miss Eastlake's lover? Might not this explain the ambivalent devotion Fancy had to have to remain with someone she professed so vehemently to hate?

But, then, what of Jimmy Flame and the ridiculous jealousy he inspired in them? A cover? And what of this playful interest she had in him, in Alex?

Alex was suddenly touched to think that these old women might have lived with the stigma of a homosexual "secret" for so long. It was the kind of emotional and psychological burden a great star would have to conceal with extraordinary care, and the star's lover or lovers would likewise be bound to secrecy.

But had anything changed? Didn't Frank cover up his real identity in exactly the same way?

From "Lady, Be Good," the music changed to "Night and Day."

Alex, glimpsing a vaguely familiar face in another picture frame, examined the photograph. "Who is this? I saw him today in that film footage."

The subject was a fair-haired and mischievous-looking man of about twenty, his face pretty, bold and conceited. Wearing nothing but a pair of loose shorts, his hair slicked back, he stood with one long leg resting on a step. His hairless, bony chest was bullishly thrust out to make it appear larger, pouter-pigeon style. Sharing some secret joke with the camera and himself, he smiled mysteriously, squinting into the sun.

Fancy took the photo and focused on it with distant amusement. "That, darling, is none other than Abe West."

Alex looked up into the mirror and back down at the photograph. Abe West. Cygnet had said he looked like Abe West.

"The only photo of him left. Taken back in 1930, on the steps of The Black Orchis where we all worked before Mabel became famous. Becoming famous changed everything."

Alex was intrigued by Abe West's face, in part, of course, because of his own supposed resemblance. But there was something else in that face, something buried in it, something that kept chiming in his thoughts as he looked at it, but never striking the hour. Yes. Cygnet had told him that Abe West was Mary P's father. Fancy had told him that Mabel Eastlake was Mary P's mother. But even knowing this there was something unresolved, some visible or nearly visible mystery.

"What happened to him?" he asked, chewing on a fingernail.

Fancy quickly refilled their champagne glasses. "Abe West? Well, he disappeared, darling."

"Murdered?"

"No, although it might have been better for everyone if he had been." She gingerly took the photo from Alex. "It was a long long time ago. She was in love with him once, you know. Even followed him to The Black Orchis. Love can turn a woman into such a fool!" she cried suddenly. "Abe West is one of those important people in the great Miss Eastlake's past, but she'll never talk about him. Just as she'll deny that Mary P was her child. To know Mabel Eastlake, darling—the real Mabel Eastlake—you'd have to know Abe West. Without him, no matter what the bitch says, her story is incomplete. And guess what . . . " Fancy smiled. "She's afraid he'll come back to kill her, kill Cygnet, kill all of us. Why not? Abe West is no stranger to murder, darling. And when he does come back our little Greek tragedy will be complete. Our blood will flow like champagne!"

"But how could he get in?" Alex asked nervously. "Past all the walls and security?"

"Darling, do you think Miss Eastlake's walls and cameras could keep someone like Abe West out? He'll find a way."

"Mr. Sackville said that Abe West is here already . . . that he haunts Glass House."

"Yessss," Fancy sounded as if she relished the idea, "I wouldn't be a bit surprised. He *could* be here . . . hiding somewhere . . . biding his time . . . waiting."

"Fancy, look, *is* there a way out of Glass House?"

She pursed her lips and smiled before answering. "Glass House is filled with secrets. Tunnels and doors you can't see even if you're looking right at them. Cygnet knows all of them. He's like a rat, he can scurry around in the dark, up and down and all around, get from one room to another without ever showing his face. Perhaps he *has* run into Abe in some dark, forgotten corner."

"Do you know where any of them are?"

"I know there's a secret connecting passage between Miss Eastlake's boudoir and the projection room. Did you know that?"

"No, where is it?"

"Back in the storage area behind the screen. It winds right up to her Throne Room." She paused, tantalizing him. "And in the library there's another secret door. Cygnet uses it a lot. And . . . somewhere outside . . . is Miss Eastlake's Hole. That's what I call the secret entrance, darling, in honor of my employer. But even if I could remember where it was, I don't think I'd tell you."

"Why not? *Please!*"

Fancy considered. "If you leave, darling, I'm afraid

of what will happen to me. I'm afraid of what she'll do to me, what *they* will do."

"Then leave, leave with me, I'll help you."

"There is no way out of Glass House!" Fancy cried. "And . . . I'm afraid of what's out there. There's *nothing* for me out there. Everyone I knew is dead. People would look at me, judge me. I can't leave."

"Then help me to."

"I told you not to come here!" she hissed at him, drawing back. "No one escapes from Glass House. Don't you know that by now? The past traps us here, holds us. The past haunts us, comes back like those migraine headaches Miss Eastlake used to get on the set; those fearful, terrifying headaches when she'd have to break free of her body to escape the pain of her life. Glass House is just that kind of pain, darling, and I am its slave."

"*Their* slave," Alex said bitterly.

"Yes, their slave. They are my past, my constant reminders of what I was and what I did. And what I did makes me what I am. Who I am. And *I* was Mabel Eastlake, darling, no matter what she tells you. Yes, she's the lie, and I'm the truth. My voice, my smile, my style—all stolen. Well let that imposter spin her lies, let her film herself for no one to see and pretend she's me for the little while she has left. Soon, very soon, I'll have that view again. I dream of it! To possess it again, even for an hour, that view out over all space and time. Glass House will become mine again in the end and I'll put things right. And I won't have to hear her laugh any more because her foul mouth will be packed with the dirt it deserves!"

Hearing the savagery in Fancy's voice, Alex drew back as she approached him.

"Does *your* life terrify you when you look back at it?" Fancy asked, grabbing his shoulder and giving it a vehement wrench. "Mine does. Jimmy used to say that if life doesn't terrify you you can't be certain you're alive! And we always lived on the very edge, Jimmy and I. The fast lane, back when Miss Eastlake *drove*." She laughed and pointed to a framed newspaper photograph showing the wreckage of the Duesenberg. " 'Fate Catches Up to Miss Eastlake,' that's what I call it. But Jimmy, ah, Jimmy!" she cried. "Fate caught up with him too. With all of us. And he left me behind to face life without him. With *her*. Why did Jimmy have to die? What was he doing in the car with her?" And she clutched Jimmy Flame's photograph to her breast, rocking it tightly back and forth, tears dripping from her false eyelashes. She looked vulnerable and ridiculous, but sidestepped suspiciously away when Alex tried to touch her shoulder and acknowledge her pain. A sweet and sad old rendition of "Our Love is Here to Stay" played on the radio.

"I saw him last night in my dreams again," she said, her voice a low haunted croak. "And I saw Abe West, too. It must be because you're here and look somehow like him and like Mary P. You're making this happen."

"Tell me your dream."

"It was so intense. I dreamt of the time when we were all young. Before everything changed. I was at a costume party that Basil and Ouida Rathbone gave. It was a big affair because it was the first time Mabel Eastlake was to meet Marlene Dietrich face to face." She wiped her eyes and paced the floor wringing a small wet hanky. "They tried to call Mabel the American Dietrich, you know; and they called Dietrich the Kraut Eastlake. And Dietrich came to the party as Leda *and* the Swan. She was a sensation, let me tell you. Every feather on her costume had been dyed the exact shade of her blue eyes. And everyone wanted to know, of course, if Eastlake could top it. It's deadly making appearances in Hollywood, when your reputation is so large and people expect you always to be larger than life instead of the scared little nincompoop you really are. Terrifying, those Hollywood entrances."

Now, caught up in the memory of her dream, she excitedly screwed one of her pink cigarettes into the red holder.

"Everyone was waiting for Mabel Eastlake to arrive. I was standing in a corner watching and Jimmy and Abe West were watching on the other side. Then she was announced. The room fell silent." For emphasis, Fancy did too, momentarily.

"She entered. And she had come as Death, darling, with huge X's drawn across her eyes. No one dared to utter a word as she slowly came down the stairs, her face furious and ghastly white with those insane X's that meant nothing, that meant annihilation. She was wearing a white jersey gown, cut in a classic Grecian style. And we all knew what those eyes meant, but we didn't know what she would do with them, which of us she'd look at.

"People parted, afraid of her, afraid of Death wearing a beautiful gown. Then she stopped and slowly . . . ever so slowly . . . began to search the crowd . . . and she saw me!

"I ran to try to hide behind Jimmy, but Abe wouldn't let me. He wanted me to be seen, he wanted her to stare at me. He pushed me forward and then I saw those horrible eyes . . . and I knew that I was staring at Death . . . and that Death was Mabel Eastlake! Suddenly I *wanted* to die. I was ready. I wasn't afraid. I *wanted* to. I held out my hands, wanting to be taken. I closed my eyes and waited.

"But something went wrong. When I closed my eyes, something changed, something tricked me. I opened them, but it was to see Jimmy walking slowly out with Mabel Eastlake, staring deeply into her eyes, hand-in-hand with her."

Alex could think of nothing to say. He tried to rub some warmth into his own chilled flesh. "You must have loved him very much."

"*Loved* him!" She dismissed this inadequate description with a disgusted laugh. "Loved him, he says. Have you ever loved a man so much that fucking him becomes an honor? Love, little modern man, is chemistry, and Jimmy and I were explosive ingredients. We burned holes in one another. We couldn't keep our hands off one another. We couldn't reason with it, we simply let it devour us. Every time Jimmy walked into a room my tits stood on edge, my hair rose. Do you understand why I can never forget him? He made my body come alive, he mastered everything in me there was to master. No matter what she says, Jimmy was *my* man. Mine! I was working at The Black Orchis before she ever came. That's where Kranzler discovered the great Mabel Eastlake, you know. Ah, The Black Orchis. And when she couldn't get Abe West, no matter how hard she tried, she had to go after Jimmy, *my* Jimmy. Ha! Did I love Jimmy?"

Alex took the photograph of Jimmy Flame with some trepidation, fearing to see someone whose image wouldn't meet the expectations Fancy had built up. Sheer sex, that's what she had been talking about. Alex could still hear the growl of it in her voice. And he thought of his own untapped sensuality, his own craving to meet his equal in passion, in capacity for abandon, in the whole-hearted ability to love.

Flame's photograph was in a cobalt-blue frame. He had a dark, brutally handsome face, slightly scarred on one cheek. His thin mustache was so meticulous that it looked drawn in by hand. Strange to have seen him "alive" in the film footage, although there he had refused to look at the camera. In one ear Jimmy Flame wore a small black pearl.

"Did Flame really sell Mabel Eastlake to Otto Kranzler?" he asked.

"Who told you that? If he did, he had his reasons, and realized his mistake later and wanted her back." Fancy paced back and forth. "Jimmy knew Miss Eastlake could go far and since she was his original creation, he was vain enough to want to see his beautiful monster take the world by storm. And she did, darling, believe me. She caught them all with their pants down. Kranzler was a swine, but Miss Eastlake wasn't kosher so they had quite a time of it. That's Kranzler, taken when he and Mabel were filming *Two-Faced Woman*."

Massive, commanding, coldly Teutonic, Otto Kranzler stared down the camera with a glaring authoritarian stare.

"Miss Eastlake and I worked Otto's whorehouse together too, you know. Kranzler's was called Paradise Studios. Owned by Harry P. Franklin. That's P for prick, darling, and don't think old Harry didn't show us that he was a big one every chance he had. Harry brought Kranzler over from UFA in Germany. He thought Kranzler was a genius. Unfortunately Kranzler was, in his own demented way. So Harry told Kranzler that Kranzler could have carte blanche at Paradise Studios, and that meant carte blanche with Miss Eastlake too. She had to let him, but it was like fucking a fat pink hairless pig." Fancy shuddered, pursing her face with disgust. "God, how we hated Kranzler and his abuse. It could be so subtle, so meanly subtle, playing us off one another. Manipulative. He tried to get Mabel to love him, but he disgusted her. Jimmy was so different, raw and hard, and on his own since he was ten. But he could love, it came through somehow. And I know his record is not exactly smirchless, darling, but none of ours is. Jimmy had a beautiful stable of whores, and was mixed up in sulky racing and drugs and all the rackets. But Kranzler had been born into the Prussian aristocracy and had always had everything exactly the way he wanted it. Until—ha!—until he met Mabel Eastlake. Kranzler always said, 'Women love emotional violence and men love the physical kind.' But I don't believe that, do you? I think women love physical violence as much as men."

"I don't. I don't think violence comes naturally to a woman."

Fancy laughed at his naïveté. "Then how, darling, do you explain Miss Eastlake up there? How do you explain Abe West's mother? He would tell everyone how she would tie him and his sisters to a pee-soaked mattress and hit them and burn them and let her drunken tricks do whatever they wanted to them. Some women thrive on violence, darling. It's all some women have ever known. An addiction, I suppose, like any other. Just watch next time she feeds Cocaine a sweet little rabbit from Belgium, or some other little creature."

Or big creature, Alex thought with a shudder, seeing again Hilda Hatter's body . . . the panther plunging its teeth into her stomach.

"She lets it go at the top of the stairs and watches, laughing, as Cocaine bats it from room to room. It gives her a feeling of power. It keeps her young."

The photograph she now handed Alex was a Hollywood glamour portrait of Mabel Eastlake shot by George Hurrell. Alex had seen it in many movie-memorabilia stores. One hand clutching together the flimsy, delicate fabric of her dress, Mabel Eastlake was posed half-sitting, half-crouching, one of her long, famous, strong legs exposed, her blonde head thrown back and even the shadows of her eyelashes casting a violent, hypnotic spell on the viewer. Had her dress been torn? Was she, in fact, meant to be seen as the victim of some sexual outrage? Or was the dress a negligee and her pose meant to entice the viewer into her boudoir?

"Taken at the time of *Fast and Loose*," Fancy said, adding with a frustrated groan, "God how I've wanted to talk to someone! The burden of memories, the burden of the soul when it can't talk! You don't know what it's like living with murder all around you . . . "

Alex kept his voice low and calm. "You know who killed Kranzler and Boyd Powers, don't you?"

"Of course I know!" Fancy cried, smashing her glass in the fireplace.

"And you know about Hilda Hatter. You know that she's been killed, don't you."

"I didn't do it." Fancy let out a nervous whimper and paced her room, stopping in front of another photograph. "Hilda was terrifying. She knew too much. She knew everything and she made us pay and pay and pay."

Her photograph signed with a confident flourish, Hilda Hatter had posed wearing one of her famous hats, this one a head-hugging wingless version of Mercury's visor, one sharp quill of a feather jabbed into its inky fabric. Rising over one ear, the hat revealed a gleaming, marcelled mass of dark hair. Miss Hatter's dark, penetrating and powerful eyes saw everything, brooked no disagreement, and knew exactly what their vision was worth. A fine gossamer scarf was draped artfully across her neck and over one shoulder.

"Just what's in that film footage that made it so valuable to her?" Alex persisted.

Fanny looked at him intensely. "The Secrets of Mabel Eastlake," she whispered. "Film that could change the course of motion picture history if it ever got out."

"How? And how did Hilda Hatter get it?"

"She stole it. The night . . . the night of the accident. Jimmy was going to show it. The film belonged to him before she got it."

"Tell me what happened!"

"I can't! I can't remember that night—only pieces of it."

"You were here in Glass House that night."

"Of course I was here! I *lived* here."

"Mabel Eastlake was not telling the truth when she said Flame killed Boyd Powers and Otto Kranzler, was she?"

"Miss Eastlake above is incapable of telling the truth. She is falsehood incarnate!"

"Someone here in Glass House killed Kranzler and Powers."

Fancy looked at him with wide, terrified, pathetic eyes. "Darling, I can't tell you. I simply can't. Don't make me."

But Alex was tracking her now and wouldn't stop. "Was it Abe West?"

"Don't ask me these things!"

"Tell me what you remember of that night!" he insisted.

"I—I don't know anything except for what they told me." She turned, hands clenched. "Jimmy came to show the film. He was going to blow the whole Eastlake empire and everyone in it. He was going to *destroy* the image of Mabel Eastlake. It was the night *Desperate Woman* premiered. And he invited Kranzler and Boyd and Hilda to watch it—without telling them what it was they were going to see . . . "

9.

The talk in Hollywood was of nothing but Mabel Eastlake. Whispered rumors about her behavior on the set during the filming of *Desperate Woman* were beginning to take on the sharper and louder tones of certainty. Too many people on the set had seen things, heard things, and Hollywood, when it came to gossip, was smaller than any small town, and twice as vicious.

Notorious for the way he guarded sound stages where she was working, Otto Kranzler was said to be furious with the star he had created. Countless ruined takes had shot production costs up to nearly a million over budget, and Harry P. Franklin, personally producing *Desperate Woman* for complicated reasons that had to do with the internal management warfare then rife in Paradise Studios, started to panic. Losing his faith in Kranzler's genius had more to do with the escalating budget of the picture than with any deterioration or visionary change in Kranzler himself.

Desperate Woman was Kranzler's most ambitious picture to date. Unlike many of his American counterparts, he considered himself an artist in his field. He could think this way only as long as Paradise Studios, wanting what Harry Franklin called "some class" in their pictures, bankrolled his ideas. Surprisingly enough, Kranzler's pictures, all of them starring Mabel Eastlake—and probably because of her—were money-makers. Not always great money-makers, but money-makers.

Just as a painter might migrate to Paris for its light and artistic vitality, so Kranzler found his way to Hollywood. Here at his disposal was exactly what he wanted: technical equipment of the very highest caliber. Nothing was impossible here. He was proving that with his Mabel Eastlake movies.

To finish *Desperate Woman*, which he considered his most subtle, powerful and subversive film, the last thing the mighty Prussian Kranzler needed was Harry Franklin—his source of capital—undermining his confidence and undisputed authority. This had never happened to Kranzler. Until now he had been living a charmed existence.

For any number of reasons, then, the shooting of *Desperate Woman* was overloaded with tension: creation, psychically at war with the final reality of a ledger book, became a battle of personalities and personal power.

But how desperate a woman was Mabel Eastlake really? Was she caught in all this, or was she merely its catalyst? Hollywood said that she was preparing for a new role—as a patient in Glenwillows, that quiet and discreet "rest home" where stars went when, like the overworked horses they generally were, they simply broke down after too many years in the harness. Those who made it their business to know the secret dramas of a star's already overpublicized life topped one another with Mabel Eastlake stories. There seemed to be no end to them.

On the night of *Desperate Woman's* premiere, some astrologers later claimed, a particularly strange and malignant conjunction of stars and planets foreboded dire events. That was the same night that Jimmy scheduled the private screening of his own, personal film footage. "A private premiere," he called it.

Within the Industry *Desperate Woman* was rumored to be a bomb, which only added to the intense interest surrounding it. Mabel Eastlake, riding high on this crest of prurient speculation, appeared an hour late at Grauman's Chinese. The crowd had been growing increasingly restless during the long interval. But when Miss Eastlake finally did appear and stepped out of her white Duesenberg with Boyd Powers, the agitated crowd went wild. She was dressed in a costume from the picture, a tight white satin tuxedo and a white top hat. An enormous black orchid looked as though it had burst from her shoulder. Her tightly waved hair was greased and her thin eyebrows had been redrawn by Cygnet at a slightly malevolent angle. Not red but carmine, her lips were not meant for kissing so much as for sucking. The high cheekbones, the strong, cleft chin, the walk and the famous Voice: this was Mabel Eastlake. "The finest ass in Christendom," as Benchley once told Dorothy Parker.

Mabel was terrified of crowds, but had been forced to learn how to act as though she loved them. Tonight she was the object of their blind delirium. "Pretend that I can lean on you," she said to Boyd Powers through smile-starched lips.

For quite contrary to what Hilda Hatter's feature articles in "Movie Play" claimed, Boyd Powers had not married Mabel Eastlake for love. Nor she him. Their marriage, like many others at the time, had been feudally arranged by the highest powers at Paradise Studios. Boyd's floundering career desperately needed some sprucing up. Like Mabel's, his was a life of public adulation and private malaise; a life protected at all costs by the studio publicity department. As they smiled for photographers immediately after their faked elopement and wedding, Boyd's new wife said through perfect false teeth, "Don't believe for a second that this is anything more than a joke for me or for you."

Mabel detested him. They led emotionally and sexually separate lives. Mexican houseboys, and the drugs supplied to him by Jimmy Flame, increased Boyd's secret desire for humiliation, for annihilation. Mabel discovered that her husband had no internal direction, never quite knew who he was. Paradise Studios had purchased him in his teens, jealously guarding his secrets while it robbed him of any ability to act on his own. Boyd felt impossibly remote from his own life. What he projected on the screen, he knew, had nothing to do with who he was. And who he was had nothing to do with what *they*—the powers—wanted him to be. His image could never meet his soul.

But Boyd had far more in common with his emotionally estranged wife than he ever knew. He only realized it after he had seen Jimmy's film, but by that time he was slumped over and dying in the projection room, his skull smashed from behind.

For weeks before the premiere Mabel Eastlake's dreams had been vivid and frightening. She would wake up sweating, weeping. For weeks she'd lived in a state somewhere beyond exhaustion. "Reality" was lost to her. For weeks she'd had a stabbing migraine. Kranzler was pushing her beyond her limits. Everyone in this city of delicious stink and malevolent glitter, this city of Lost Angels, had become an enemy, wanting more and more of something she felt increasingly unable to give. Hilda, for instance.

And if Mabel's dreams had been strange, what could have been stranger than this extraordinary public adulation? She was worshipped. Here she was with the hoaxed image of love beside her. Here she was, dazed, with Boyd, the fake husband, while Hilda, her fake lover, waited for them in the lobby of Grauman's where *Desperate Woman*, Kranzler's own form of torture, was about to be shown.

And here was Otto Kranzler himself, who on that

balmy moonlit night was to fall face down in Mabel Eastlake's famous black bedroom, the same bedroom featured so lavishly by Hilda in "Screen Stars." Lodged in the mirrored wall beside his creation's black satin-covered bed, shattering the wall's specular surface, the bullets that had exploded into Kranzler's massive chest and out the back of his rib cage would be found. The murderer would see his face reflected once, then a thousand times in a kaleidoscope of silver fragments smeared with the blood of the tyrannical genius. Otto Kranzler, who knew all of the secrets of Mabel Eastlake, was to be added to their sum. The maker of Mabel Eastlake would go off to meet his own.

Taking drugs and alcohol to sleep, and combining them with cocaine to stay awake, and arsenic tablets for her migraine—all doled out by Cygnet, her trusted pharmacist—Mabel Eastlake was used to hearing strange sputterings in her head. But tonight, the night of the premiere, it was a low, constant, dangerous buzz, almost a voice, that made her feel wild, like screaming, like unzipping her weary flesh and running naked and free away from it. Since the camera always adds ten pounds to a filmed image, she had on top of everything else gone back to the Judy Garland diet of chicken soup and Dexedrine. She was speeded up like an old movie.

But she kept her face and eyes professionally open and alert despite the blinding, popping lights. There was that Eastlake smile to maintain; "Miss Eastlake's Killer Smile," as Kranzler dubbed it. Powerful arc lights swept back and forth across the moonlit Hollywood sky, signaling that this was a great event, an important event. The crowd howled and shrieked as Mabel Eastlake was led to the cement.

"Do they want me or you?" Boyd drunkenly whispered to her.

"If they knew the score, darling, they wouldn't want either one of us."

"You're being given to them," Boyd said.

Mabel eyed the fresh cement. "Sacrificed, darling." And then laughed her deep, artificial laugh—meant to sound so genuine—and stepped in the cement, raising and showing her splendid rump, like a she-cat in heat, as she bent over to impress her hands. A roar of approval went up on all sides.

Hardly able to see, she wrote her message to the world: "Thanks a heckuva, Sid," wondering for a moment who the hell Sid was, and plugged *Desperate Woman*. It took every ounce of concentration she had to do this, to remember where she was, let alone why. She shakily pressed in her feet and then groped blindly for an arm, found Boyd's, and together they entered Grauman's.

Hilda, spotting her at once, opened her eyes wide in amazement and appreciation of Mabel's white satin tux. She headed right for her, greeting, kissing and dismissing the usual Industry people along the way.

"Let's take a powder, darling," she said, "straight to the ladies' pissoir so you can change your shoes and wipe that cement off your hands."

And once inside, Hilda stood regarding Mabel, her Mabel, who was looking at herself in the mirror with nervous, dog-whipped skepticism. "I remember you at your first premiere," Hilda said nostalgically. "You were so frightened you threw up in your bag."

Mabel, silent, biting her lips, watched Hilda working expertly with her cocaine apparatus, all if it tidily hidden in a small square compact. "You were born with a silver spoon in your nose, darling. I wasn't. I've never stopped being afraid of the public."

"Darling, don't give a shit unless you've been given an enema," Hilda said. "What do they know of you? What I tell them. And haven't I been telling them only the best for years now?" She sucked the white drug deeply into her nostrils, sniffed and patted her nose with a smile, and was handing the apparatus to Mabel when the ladies' room door opened. They looked over to see Joan Crawford watching them, an amused smirk on her face.

"You girls powdering your noses?" she asked, swaggering in. "Say, I hear Paradise is almost bankrupt and no other studio'll touch you, Mabel."

Miss Eastlake and Miss Crawford had a strange, half-sympathetic regard for one another that made their rivalry almost enjoyable.

"Joan darling!" Mabel said effusively. "What an honor and surprise to see you at my premiere."

"Couldn't get out of it," Miss Crawford said, pulling out her lipstick. "Hello Hilda. This your new office?"

"Where else, my love, could I get so much poop from so many assholes?"

Miss Crawford laughed appreciatively as she lipsticked her lower lip. "How *is* this new picture of yours?" she asked Mabel from the mirror. "I heard that artsy-fartsy Kraut Kranzler kept your beaver mighty busy."

"The fiend is busting her balls," Hilda said indignantly, motioning for Mabel to pass the hop on to Miss Crawford.

But the star of M-G-M waved it away and pulled a slim flask from her purse, drinking deeply from it. "Speaking of balls," she said, turning Mabel around so that she could see the tuxedo front and back, "when is that priss-ass dresser of yours going to talk you into looking and acting like a real lady for Christ's sake?"

"I think it's quite chic," Hilda said, "although there are those who'll say it's another example of her penis envy."

"What's that?" Joan asked.

"Something this Austrian dreamed up," Hilda explained. "He says we women can't stand the fact that men have the cocks."

Miss Crawford laughed again. "Speak for yourself, Hilda. What a woman doesn't have is just one thing less that can be taken away from her." She found nothing wanting in her appearance and left after chucking Mabel under the chin.

"Don't come to Glass House tonight, Hilda," Mabel said, losing her balance against a sudden dark wave of foreboding.

"Think I'm afraid of that cheap greaser Flame?"

"Be afraid tonight, darling. Be afraid and please don't come—please—" Mabel began to cry. Thick tears slid heavily down the powder and grease on her cheeks.

"I've heard just about everything, darling," Hilda said. "Don't think I haven't informants very eager to tell me everything I don't see for myself. That's how gossip goes here. And I know you're living very dangerously these days, close to tilt." She took Mabel by the shoulders. "Now look, baby, sinning is what we all do. Sometimes it's what we have to do. You live here awhile and sure enough, sin comes over and asks you to dance. So dance, but watch your feet. As I do. Don't leave any tracks when you step out of the mud." She tried to draw Mabel's eyes to her own. "I've been a kind of guardian angel for you so far. I could have smeared you ages ago, you know, but I didn't. I couldn't."

Mabel stiffened as Hilda's lips pressed against her own.

"My angel. My darling Mabel." Hilda trailed eager kisses down Mabel's neck.

"No, don't," Mabel cried as Hilda's hand moved down her leg.

"Let me love you. I'll protect you. Let me take care of you."

"You can't!" Mabel pushed her away, harder than she intended.

Hilda instantly froze and her voice turned to ice. "*I*

can't? But that greasy dick of Flame's can any time he wants?" Turning suddenly into a remote, professional woman, she dabbed at her face in the mirror. "Don't lead me on too much, Miss Eastlake my dear, unless you're willing to dance. And when we dance, remember I'm the one who'll lead. That way I keep my feet from being stepped on. The last thing you need is to have me as an enemy. And believe me, nothing would stop me from coming to Glass House tonight. I want to have it out with that dago pimp of yours."

Mabel held on, held herself together, until the lights went out in Grauman's and *Desperate Woman* began. She then broke down as quietly and completely as she could. Boyd, no stranger to such scenes, managed to sneak her out of the theatre and back to Glass House. There, Mabel was put to bed and Fancy was told to watch over her.

Kranzler was already there, pacing back and forth like a large, penned animal, when Jimmy finally appeared with the film he had promised to show. Hilda arrived, roaring up in her Stutz. Boyd was drinking. Cygnet Sackville, sensing that something catastrophic might be about to happen, moved furtively and uninvited into the projection room with the other guests.

Jimmy Flame was a corrupt man even by Hollywood standards, and Mabel, in tender moods, always told him they'd better send their souls to the cleaners before it was too late and the stains became permanent. Because of Jimmy's connections, and because of the times, and because it was Hollywood, he and Mabel frequently joked about death, knowing that it could overtake them at any moment, could separate them forever. Perhaps it was because their lives were so filled with violence, Jimmy's physical, Mabel's primarily emotional, that they seemed to set the sheets on fire whenever they made love. Whatever its sensual basis, Jimmy's and Mabel's love was inflamed chiefly by their shared sense of impending doom. Something in both of them demanded it be that way.

Flame was not a man given to rescuing imprisoned women from towers, but he was planning an escape with Mabel Eastlake that night. So he had told Mabel, but he had not told her how. That was to be the surprise. It involved destroying the screen image that surrounded her, destroying thereby the Mabel Eastlake she had become. And gladly, for him, would Mabel have discarded the identity that had taken form, ironically enough, with *him*, at his instigation, at The Black Orchis. The only problem was that the Eastlake image was by now worth a fortune, and the rights to it were in the hands of the powerful.

So who was Mabel Eastlake on that night of her last public appearance? Who was this "woman even women adore," who had been handed her official personality on a sheet of paper bearing the insignia of Paradise Studios? Knowing herself to be created by others, a beautiful Frankenstein's monster, what would life be like when she was no longer what she had become? Did she have any other image?

One, Jimmy said, that he had on film. And the existence of Mabel Eastlake's true past, as it existed on this film that Jimmy now proposed to show, would ingeniously destroy not only Mabel Eastlake's screen image, freeing her from its bondage forever, it would destroy her enemies as well. *My* enemies, Jimmy might have said, for anyone who blocked his access to Mabel was an enemy.

Kranzler, if the secrets of Mabel Eastlake were shown and became known to the public, would be dropped instantly by Paradise Studios and forced to leave America. His adopted home would not want him if it knew what revolutionary visions his pictures actually contained, an entire visual subtext legible only in a series of double images. What was seen as provocative and European in his art would, if Jimmy's film were shown, be reevaluated with the eyes of puritanical American outrage and condemned. His charmed life was over if Jimmy's film were shown. For Otto Kranzler happened to be Miss Eastlake's co-star in this particular footage, footage Jimmy had retained from the early days of The Black Orchis.

Hilda Hatter was invited because she would be the perfect person to broadcast to the world the secrets of Mabel Eastlake. Miss Hatter would, at the same time, get her final comeuppance from Jimmy. They hated one another with the intense, intuitive hatred of rivals. Miss Hatter had been flirting with and flattering Mabel for years, attempting by slow degrees to move in and take over. Mabel, for the sake of her career, flirted with and flattered Hilda in return. Hilda, however, took her loves very seriously and worked with the fierce and dedicated patience of an animal trainer to subdue her wild-hearted Mabel. But now Jimmy could show the Mad Hatter once and for all the *folly* of loving Mabel Eastlake when Mabel Eastlake belonged to *him*. It was he, Jimmy, who held the snapping whip of power and was in charge of this particular menagerie.

And finally, Jimmy invited Boyd Powers. As Mabel's husband, did he not deserve the final humiliation of seeing with his own eyes his wife's carefully guarded secret? Jimmy never treated Boyd with anything less than contempt. He despised Boyd's weaknesses and had always turned them to his own financial advantage.

But there remained uninvited two people closer to Mabel than even Jimmy knew. Two players she had come to rely on absolutely, two who were always and forever "backstage" with her, helping to preserve her image and protect it from public scrutiny. Knowing her secret, both had become richer, closer to her, and more daring in what they would do to guard it.

Cygnet Sackville was there in the projection room that night, a slender shadow in black, able to efface his presence to the point of near invisibility. Cygnet, the man who prepared Mabel Eastlake for the ordeal of every day.

Fancy Barlow was upstairs with the unconscious Miss Eastlake. Fancy, the woman who doubled for the star on the set and who could, in a pinch, if Mabel Eastlake were attacked by one of her Panics, appear as Miss Eastlake at non-Industry functions.

A small, neglected child, Mary P was also in Glass House that night in 1939. She was quietly watching the moon from her bedroom window. The moon, in turn, watched Glass House—like the cold, impassive lens of a camera—as the drama that had been slowly unfolding reached its violent climax.

When Jimmy began to run the footage—and at first it was recent home movies shot at Glass House and featuring all the principals now gathered in the projection room—Jimmy stood protectively close to the projector. The images he directed onto the small, private screen belonged to him. This was the world-famous woman who belonged to him. "Not quite as technically perfect as your pictures, Otto," he said as the footage unwound, enjoying the director's visibly mounting anxiety.

Jimmy had spliced a title into the last and most important part of the footage: THE SECRETS OF MABEL EASTLAKE.

In the darkness of the projection room, the raw, grainy images of Otto Kranzler and a younger, coarser Mabel Eastlake appeared. Jimmy was aware that Kranzler immediately left the projection room, and did not try to stop him. "Afraid of what you'll see if you stay longer?" he called after him.

A few moments later gunshots were heard and fate, like a camera, moved in for a close-up of Glass House.

Fearing that Kranzler had shot Mabel, Jimmy ran

out of the projection room and up the great black staircase to her room. The door was locked. He pushed and hammered and finally used his own gun to shoot through it. Mabel's bedroom was rank with the smell of blood; that much he could sense with the quickness of an animal. He had to think fast. He stepped back outside. It was then that he caught a glimpse of a woman dressed in a blood-spattered white tuxedo running across the foyer below him, and outside. Simultaneously, through the open front door, he saw Hilda's Stutz roadster tearing away.

Calling Mabel's name, screaming it as if his heart had achieved a sudden, startled, unforeseen need, Jimmy ran after the Duesenberg, now on its ponderous way down the drive but gaining speed. Catching up to it near the front gate, he grabbed hold of the doorhandle and leapt precariously onto the running board. He banged on the car window, calling Mabel's name, telling her to stop, to listen to him. The car throbbed into a higher gear and sped through the gates.

Slowly he managed to get into the car. He knew there was a blood-crazed woman inside. He gave the steering wheel one strong, infuriated pull to frighten her into submission. The Duesenberg shrieked like a shot animal, spun sideways off the road and hit a tree. Until the police came with their lights, it was only the moon that looked through the shattered windshield, coldly surveying the human wreckage inside.

Mary P, for the rest of her life, would associate the full moon with that night of death and horror. She never forgot the sound of gunshots—those short, explosive, echoing sounds of doom. She remembered trying to get into Mabel Eastlake's room, finding Kranzler's body, and seeing Cygnet with someone sobbing in white. He rushed her out, screaming at her like an enraged bird. And always she remembered that high bright full moon of light from

the projector in the projection room. Under it she saw th
body of her vague "Uncle Boyd" neatly folded in two in
very bloody chair.

10.

These were the details of Mabel Eastlake's life leading directly up to the ill-fated night of the premiere of *Desperate Woman*.

Putting the pieces together much later, when he had harvested all the loose ends to his own satisfaction, Alex would remember this evening with a terrible poignancy. How many hours had they spent, he and Fancy? The burden of telling even part of the story lay heavily on the old housekeeper, and when she had waded as far into it as she dared, full of passionate outbursts and tremulous asides, she suddenly stopped and stared into the fire.

Alex, having come this far, pressed her to continue. "If Jimmy didn't commit the murders, who did?"

Fancy uttered a sharp, high, panicked cry. "Darling! You don't know? It was Mabel Eastlake!"

And something in Alex snapped then, and instantly he was filled with a dark sense of elation. Hadn't he now been vindicated, and his trip to Glass House made successful? The only thing left was to get this information out of Glass House and onto paper. Mabel Eastlake had framed Jimmy Flame for her own crimes.

Thinking of his story, Alex's heart began to race, incidentally sending out a low throb of Fancy's perfume. *He* would reveal this story to the world! Mabel Eastlake . . . a murderess. To think that underneath the sympathetic ambiguities of the celluloid image that Alex so admired, there lurked this murderous reality. . .

"Fancy!"

The housekeeper was hunched over, a quivering gloved hand to her mouth, her eyes straining wide with what looked like terror.

"Don't!" she hissed when Alex put a hand out to touch her.

"What's wrong? What is it?"

"I told you! I've never told anyone! In all these long hellish years I've never told anyone!"

Seeing the frightening change in her face, Alex backed away.

"I shouldn't have, darling, I shouldn't have told," Fancy whispered in a low, frightened voice. "I told her that I would never tell. You made me tell you!" she cried. "I'll tell her that you made me!"

"She'll never know," Alex insisted.

"Never know? Never know, he says!" She seized him by the shoulders and gave him a shove. "She knows everything! She finds out everything!" Panic distorted her face. "Darling, she'll kill you. If her story got out she'd kill you. They'd come to take her away. All of her life would suddenly come to nothing. They'd take all of us from Glass House. We can't stay here unless we keep her secrets. And now *you* know." She stood, crimson and seething, a finger pointed at Alex.

And it was true. Alex at that moment felt he held Mabel Eastlake's fate—perhaps the fate of Glass House—entirely in his own hands. As the only outsider who knew this terrible secret of Mabel Eastlake's, he could use the information, if he chose, for his own ends. And that was precisely why the longer he stayed here, the more vulnerable he became. If the secret had been protected so elaborately for these many years, what might they not do to prevent it from getting out *now?*

"You don't know what her guilt has done to me over the years," Fancy groaned. "And by staying in Glass House, I accepted Mabel Eastlake's guilt. I became a part of it. I didn't know what else to do. And the longer I stayed, the worse it became—not being able to tell anyone. I need to confess, darling. That's why I had to stay away from the witness box. That's why it was fixed so the D.A. never knew I was here that night. She said Jimmy did it, and I never once opened my mouth to call her a liar. The D.A. got a convenient solution, Hollywood got its scandal, and I got their word—I could stay in Glass House in exchange for my silence. Silence!" She looked around her with a bellowing, disbelieving laugh. "You don't understand why I stayed here, do you? You of today, you who've never known the tyranny of really expensive tastes. Luxury is sweet, Alex darling, and once you've had it you don't give it up easily. You fight to hold on to what you had, what you created out of nothing. You'll even kill for it."

It was then that Alex saw the silver doorhandle slowly turning. The door behind which Kilimanjaro, stuffed and mounted, rose in furious attack. "Fancy," he whispered, "is that door locked?"

There was no need for her to answer because by now it was ajar. They both stood staring.

It flew open. The terrible beast appeared. Alex dove for the mirrored alcove. He could see the blurred reflection of someone entering the room but was too terrified to look. "Fancy!" he shouted. Overcome by the violent and sinister atmosphere of Glass House, he thought, don't trust any of them, not even her. This could all have been prearranged.

A moment of silence. He lay with his ears covered, waiting for the bloody scream, the gurgle of death, the blow to his own body. Nothing happened. He looked up.

"Ah, darling, I'd forgotten about my pedicure," Fancy said, as she swooped in her old dramatic manner to greet the visitor. "Alex darling, why are you hiding in the liquor closet? The champagne's out here. And look who else . . . our zoo-keeper, darling, here to trim our cloven hooves. And he's brought six extremely gorgeous and very sexual-looking calla lilies for us to munch on while we're declawed." Her sudden excitement dispelled the troubling mood of moments earlier. "Come in, darling, come all the way in," Fancy said, pulling the Child by his arm. "Alex is here, and he'll put these phallic fellows in some gin, won't you, darling."

Alex took the flowers as Fancy settled herself happily, girlishly, on her giant bed, a Fabergé tray of Russian jade loaded with sweets beside her. "This is enough to turn any girl into a foot fetishist, darling," she said to Alex, smiling with terrible rapture as the Child slipped off first one, then the other of her feather-toed slippers. "Just imagine how those itty-bitty geishas must have felt when some giant samurai warrior licked their little bound feet."

Alex filled a crystal bowl with water and grimly arranged the lilies, their thick golden spadices thrusting themselves out in a merry parody of sexual symbolism. The Child's presence made him nervous, unsure, light on his feet, ready to spring away. Wearing nothing but loose-fitting shorts, the Child was eyeing him with intense interest. It's these clothes, Alex thought, embarrassed. Do I look too feminine? He removed the jacket to show off more of his own gym-trained body.

"You know what I think?" Fancy said to the Child. "I think he's a prude. You're a prude, Alex, just like Cygnet . . . but hasn't anyone ever told you it's the prudes who have the filthiest minds?" She laughed. "Haven't you ever had any just plain silly fun in your life? Just because we all suffer, darling, doesn't mean that we can't have a little fun on the side. Now don't tell me that a man's never bathed your feet in rosewater and wiped them dry with his toupee?"

"No, not recently," Alex said.

"Well, I believe in the luxury of the senses," Fancy said. "For my hard labor in Glass House I reward myself amply and luxuriously. A prisoner, yes, but a comfortable one. Accommodate yourself to your sins, that's what I say."

"How much of his past does he know?" Alex asked of the Child.

Fancy stroked the Child's head as he crouched on the bed by her feet, his back to Alex. "It's difficult to know how much he knows," she said. "Sometimes he's more like a funny and beautiful pet, just silently around. I don't think time feels the same way to him, or that he *could* understand his past if anyone told him. Like Mary P. It's better for him if he doesn't know. The world's too confusing."

"So he doesn't know that Miss Eastlake is his grandmother?"

"No, darling, *I'm* his grandmother." Fancy whispered, a blissful, possessive look on her tightly taped face. "I'm the one he knows to be his real old granny. Ooh, see how he's massaging granny's poor tired dogs?" She sighed sharply. "To relax her before her clipping . . . just as Cygnet used to relax Mabel before the ordeal of her face began. I taught the Child how to do this, and Cygnet taught me. He didn't like to actually touch her body, so I'm the one who had to massage Miss Eastlake. And believe me, darling, I learned all the strokes that break down a cold person's resistance and make them a prisoner to your touch. I used them on Jimmy, too. I've never told her that the Child comes and does this for me, of course. Miss Eastlake turns nasty when her pet pays too much attention to anyone else."

But how could the Child not pay attention when it

was nothing but pampering he received from Fancy? Alex watched, hardly believing his eyes, as the old housekeeper stroked the Child's arched body, long firm strokes which his flesh at first appeared to resist, as a cat's would, but to which the muscles slowly surrendered. Alex could see the Child sinking deeper into a state of physical contentment . . . Fancy too. He felt displaced, intrusive.

"Would you like to pet him?" Fancy asked.

"What? Of course not."

But the bemused expression on her face told him that she saw exactly what lay at the heart of his denial.

She popped a chocolate into the Child's mouth. "Now get the oils, darling."

With the reverence of a small boy delighted to participate in mysterious, grown-up rituals, the Child carefully removed a tray of precious ointments from Fancy's dressing table and brought it to the bed.

Following her part of this timeless ritual, Fancy was preparing to "puff bamboo," her old-fashioned term for smoking opium. From a hidden recess near the head of her bed, she withdrew a long, handsomely carved pipe and apparatus tray. "The secrets of the poppy," she whispered to Alex. "Have you ever let the voice of the flower speak to you?"

Alex shook his head.

"Some call it devil's jam," she said, picking up with long steel needles a tiny droplet of opium, "but I think of it as the tears of angels." She heated the precious seed of pleasure over the scented flame of a small lamp. "Pity we don't have Chinese servants to do this. In the old days they prepared the pipes with a special Asiatic ceremony. You can't tell me you'll ever get a computer to do *that* for you!"

Now the tiny glowing eye of dreams was ready. Fancy put it into the pipe and inhaled, passing it on to the Child. After smoking, he in turn offered it to Alex. Alex shook his head, afraid of succumbing to something stronger than the sensual languor of marijuana. If he didn't keep his wits about him Glass House would swallow him up. "Thinks he's too good for us," Fancy said to the Child. "We're too common. But if the famous and all-mighty Miss Eastlake offered him a smoke, a snort, or a syringe, wouldn't he just jump at the chance."

"That's not true," Alex said. "You just don't seem to realize the danger. . ." He broke off, seeing how the Child's eyes were on him, a little taunting, a little amused.

While Alex watched, the Child slowly stretched his massive body out on Fancy's bed. Alex couldn't take his eyes from that extraordinary form. If the Child had been an animal he would have gone over to stroke the beautiful hard curve of the belly, the slope of the shoulders, those sculptured arms, those high-arched feet.

"Lock the door and relax," Fancy said. "What can happen to you when the Child and I are right here?"

Which sounded reasonable enough, except that it also seemed crazy to take the time to enjoy himself in Glass House. The compressed sensation of underlying fear, that sense of being pulled downward in a steadily tightening spiral, hardly left him in the mood to relax. By relaxing, by letting down his guard for one moment, he might end up like Hilda Hatter.

At the same time, he was no doubt safer in here than outside. These two had protected him. And what *would* he do if he were out in Glass House? Go to the useless protection of an unlocked room?

"That's a boy," Fancy said as Alex locked the door he'd come in by. He stood for a moment contemplating Kilimanjaro, frozen in his leap. "Leave that one open so he can be here with us in spirit." She gave Alex the pipe and he inhaled for the first time the sweet breath of the flower.

"I want us to have fun tonight, like girlfriends who tell one another all their secrets, all the hearts they've broken and all the hearts that've broken them. A cozy little threesome. Miss Eastlake is hardly a fun person, as you know by now. But she used to be. . .years ago, at The Black Orchis. Darling, the jams we got into! Back before our lives became a Greek tragedy. You know, darling, wearing those clothes you really do remind me a little of what Mabel used to be like. And look, my Child can't keep his eyes off you."

Alex again caught the Child's eyes, this time in the mirrors of Fancy's toilette table.

"Olive oil tonight," Fancy whispered to the Child. "Tonight I want to remember Jimmy."

The Child began to massage Fancy's thick and surprisingly large feet with the oil. Alex stared at the soft, mysterious tuft of black hair that appeared above the waistband of the Child's shorts and rose from his buttocks part way up his back. The hair was a different color from that on his sun-gilt head, and seemed to emphasize some compressed, waiting energy stored in his lower back.

"I want you to forget all the gruesome things we've been talking about and come join us here, darling," Fancy said, patting the bed beside her. "Your feet could use a pair of strong hands on them, too, I'm sure. A two-for-one sale tonight. And here, just one more suck on Barlow's Best and even your toes will feel shapelier when the Child finishes with them."

"What the hell." It was useless to protest against the inviting voice of this old sinner, especially after another puff of opium. Trying not to appear as dizzy as he suddenly was, Alex primly sat down next to the housekeeper.

Why had he smoked this? His fear flared up again. It was like pot, only deeper, pulling him into his own body and the strange mystery of the present moment. It unglued all of his tense resolves. And it made him think of sex. A deep wave of heat washed through his body and the rare scent of *Forbidden!* rose and lingered around him.

When the Child, as if in response to the scent, slowly looked up at him, Alex felt his passion being teased awake. It was ridiculous to pretend that it didn't exist . . . yet it made him fearful. How open could he be, here in front of Fancy?

"Doesn't Barlow's Best make escape seem less urgent?" Fancy asked, languidly eyeing him. "You've looked like a totem pole all night." She came dangerously close, a breath away, and whispered, "Having a man serve her is a woman's greatest pleasure, you know . . . and sometimes having a woman to serve is a man's secret craving."

"Is that why Cygnet stays with Miss Eastlake? Because he enjoys serving her?"

"I suppose it's his way of being religious," Fancy said. "The Virgin of the Temple, as it were. *Jimmy* wasn't that way with his women, let me tell you. That's why all the Hollywood lesbians hated him so much." She threw her head back and laughed. "Mabel used to joke that she ran around with women who were butcher than her leading men. And Hilda was the Prince of that Secret Society. She was always getting others to compare sizes with her, if you get my drift."

"Dress sizes?" Alex asked.

"What a naive little darling you are!" Fancy laughed, snuggling closer. "I mean slit sizes. Hilda claimed to have the biggest, of course. She said she could fit a Grade A Extra Large egg into hers without cracking it—the egg, I mean. Imagine."

"Imagine!" Alex let out a nervous laugh.

"Could you do the same thing with your you-know-what?"

"Are you kidding? Could you?"

"Don't get fresh, my dear. You might accidentally put thoughts into my dirty old head."

The Child gently cradled Fancy's oiled and massaged foot between his knees and began to clip her toenails.

"What greater trust can a woman show than to put her nails in a man's hands?" Fancy said, touching Alex's hand with her own dark crimson nails. Alex stared at them with fascination.

"Does he ever go out by himself?" he asked of the Child. "Does he ever get to leave Glass House without Cygnet or Miss Eastlake?"

"One or the other nearly always accompanies the poor boy everywhere outside the gates. Overly protective, you might call them." Her voice turned sly. "But us has our little ways too, hasn't us?" she purred, stroking the Child's hair and withdrawing a pale lavender envelope from a drawer beside her. "When Miss Eastlake takes him out for his drive tomorrow, he'll manage to get this into a mailbox without her ever seeing him. Won't you, darling."

The Child took the envelope—guiltily, Alex thought—and tucked it in his shorts.

"My man of letters," Fancy said.

Instantly Alex conceived a plan and had to fight his altering consciousness in order to hold onto it. The Child could get him out of Glass House by the U.S. mails. "Who's it to?" he asked Fancy.

"An old fan of Miss Eastlake. I've been writing to him on her behalf for ages. A little joke I have going with the outside. I write this stranger the most incredibly filthy letters I can think of, all in Miss Eastlake's name. I slander her endlessly, make her the most perverse character who's ever lived . . . and she never even knows!" The joke was lost on Alex, but Fancy found it hilarious. "What must this old fan of hers think?" Wiping the tears from her eyes, she fed a petit four to the Child. Alex was told to fetch the brandy she had warming near the fireplace.

He confronted Kilimanjaro on his way, trying to defuse the deep panic the very sight of the rearing, attacking body put into his bones. Hilda Hatter. . .

The old brandy spread across his tongue and eased its warmth into his throat. The Child gulped his.

"Ah," sighed Fancy, closing her eyes, "I love it when he gets to my big toe. The nail's so tough it's like shoeing a horse for him, and he patiently works on it for hours. . ."

It happened so quickly that both Alex and Fancy were startled. The Child, dropping Fancy's foot, suddenly moved over and took Alex by his ankles.

"I've never had my feet pushed aside that quickly!" Fancy complained peevishly. "Don't do anything to make Granny jealous, dear." She watched as the Child began to press Alex's feet with his fingers.

"Oh God," Alex sighed, his shoulders dropping, his eyes closed.

"Divine, ain't it," Fancy said approvingly.

The opium, champagne, brandy, firelight, perfume, silver, silk, music . . . the Child's hands . . . the combination floated Alex into a state of aroused sensuality such as he'd never before experienced. That palpitating sense of powerful, violent danger lurking all through Glass House flitted like a warning through his darkened consciousness.

"He never massages my legs like that," Fancy complained, observing the two of them through a suspicious squint.

The Child's touch was superb. Alex let himself rejoice in it. Already his legs felt lighter, glowing with a flow of energy. When he felt this way he wanted to move, run, dance, somersault, chin himself. Through half-closed eyes he watched as the Child took his foot and cradled it firmly between his knees. He began to rub into it a light, scented oil. His deep, sunburnt smell reached Alex. They smiled at one another as the secret, silent voice of the flower began to speak.

11.

They left, through the door guarded by Kilimanjaro, into a corridor reached only from Fancy's room. They entered the dark bowels of Glass House, its complicated intestinal network of secret passageways built so that a vast, invisible army of servants could keep the place going. Alex had no idea where they were and simply followed the Child.

With a monastic gesture of silence, the Child slowly and with hair-raising exactitude opened a door so that not a sound was made. He motioned Alex over to it.

A desiccating blast of hot air hit Alex in the face as he peeked into the room. Cygnet Sackville was inside, lying naked and perfectly still on a narrow boardlike bed. There was nothing else to be seen in the empty, roasting-hot room. It was a weird, disquieting sight and Alex turned away from it.

The Child took his hand and led him away. They entered rooms Alex had not known existed and stepped out into secret walled gardens mortared into silence by the light of the moon. How different Glass House felt with the Child at his side. If its past could be erased or laid to rest, one could live and make a claim on these great, aesthetically peerless rooms. Glass House needed the simple grace of love to show off itself and its perfect proportions. But was that possible, when the past haunted the present and a burden of guilty secrets weighed upon the atmosphere? Mabel Eastlake . . . a murderess.

Hilda Hatter, dead, her body somewhere in Glass House or out buried in the grounds.

The mystery of Abe West . . . someone whose untold story and connection to Mabel Eastlake had yet to be unraveled.

Even the Child . . . even he, the moment he left Alex's side, had to remain suspect. The Child could not yet be absolved. His allegiance to Mabel Eastlake, unconscious or not, implicated him.

The Child showed Alex an enormous antique gym faced with mirrors and glass. A terrace and another walled garden lay beyond it. Alex stepped into the dry scented balm of the night, but as he did so the floor began to vibrate beneath his feet. He leapt off as it rolled away to reveal a pool. The Child, laughing at Alex's surprise, stripped and dove in, bobbing up at the far end, waiting.

"What the hell?" Alex showed off his own dive.

As they walked on, the Child revealed to Alex the secret ways of Glass House. He would open a door and they would suddenly enter a room Alex knew only from another perspective. In one of the gardens the Child pulled down his shorts and let loose a powerful stream of piss. His eyes were pleased, mischievous, wild. The golden spadix of the lily, Alex thought. He pulled out his own cock and there under the moon pissed as mightily as he could. If Frank could see this, he'd die.

Finally the Child escorted him back to his room, where he made it clear that he wanted to remain. At Alex's door his look changed to one of dark, hopeful longing. And Alex half-teased himself with the remarkable sensations inspired by the Child's hands, and then his mouth.

The Child did not want to let him go but Alex eased him away. His own power came from controlling this mutual sensual urge, not from giving in to it. The Child must be handled gently, like an animal that could turn at any moment. Alex told him he could return in half-an-hour.

Once inside his room he went over the plan that had occurred to him earlier. He would write a letter to Frank explaining everything and insert it with Fancy's letter that the Child was going to mail the next day. But would Frank believe him? He couldn't send a separate letter to Frank or even to the police because absolutely no suspicions must be aroused that he was communicating with "the outside." This fan of Miss Eastlake's, receiving Fancy's obscene letter, would either mail *his*, or call the L.A. police department. A ridiculous chance, but also a ridiculous situation to be in!

Every possible escape route had to be tried. He would have to get out and examine the circuit of the walls to see if Mary P's secret exit still existed. And he had to try to reach the telephone in Mabel Eastlake's boudoir. Until he was out of Glass House, he simply had to stay alive.

But now his sense of isolation in this strange place rose up to paralyze his hand. The secret voice of the poppy flower, that voice of sensual reflection and mysterious reality, expanded every moment, enlarged the meaning of every word. The letter needed to be written quickly, forcefully. He wrote it. But when he went to his suitcase for an envelope he drew back, panic-stricken. Someone had gone through his belongings. The two books by A. Liddell were gone. Gone too were all of his Eastlake research materials and the letter from Hilda Hatter. Someone in Glass House knew that he had not come innocently, as he claimed, but to gather information. A spider caught in its own web.

"All right, Mabel darling," he said in a low voice, turning to look up at the camera in his room. The black underwear still hung from it, blocking its vision. "All right, we'll see who's smarter. We'll see who gets to keep your secret."

But half-an-hour passed, and then an hour, and still the Child had not returned. Had he understood? Had something happened? Alex was impatient and frightened. He would have to find the Child.

Violence seemed to gather itself in every corner, waiting cunningly around every turn in the corridors. From the domestics' wing Alex reached the small anteroom to the right of the foyer. He'd become lost trying to follow the inner passageways. The library was just beyond. From there he could enter the projection room, and from the projection room the galley with the glass wall looking into the Child's inner garden. He found the library and stopped, patching up his resolve, listening hard to the vast silence of the place, ready to register any and every drop of sound.

The library was unexpectedly vast. Fancy had told him that when Cygnet had the house built he wanted to impress the fact of his literacy upon the guests. "Not unusual here in the Hills, darling, where they're always amazed if you can read more than the figures on a check."

A great curving bookcase patterned with an appliqué of rosewood, beech, ebony and cherry covered three walls of the room. Two fragile-looking wheeled ladders were attached to a track running its length. The roof was glass set in hand-blown sections forming a modernist design of intersecting arcs and lines. The quiet aroma of leather rose from a floor that was padded with it.

The wrong door. He suddenly found himself in the shadows of the foyer. And his heart nearly stopped when he saw, near the door leading down into the Black and Blue Room, the Child. He was dressed in evening clothes and staring upwards as if entranced. Alex followed his gaze. Standing at the top of her black curving staircase, with Cocaine on a leash beside her, was Mabel Eastlake.

The foyer was gently lit for an old star about to make yet another of her legendary appearances. No one in Old Hollywood knew better than she how to make an impressive entrance. And no one, Alex was later to learn, no one except Fancy and Cygnet ever knew the toll these appearances took, how for her they were exercises of sheer willpower, how she would fret and anguish for hours before each materialization.

Dressed and prepared by Cygnet, she would suddenly be there at the top of her black staircase. There she would remain, immobile, until everyone below was quiet and devoted wholly to the vision she was consenting to offer them. The men stared hard, the women harder.

And then down she would glide—click, click—a cigarette holder, always, and rings over the fingers of her three-quarter length gloves. Not one missed step, not one moment of hesitation as she conquered her terrifying staircase. Furs, feathers, hats and an ass with class: Mabel Eastlake. On a leash, something white, something ferocious. Her eyes then shone hard, glazed, half-wild. You never knew if she was going to be a bitch or a lady or that strange mixture of both that gave her style such an edge, such a bite.

Yes, you'd see those famous eyes, eyes created by Cygnet Sackville in the makeup laboratories of Paradise Studios. Eyes that Kranzler had approved, with a slight line in each corner to give his star the look of a dangerously seductive cat, one that rarely purred.

Mabel Eastlake, once descended, did not greet people. She accepted them into her midst. And what they never knew was that they were the ones who terrified her. They were the ones who would turn and attack . . . if they knew her secret.

A famous scene from *Moonstruck* played itself out in

Alex's thoughts as he concealed himself. In it, Mabel Eastlake enters a party alone. She stops in the doorway, wearing a silver fox jacket over a long, tightly draped black crepe gown. The inevitable cigarette in a long holder remains unlit as she surveys the assembled party. They are socialites. She is a tramp. She's here because one of them invited her. There he is. Seeing a young John Wayne standing near the terrace doors, Mabel Eastlake glides over to him and puts her cigarette, in its long holder, to her lips. Staring at her, John Wayne lights her cigarette. Eastlake takes a drag, flicking the tip of her tongue in a provocative manner. Dance music is playing. The crowd is silent and observant. Eastlake looks her partner up and down. She tosses away her cigarette, slides out of her fur jacket, and stands before him with her arms subtly beckoning. Pulled towards her as if by an irresistible magnetic force, Wayne steps into those arms. They do not speak a word, but what is unspoken is highly charged.

Mabel Eastlake was wearing that same black crepe gown tonight. The veil, thickly patterned with velvet chenille dots, put her face slightly out of focus. Alex was still able to recognize the face as the same one he had seen earlier. The face of Mabel Eastlake turned to stone, devoid of emotion, frozen into the perfection of a classic. Not the Mabel Eastlake of the movies.

Cocaine perfectly timed beside her, the two of them never missing a beat, Mabel Eastlake slowly began her descent. Staring straight ahead, her immobile eyes apparently seeing nothing, she had the terrifying look of a sleepwalker, a catatonic, a zombie. Her connection to this world was gone. The heels of her shoes sent out a faint clicking—click, click—slow and inexorable as the sound of a deathwatch beetle.

She carefully turned at the bottom and approached the shrine she had erected to herself. She walked slowly to the Vargas portrait and stood for a moment gazing up at it. Then she turned and held out an arm as she approached the Child. "Walk with me," she said. Her voice was old, withered, tired. It had nothing to do with her uncannily youthful face.

Alex waited until they disappeared into the anteroom that led into the east wing. Then, not allowing himself to think of repercussions, he slipped off his shoes and made his way up the staircase. If Mabel Eastlake were gone for even a few minutes, now would be the time to find and use the telephone in her room.

Suddenly he slipped. Looking out he saw only a black void, and a dislocating attack of vertigo sent a strum of panic through his bones. His stocking feet on the polished glass stairs were like skate blades on ice, and one foot shot out from under him. His body pitched forward, and only by grabbing hold of the step above was he able to keep from plunging over the edge to the floor.

He hung there for a moment, sweating and absurd in that huge black space, trying to balance his body before chinning himself back up. Wet fingers on polished glass . . . slipping. . . "Do it, Alex!" he ordered himself.

He began to swing his body for momentum. A clapper in the great silent bell of Glass House. At the right moment, with a sharp intake of breath, he pulled himself up to his waist. Poised, gathering still more control, he slowly raised a leg until it rested on a step. For a moment he had to let go altogether and grab for more stability in the center of the step. It worked. Knees weak, his body fired, holding on to each step with his hands, he got to the landing and slid over to the recessed doorway.

Locked.

Then he was back down, wishing he could fly, wishing he were invisible instead of so highly visible to Miss Eastlake's monitors, even if Miss Eastlake was not viewing them.

Peering around the door into the anteroom he could see, down the enfilade, Miss Eastlake, Cocaine and the Child slowly walking. Alex dashed through the bar, and into the room that had access to the Child's world.

The briny moonlight gave objects a terrible significance as it sifted down into the inner garden where the disfigured stone statue of Mabel Eastlake watched softly, ominously, from the ruination of her marble face. Alex stepped in.

The still, humid air was sharp with the smell of cat. Some kind of night-blooming flower sent out a lurking, musky perfume. A bird disturbed the thick silence with a sudden shrieking call. Alex entered the hut.

With one gaze his fantasies about the Child were both destroyed and made newly mysterious. Books lined the walls. There was a single narrow bed, carefully made up with an old patchwork quilt. A green-shaded lamp sat on a desk.

Two books by A. Liddell lay on the desk, under the light, but Alex did not have enough time to take it all in or to worry about the theft. He found the Child's shorts, pried open Fancy's envelope, and inserted his message. It would not reseal properly. It would have to do. Now it was time to go.

But his attention was caught by a thick leather-bound volume under a jar of flowers. Inside, words were scrawled across the pages:

> I see him. I want to love. I see her. My heart follows. Do I love him or her? Her in him or him in her? Him alone? Her only? My tongue is dumb, but he hears me speaking my silence.

In a moment Alex was back outside. He saw Miss Eastlake's balcony, with the steplike branches of the banyan tree rising up to it. If Miss Eastlake's front door were locked, he would get in through this back entrance.

But not tonight. He dare not tonight. He was almost certain that a dim, slender figure, arms crossed, was pressed back in the shadows of the balcony, watching.

Quickly and stealthily he went back into the foyer and was already slipping his shoes back on when Mabel Eastlake's voice said in the distance, "Take her off the leash. Let her have a run."

Alex shot a glance down the east wing. The panther was standing on the dining table. The Child was removing its leash. The panther saw Alex and leapt from the table.

He ran to the door he'd come from earlier. Locked. No choice but the anteroom before the library. Glancing back, he saw Cocaine appear in a far doorway and when he looked back again the cat was standing in the foyer. The diamonds in Hilda Hatter's choker glinted softly around her neck.

Quiet. He must be quiet. No fast movements to startle the cat. Feeling behind him with one hand, all his senses painfully alert, Alex found the door of the library and inched it open. The cat darted into the anteroom. Fear of it, and a blinding sense that he was powerless before it, prevented Alex from thinking to shut the library door. The cat stood tensed, watching him. It moved towards him.

Alex felt his way along the bookcases, deeper into the library, towards the door he'd used earlier.

Casting a huge shadow, the white panther stalked into the room.

They looked at one another.

It was difficult to think, to plan. As slowly as he possibly could, Alex edged his way towards one of the ladders.

The cat stopped, watching him. Opening its mouth, it made the motion of a sound, a low warning growl, perhaps, from deep back in its throat. But nothing was heard.

The diamonds sparkled maliciously.

Alex carefully raised one foot to the bottom rung of the ladder. He did not dare turn, fearing the cat would lunge if he did. It took another step towards him. With the light of the moon pressing down through the patterned ceiling, with the oppressive silence of Glass House all around, capable of absorbing him if he did not conquer his fear, Alex climbed another rung. And then . . . slowly . . . another.

A few rungs higher and he turned to clamber to the top. Out of reach, he surveyed the room. Below him Cocaine was poised in an excited rear-wiggling crouch, the preliminary to a kill.

With a sudden leap, she came straight for the ladder.

Teeth that could tear off a limb, lacerate flesh as though it were paper. Alex felt his mortality, the sad frailty of his body. Another attack of vertigo began to play havoc with his sense of perspective. For a horrifying moment he looked down and saw the panther's open mouth mere inches below his feet. He could feel the animal's hot breath. He tightened his hold on the ladder but it felt suddenly as insubstantial as a twig.

Cocaine reared up, stretching full-length, her powerful body shaking the ladder with its weight.

Alex could do nothing but climb the few remaining rungs to the very top of the ladder and stay there, clinging to its sides.

Cocaine backed off, but kept her eyes on him and bared her teeth. In the moonlight, set off by the shimmer of diamonds, the eyes of the cat had an unearthly glow. They were intense, terrifying, incomprehensible.

And then, as if parading the proud, glorious pleasure of her strength, the cat ran in a long, wide circle around the room, increasing its momentum until again it leapt at the ladder, this time with the full force of its motion.

The ladder shook and began to roll down its track. Alex was nearly knocked off by the impact. One of his feet slipped from the ladder rung and his shoe dropped with a clatter to the floor. Cocaine jumped on the shoe, biting into it, shaking it back and forth in a frenzy and then excitedly hurling it into the air.

Alex tried to prepare himself for the pain, for the moment when it would actually happen, when the teeth would crunch mercilessly through to the bone, and his flesh would become food.

The enraged cat backed off once more, making ready to repeat its running leap. As the full force of Cocaine's strength slammed against it, the ladder buckled and sped on to the end of its track.

From then on it was sheer willpower. One against the other.

Cocaine crouched in the center of the room, her whiteness crisscrossed by a net of lines and arcs cast by the patterned ceiling onto the floor.

Finally it happened. Cocaine ran, leapt higher, a strong, callused paw hit Alex's leg. He heard the splinter of the breaking ladder and fell with a cry onto the bristling excited animal. Instantly he gave himself up to attack, trying to keep his face covered, refusing to believe that this was how he had been fated to die.

The terrific weight of the cat was on him and then off, and the Child was there struggling to calm the infuriated beast, wrestling with it, trying to hold it still. They fought until the Child had the cat under him and had managed to soothe it with the force of his greater strength. When he had subdued her, the Child took Cocaine by the diamond choker and led her from the room.

Alex tried to keep from sobbing, but the intensity of his relief demanded some form of expression. He lay on the floor drawing in shallow, shuddering breaths. The

Child reappeared. In his evening clothes he reminded Alex of someone else . . . but who? Then he knew—Abe West.

He felt very small as the Child approached him. He did not want the Child to see him so vulnerable, but he could not move.

The Child was there crouching beside him, gently touching his face, holding him by the chin and staring intently into his eyes. He took Alex's hair and crushed it in his fingers. He buried his nose in its wet thickness. Alex made the motion of a cry as his shirt was torn open and the Child pressed his hand to Alex's chest and neck.

The mysteries of the past and the dangers of the present were obliterated in the pressure of the Child's powerful body against his own. Alex wanted finally and absolutely to enter into whatever their fate was to be.

The Child helped him to his feet, took him in his arms, held onto him. Some natural instinct brought them to the inner garden. There, on the Child's bed, he felt the Child's lips, heard the hot pleasure of his breath. Wanting to make his own strength known, Alex clasped the Child's powerful back as hard as he could, absorbing its strength into his fingers. He could feel himself letting go, wanted to. His legs were held by the Child's thighs. His clothes were torn off. Large, hungry lips were on him. The sweet faint pull of teeth on his nipples. The Child's fingers traced warmth, kindled fire along the length of Alex's body. And Alex let himself go. He gave himself up to this strange silent creature. His flesh felt the burr and lap of the Child's tongue. He reciprocated every thrust, every stratagem that passion suggested. The Child's smell came in waves and Alex wanted to gulp it down, gulp down that smell of musk and flowers, that intoxicating smell of male strength, male passion. The Child cradled Alex's body in the hard smoothness of his arms, looking deep into Alex's eyes. For a moment they were lost to everything else. A deep kiss. Then he resumed his desperate, tender embraces, convulsed by the force of pent-up, and returned, longing. Alex was frightened by the intensity of the Child's passion, but more frightened by his own. He made an attempt to resist, but the Child had clearly determined upon his complete surrender. At last Alex gave in, gave himself up with a kind of wild, self-dissolving joy. In another instant he was devoured.

12.

I could tell you stories about Mabel Eastlake, boy, that
I would turn this hair of yours platinum." Cygnet fingered a dark strand of Alex's hair with interest, testing its fol-
licular resiliency. "A star has no greater friend than her
personal makeup artist and dresser, you know, and stars
tend to cling to those who know how to create them."

"Miss Eastlake doesn't strike me as the clinging
type," Alex said.

"Weak and dependent," Cygnet sniffed.

"Well, that's certainly not her screen image."

"Weak and dependent, boy, *vulnerable*, just like
you." He cast an inquiring glance at Alex. "Why do you
suppose it is, after all, that women are so vulnerable and
persistently let men make such fools of them?"

"Women are more trusting," Alex said.

"But not, I think, to *be* trusted."

"Then why spend all your time serving them?"

"Because I find them far more fascinating to observe than men. A different species from us entirely."

In the same way that Sackville himself was of a different species of man. Alex tried to place him in some iden-
tifiable age group, connect him societally with a people and
a culture. It was impossible. Pure Hollywood, he thought.
A nonperson in a nonplace, a character of his own inven-
tion. Looking not younger than he was, but different from

what nature would have had him be. That weird, masklike look that lifted faces inevitably assume, a stiffness that effaced the human play of emotions and eventually the human character itself.

He tried to imagine Cygnet young, as young as himself. "Mr. Sackville," he asked, "have you ever been in love?"

Cygnet let out a high wavering laugh. "In *what*?"

"In love."

Sackville stepped back, as from a too-hot fire. "Oh yes, boy. Once I was in *love*." He theatrically mocked the word by rolling his eyes up and clasping both hands to his skeletal breast. "Yes, once that divine spark set one on fire. But one was smart and put it out at once. At once!" he said intently. "Do you know why? Because one could feel oneself slipping away. One could feel oneself losing one's sense of who one was. One's identity."

"Who was it? A man?"

Cygnet's gaze turned sharp as he lifted the razor he was stropping. "How dare you make assumptions about me!"

"Sorry."

"Anyway, my real love is Glass House." His face flashed a look of amusement. "But even Glass House, you know, can be jealous. Oh yes, insanely jealous of any rivals that may try to come between me and it."

Reclining on Mabel Eastlake's sumptuous makeup chair, naked under a thin white hospital gown, Alex tried to sober his body from its residue of passion. An intense physical memory of the Child's flesh, reluctant to displace itself into memory, still hovered about him. He could feel it like a light second skin. Never had his body been so aware of its own longings. What had the Child awakened in him? And where had the Child learned so thoroughly the fine art of sensual persuasion?

Strange, now, to be shaved by the epicene Mr. Sackville while still floating in this languid state of utter contentment. With his unisexual clothing now covered by a long white clinical gown, Sackville had the look of an outlandish surgeon or mortician. Despite the hot intensity of the makeup lights, his own face maintained a tight poreless chill. But it was his touch, so professional and sexless as to deny any involvement with Alex's physical reality, that Alex found particularly repulsive. The tips of Cygnet's long and very white fingers, as he turned Alex's head this way and that, felt like cold, metallic, medical instruments. Every few moments he would clean and then vigorously strop his razor; his stroke was painstaking: he found and severed every hair on Alex's face.

Alex hadn't dared say no when told to "report" to his studio. "Alone," Cygnet had added significantly.

Adjacent to the Deco-Baroque entrance to his secret domain, in the west wing of the house, Cygnet's studio, as he insisted on calling it, had the same heartless, sound-and-self-absorbing atmosphere as the rest of Glass House. Another room created to frame drama. "Drama must exist in the art one creates for it," Cygnet had said, referring not only to Glass House, but to the beautiful screen image of Mabel Eastlake. He had created both.

"For she was created, boy," Cygnet oracularly intoned when Alex entered the studio. "In this chair, in this studio, under these lights, Mabel Eastlake has been created over and over again. An Eve from Adam's side, as it were. A Hollywood goddess, springing forth in full makeup and costume from the head of our mighty Zeus, Otto Kranzler. But it was I, boy—I, her beloved Cyggie—I who breathed life into her, into that image. It was I who ultimately perfected her."

Amused by Alex's naïveté in these matters, Cygnet had shown him the cosmetic formula of Mabel Eastlake:

seven pages of finely detailed instructions outlining the exact and incredible makeup procedure to be used on the new star at Paradise.

"A star is randomly chosen by the gods, boy, but once chosen a star will do anything to stay that way. A star can never forget the touch of a god's finger, the breath of the divine summons. And to remain a star, appearance is of the utmost importance. An enduring, recognizable image. Because a star is not hastily assembled from the elements at hand—with a tube of cheap lipstick and some powder. No, a star must be perfection, a perfect vehicle of her screen image. And perfect materials must be used in her manufacture."

The amount of makeup used on Mabel Eastlake over the years was prodigiously reflected in the extraordinary number of bottles, tubes, jars and containers on the laboratory shelving. Many of these ointments, unguents, pastes and powders had been invented by Cygnet, and were based on arcane research in the field of ancient herbal cosmetology.

And it is a laboratory, thought Alex. Impressive but in a soulless, anonymous, clinical way. There was nothing to distract the attention of the chair's occupant—no art on the walls, no music for the ears—and so whoever endured Cygnet's ministrations in this studio of his was pushed by the intense concentration of the lighting into a state of high inner self-consciousness bordering on lunacy. Any woman subjecting herself to this routine for several hours a day deserved all the stardom she got.

"You have a good neck, boy," Cygnet said, drawing his razor down to Alex's clavicles. "We'll show it off." The closeness of his shave made Alex feel cleaner, lighter. His face was wrapped in steaming scented towels.

When Cygnet finished his preliminary inspection of Alex, using a magnifying glass and a small moving beam of light, trying the firmness of his facial structure, noting with unnervingly professional precision every wrinkle, every line, every physiognomic expression of character and individuality, he stood back to size up Alex's case. "Yes, I believe one can do it," he said finally, a tremor of excitement in his voice.

The intensity of the lights was quickly reduced and, before Alex could react, Cygnet had bound his wrist to the chair with a silk strap. If he struggled now, Sackville would see it and use it to his advantage. Alex said nothing and allowed his other wrist to be secured. Sackville threw him a flirtatious glance as he did this.

"You're panicking, boy," he said, "just as Miss Eastlake would panic when I strapped her down. I can feel it coming out of you in great waves."

Alex forced his face to assume composure, like a prince meeting his executioner. Cygnet's spidery fingers trod on his neck, tying another wide silk strap around it. The strap was tightened to the exact limit of Alex's ability to tolerate it. Another centimeter would have set off the panic reaction accompanying suffocation.

"Sometimes one hated to see her face as one tied this strap," Cygnet said, his dry scented breath in Alex's face. His mouth smelled like an old woman's closet. "It made her feel claustrophobic, trapped, especially when I tilted her head back." He suddenly tilted the chair so Alex's head was lower than his feet, explaining that it "brought the blood up." "You understand. But she could never conquer the terror she had of the Straps, as she called them."

A stinging cold liquid was suddenly brushed on Alex's face. With a faint orgasmic sound, Cygnet began his work. With his fingertips he sharply pressed the cold substance into Alex's pores. Alex could feel some tingling, anesthetizing transformation taking place and cast his eyes about for a mirror. The chair was angled so that he could not see any reflection of himself.

Now the pad his head rested on was angled back another inch, stretching his neck, and before he could move,
a needle had been inserted under his jaw. When the needle
was withdrawn he could barely open his mouth, so it was
too late to protest and rage was useless. Too dazed by the
first anesthetic to object to the second or the third, he simply watched as Cygnet inserted two more needles, one in
each cheek. Part of the horror was that whatever drug Cygnet used instantly wrapped Alex's head and neck in a
numbed state of acquiescent bliss.

"Soon you won't be able to smile at all," Cygnet said,
watching impassively as the corners of Alex's mouth
turned up in an intoxicated Cheshire-cat grin. Just as slowly Alex could feel his flesh settling down, stiffening, rigidi-
fying.

Cygnet began to bathe his face in a mixture of
rosewater, glycerine and egg-white. "This hardens the
face, boy. And Miss Eastlake *did* have a somewhat hard
face. This mixture cakes the pores so they can't breathe,
suffocates them as it were. And this," he said, fixing a brace
on either side of Alex's head, "will keep you from moving.
You know, boy, a flinch in Hollywood can hold up production for hours. And sometimes Miss Eastlake was perverse
enough to do just that. She couldn't *help* herself, she said.
She could be a whiner, all right. But one taught her endurance, boy. Endurance. One trained her to sit perfectly still
in this chair for three hours every morning. Three hours
here, before her day at Paradise began. And after working
there all day, Kranzler *might* have a minute's worth of usa-
ble footage. You know, one always admires fellow perfec-
tionists, no matter how loathsome they may otherwise be.
And Herr Kranzler, to be frank, was loathsome. One quite
hated him."

As he worked, Cygnet told Alex about the Mabel

Eastlake Master Plan: a highly detailed and carefully or-chestrated series of public relations maneuvers that un-leashed, finally, the new star image of Paradise Studios.

Ah, but make-up was only one part of the creation of Mabel Eastlake's image. Each detail pertaining to her was as precise, elaborate and artful as emerging technology and Otto Kranzler could make it. Cygnet felt that his own contribution had never been properly recognized.

By 1933, he said, no woman dared to be photographed without deep hollows in her cheeks and dramatic shadows on her face. "And there was a slight world-weariness in the expression that everyone tried to copy."

The spacing of Mabel Eastlake's eyes was accentua-ted by affixing long, imported eyelashes only to the outer halves of her upper lids. Kranzler would then have her shot slightly off-face, using a baby spot at a thirty-five degree angle above the eyes. This blended the rather high Eastlake forehead with the painfully realigned Eastlake hairline. Stronger lights were aimed at the chin, creating a shadow to emphasize what was only a slight cleft.

The Eastlake lips were naturally large—almost as large as Crawford's blaringly overdrawn ones in *Sadie Thompson*—but Kranzler would sometimes have Cygnet stuff tissue under the upper one so that her pout became more pronounced and inviting.

In the matter of lighting, Kranzler was no less a perfectionist. Miss Eastlake was required to sit endlessly, for hours, until Kranzler had achieved absolutely the right "look" desired for each still or Studio-release shot. Mabel Eastlake was always well lit. The hot glare of Studio lights tended to melt her, however, so that her face had to be con-stantly chilled. "Otherwise, after a while she'd go rotten, like mayonnaise," Cygnet said.

Overhead lighting brought out the resculpted bone

structure of her face. Gold dust was sprinkled in her hair as a highlight. "Dietrich used the same trick," Cygnet reported, "but Eastlake's was the more naturally beautiful hair."

Alex's own hair was drenched in a foul-smelling liquid and set tightly with tingling electrified rollers attached to an old machine. Christ, he thought, I'm going to come out of this looking like Elsa Lanchester in *The Bride of Frankenstein.*

The pain of Mabel Eastlake! Alex could almost feel it. Incisions were made and paraffin poured under the parts of her that Kranzler wanted built up and changed for the camera. Even her pelvic bones, because they subtly undermined the illusion Kranzler was trying to create, throwing the curve of her body off as she stood in a certain characteristic pose, were shaved down. It was all part of the marketing of Mabel Eastlake. She must be perfect. She must be believable in her unbelievable perfection. "She must be so beautiful," Kranzler had once said, "that men will want to destroy her."

The same electrolysis used to reshape her hairline stung her flesh as her body hair was plucked, one at a time. Hot wax was poured over her, again and again. She allowed Cygnet to drug her more deeply so that when the wax dried and was torn away, any lingering hairs with it, she would not feel it and have to scream. She would feel nothing.

Hours and hours of painful and exacting dental work were necessary if Mabel Eastlake was to have her famous "Killer Smile." The backmost molars, top and bottom, were removed to create the high Eastlake cheekbones. Her capped teeth were known back then as "cheaters."

Always a new pain in her face or somewhere in her body. For over two years, during the time Kranzler was first molding her clay, shaping her form and laying the-bodily groundwork for Cygnet's final cosmetic superstructure, Mabel Eastlake's flesh was tortured daily, subjected to a barrage of cosmetic operations that made pain a daily ritual to be endured in the name of beauty. Kranzler wanted her to have a perfect body. "Aesthetically, she must be perfect," he insisted.

As an accompaniment to her physical pain, she was also rigorously coached by Kranzler into becoming a different character. She developed her High Hollywood accent—more theatrical than the voices of today—and learned to move with the swaggering grace she became famous for.

Kranzler instilled in her the fear of being observed at all times and from every angle by the camera, Kranzler's eye, the unarguable eye of God. "They'll see it on film," he said, when she was not as perfect as he wanted her to be. "It will be there in close-up."

For Otto Kranzler had a perfect vision of the new star he wanted to unleash on an unsuspecting American public; a star unlike any seen before. Mabel Eastlake! There was her name, her face, forty feet high, staring down like a goddess on Times Square. She burst into tears when she saw it, knowing the sight had changed her for life. That was when she knew in some dark, fatalistic way that she could not escape becoming enslaved to the image they had devised for her. And yet she could not keep herself from hating it.

With the alchemy of Hollywood at his disposal, Otto Kranzler took base metal and transformed it into gold. By the time he was finished, his star had been planed into perfection. "Streamlined and mysteriously ambiguous when it came to sex," Cygnet affirmed. "The oh-so-moderne modern woman, breastless, with a high, firm derriere and long, strong, beautiful legs. Kranzler gave her a little round belly, too, to make her front softer and more erotic. But that tummy was rock-hard muscle. Once she and Jimmy had a terrible fight and he punched her in the stomach. Miss Eastlake laughed and sent him reeling with a fast upper cut to the jaw."

Ironically, it was Sackville, back when he labored under the uncongenial burden of projecting a masculine image, with whom Mabel Eastlake co-starred in her first, and Cygnet's last, picture, *Hearts Aflame*. The combination of her deep theatrical voice with Sackville's thin, cultured, flutey one proved to be irresistibly funny to the movie-going public. Unfortunately, Cygnet's was not a comedy role as Eastlake's was, and whilst the bright newcomer Mabel Eastlake was showered with acclaim for being such an accomplished comedienne, Cygnet Sackville was laughed off the screen forever. The moment he opened his mouth, audiences found him completely and hopelessly unconvincing as a romantic male lead. According to Cygnet, Kranzler had had this all planned from the very beginning.

"Kranzler needed someone to act as a foil to his new star. In *Hearts Aflame* her edges were still a little rough and the vulgar guttersnipe she truly was kept peeking through, so Kranzler quite brilliantly diverted attention from her by using *me*. I was the first, you know, to be sacrificed to our dear Miss Eastlake." But he sounded as though he didn't exactly consider it an honor.

Ah, but this was Hollywood, circa 1930, made dizzy and relentless by the power of the picture. Americans—the entire world—had an insatiable need for pictures, images of what was not theirs, fantasies to help shore them up against an increasingly bankrupt life. Parched souls thirsting for water paid two-bits to drink at the fountain of Hollywood. Hollywood! Called, chosen in its queer, sunbaked way, to lead the multitudes. And it became a center with power as vast as old Rome, a locus point of great authority, holding dominion over the intense power of images. It drew more than its share of charlatans and seekers. They came hoping to reach God in Hollywood, which meant converting to the faith of the image and believing only in flesh that could be seen . . . and heard.

And so Cygnet fell, an image that could not be believed once it was heard. Mabel Eastlake's was the Voice, hers the tone of authority to be listened to, hers the image to adore. Whatever his humiliation at the time, and it must have been considerable, Cygnet spoke of it now with pinched detachment. "One of those great events in life, boy, that either make or break one."

For to be a failure in Hollywood then meant that he was instantly barred from entering the most exclusive nightclubs in the city, those parade-grounds of the temporarily elect. And when Mabel Eastlake, now shown to the best tables, heard that her co-star could no longer get into the Garden of Eden, she knew she had a chance to get Glass House.

"One's demands were not unreasonable," Cygnet said. "All one asked was a fair price and to be allowed to take over as Miss Eastlake's dresser and cosmetician. Miss Barlow had been ineptly handling it up until then. Miss Eastlake was thrilled with the idea, but Kranzler wasn't. He knew, I think, that one hated him for what he'd done to one . . . but he also knew that one could put an end to Miss Eastlake's career in a second . . . if one *chose* to do so." His thin pink lips stiffened into a smile. "For *I* knew her secret. *I* knew what Kranzler had to hide if his vision of Mabel Eastlake was to succeed. That fatal discrepancy, boy, between the image seen and the unperceived reality behind it."

Mabel Eastlake, newly riche, lusted for Glass House and the moderne sophistication of its image. She and Fancy moved in, but Cygnet Sackville never moved out. Otto Kranzler soon found out that without Cygnet there was no Mabel Eastlake. And far from harming her, Cygnet worked with enormous diligence, protecting the Eastlake image and so much refining it that Mabel became emotionally dependent upon him. She learned her style, or at least its final screen realization, from him.

"You'll want something cool about now," Cygnet said, raising the chair and putting a straw to Alex's lips. "A special herbal formula designed to calm and refresh you before I begin on the eyes and lips."

Alex eagerly gulped down the soothing, delicious liquid. The narcotic film over his senses dulled his fear, but he knew it lay in wait for him as soon as the drugs wore off. It was a confusing mental state to be in, half-paranoiac and half-blissful. "Why is it so important that you make me look like someone else?" His voice was thick, unreal.

"Miss E and I have an amusing wager, and I intend to win."

"What sort of wager?"

"That is between Miss Eastlake and myself, boy. It has nothing to do with you. You are simply the—"

"Object."

"Precisely. Now will you keep your eyelids absolutely closed and still, or must I weight them?"

"These lights—and my face feels so weird—"

"Your face is changing. Your appearance is undergoing a transformation. Tell me, boy, have you ever had an out-of-body experience?" Cygnet asked.

"*In*-the-body ones are hard enough."

"Mabel Eastlake had them whilst sitting in this very chair. This is a secret, boy, that no one else knows. I told you I'd reward you for your cooperation, didn't I? Yes, Miss Eastlake had the power and then the misfortune to dissociate. When she could no longer stand what she was, what they'd made her into, she would leave her body and its false image behind and enter into a state of nonpersonality. Imagine. It was the only way she could escape from the burden of what she was, who she was."

A form of schizophrenia, thought Alex, although others might call it mystical. The image of Cygnet lying naked in a burning hot bare room came back to him.

"Whenever a situation became too nerve-racking—and the life of a star *is* nerve–racking, boy—Miss Eastlake was able to float away, watch herself, as if she were her own home movie. Detached from the living life of Mabel Eastlake, this other consciousness she first achieved accidentally, and then by various drugs. What could be more wonderful than not to be anybody?" he asked Alex, fixing a sharp gray eye on him. "Free from the appalling weight of personality, the banality of being the sad mortals we are . . . imagine . . . to become the camera, instead of what the camera films. A form of godhood. For the camera does change you, boy. Invades your soul. Demands that you perform perfectly for it. Demands that you present a perfect image to it. No wonder poor Miss Eastlake grew to hate the camera staring at her. She had terrible eyesight, you know, but had to appear as though she saw everything 20/20. The world around her was an unfocused blur and she could only see things far in the distance. Now let your eyes relax," he said, turning away to retrieve his next batch of instruments. "This next part is very delicate and if you move unexpectedly I could put your eye out."

But when his back was turned, Alex saw that Mr. Sackville was, in fact, attempting to control one of the muscle spasms that periodically cursed his right arm. "Are you excited, boy, to be so close to finally meeting the legendary Mabel Eastlake face-to-face?" he asked as he began to work on Alex's eyes.

"I didn't know I was close to meeting her."

"Oh yes. I've kept my part of the bargain. You said you would allow one to work on your face if you could meet Mabel Eastlake. So one arranged it with her . . . for later this evening."

This was something to consider. Instead of fearing the encounter, which Alex instinctively did, he needed some way to make it work to his own advantage. The pressure of Cygnet's finger and the weight of his various cosmetic instruments on Alex's eye triggered in him a barrage of images, including the nightclub footage seen earlier. And again the face came to him, the face glimpsed for just a moment in the wardrobe vault, the face in the nightclub, the face in Fancy's suite, the face he had seen in the Child. "Who exactly was Abe West?" he asked.

Instantly the pressure was removed from his eye and he opened it to see Cygnet staring at him, inches away, revealing the dry, potpourri–scented interior of his mouth. "Why, boy, do you want to know about Abe West?" he asked slowly.

"Fancy showed me his photo," Alex said cautiously. "And I saw him in Miss Eastlake's home movies."

"But have you seen him here in Glass House? Is that why you're curious? What did the monkey tell you about him?" demanded Cygnet.

"Nothing. That he disappeared."

Cygnet burst out with a tense birdlike cackle. "Disappeared? Swallowed up might be a better way of describing what happened to Abe West. Subsumed, in the way weaker organisms are always subsumed by the greater."

"You said he haunts Glass House. What did you mean?"

For a moment Cygnet only stared at him. "Did Miss Monkey actually *tell* you anything about Abe West . . . or The Black Orchis?" And when Alex said no, Cygnet's laugh turned faint and ethereal. "Then I can see it's one's duty to do so. Part of the bargain. Miss Barlow's version of things often tends to be . . . shall we say, clouded? . . . by monkeyshine."

* * *

Even in Hollywood, where Svengalis were a dime a dozen, Jimmy Flame held a special place of honor. It was impossible to escape the spell of his eyes, the sexual power he generated. Sex was a business for him, divorced from the human emotions that engendered it. Dark, mysterious, powerful . . . who wouldn't feel the hypnotic lure of him, that sense of dark, quiet knowing?

And Mabel Eastlake loved him, and Fancy Barlow loved him, but before Mabel Eastlake and Fancy Barlow there was Abe West. This star struck fool fell hook, line, and sinker, hopelessly and ridiculously in love the moment he looked into Flame's eyes.

Those eyes overwhelmed Abe West, inspired him with both dread and longing. For some people will themselves to fall in love, and others are hit by love as though it were a shocking psychic surprise. And in Abe's case it was a double shock: the emotion itself, and the realization that the expression of that emotion was forbidden, had to remain unseen.

Abe was no stranger to sex by the time he met Jimmy, but he was a stranger to love. And once he had experienced it, he was forever lost to himself. An already cloudy sense of who exactly he was grew dim and unnecessary. Who he was was who Jimmy said he was. Jimmy, dark silent Flame, overpowered his personality. And Abe gave himself up with pleasure. Why not? Why accept the cumbersome responsibilities of life in a world you abhorred as much for being what it was as it abhorred you for being what you truly were? The Black Orchis became his home, his world. If you are going to hell anyway, you might as well enjoy the trip.

There, like a tongue of fire, what Jimmy said and how Jimmy said it scorched Abe's heart into burning submission. Jimmy's brutality gratified him, for brutality was all Abe had known. The natural windows into his heart had been barred and darkened long ago. And there, in its dark recesses, Jimmy struck those matches that illuminated their intense, secret need for one another.

Flame, of course, used everyone who loved him, turning their idolatry into the fact of cash. Jimmy despised people who believed in some kind of moral order. There was no such order. He did not suffer from sentimentality.

You see, Mr. Flame had a catalog—a very special catalog—and all the people who worked for him in The Black Orchis were featured in it. In specialty poses, of course. And guests at the club could choose from this catalog whomever they wished for the evening.

Any fantasy could be obtained at The Black Orchis provided you had the money to pay for it. The men and women who frequented its dark confines were fluent with cash. It was the language they spoke.

For many, The Black Orchis was the only place that offered a temporary respite from the blues and boredom of the outside world. At The Orchis they could be what they liked and who they liked, and with whom they liked. Identity, false or true, could be checked at the door, along with your coat. Fancy Barlow was, for a time, the coatcheck girl. How she adored handling those furs!

It was at The Black Orchis that Abe and Fancy became such close friends. Fancy wanted Abe *and* Jimmy—craved them—and became crazed with jealousy when their attention turned to one another. Miss Barlow could not manipulate love to her own satisfaction because the objects of her desire were always emotionally inaccessible, like creatures seen on the other side of a mirror. Pain and passion were one and the same for her. By the time Abe had disappeared from The Black Orchis and Mabel Eastlake had become the star of the place, Fancy's heart had curdled, refusing to take cognizance of itself.

But before that, early on, they were great friends,

Fancy and Abe. Both were actors, but in time it was Abe who became the better actress. Fancy did not realize at first just how minutely Abe was observing her. But as time went on and his effeminate repertoire expanded, she began to see herself mimicked. When her back was turned, she would be startled to hear her own voice—Abe, doing a routine, getting laughs, being more womanly than any of the other whores in the place. It was like living with a distorting mirror.

In some ways it made Fancy feel closer to him. And so did the care of his child. Abe was the father of a little girl. The story was a typical one of seduction and abandonment, of consequences disregarded in the hot flurry of a moment. Refusing to marry the child's mother, Abe had run away. The mother of the child had followed him to Hollywood. But by the time she caught up with him, Abe was at The Black Orchis under Jimmy's tutelage and irretrievably lost to her.

Barely more than a girl herself, the child's mother gave herself up to the kind of intense despair that only the young can experience. Life was too horrible and complicated. Life did not have the happy ending a picture always did. Unless you paid a dime, there were no happy endings. This was an unendurable catechism for her to learn and she died miserably, in great pain, her throat burned through by guzzled lye.

Abe had to take the child, but it was Fancy who generally cared for it, keeping an eye out for any danger. So Mary P—that was their nickname for her—lived through her earliest babyhood in various rooms of The Black Orchis.

The Black Orchis, ah, that was nightlife! That was entertainment of highly seductive order. Rich, secretive homosexuals of both sexes made it their home. Imagine! It was they who helped set the tone of the place, living out their fantasies in full, delicious view of the rest of Flame's clientele. They were good for business and Jimmy pampered them and their pocketbooks.

Mr. Flame knew how to turn unreality to a profit. At this club people could live, for a few hours anyway, and if they had enough money, as though life were a movie of their own direction.

Say a gentleman longed to vamp as Theda Bara, or the more perversely spectacular Nazimova. At Jimmy's he could find a headdress of plumy white feathers hung with strings of pearls.

There was a special wardrobe room where lavish costumes could be rented for the evening and there was always a special makeup artist on hand to assist in these glamorous transformations of image. If the makeup artist's prices were exorbitant, it was only because Mr. Flame took such a large cut.

But other pleasures could be obtained as well. In a well-fitted opium den, smokers could recline on soft pillows and take leave of themselves. In another room pornographic movies were shown, sometimes starring the most prominent current celebrities, but generally featuring Jimmy's employees at The Orchis. For those who craved violence, trained dogs were pitted against rats in the gaming room and fighting cocks ripped one another to shreds.

Upstairs there was the grand bar and ballroom, outfitted in the most beautiful and modern way imaginable. Silver, black, sleek . . . featuring live panthers in long glass pens, pacing back and forth and watching with fury as the guests on the other side of the glass ate, drank, danced freely. The dance orchestra was another draw, since it was better than the ones at the Trocadero, the Mocambo or the Coconut Grove. Mr. Flame hired the best musicians in the world to play for his customers.

Between tricks, Abe West was a taxi dancer, just as Mabel Eastlake would be. For the right price he was the best dancer in the place. He knew how to hold a woman or a man in the special ways they liked to be held.

For Flame didn't discriminate where money was concerned and there were always women at The Black Orchis, women who came because they liked to dare propriety and sample the pleasures usually reserved for men. Hilda Hatter loved The Orchis precisely because it was dangerous and off-limits to the common man. You never knew what was going to happen on a given evening. That was part of the club's appeal. More than one gangland slaying had bloodied the crisp white tableclothes and impending scandals hung in the thick smoky air.

It was Prohibition outside, but for most of the people at The Black Orchis it was *always* prohibition outside. Here, inside, the liquor was good and the drugs were even better. If the price was high, so was the clientele. The various entries in Mr. Flame's catalog were trained to peddle the right stuff—the most expensive stuff—and did so with consummate seductive ease.

If you worked for Mr. Flame, you forgot what daylight looked like. At The Black Orchis it was always night, and that made it particularly unusual in The Land of Morning Calls. It appealed to those chronically nocturnal souls who were unable or unwilling to face the relentless glare of California and were far better suited to the comforting mysteries of darkness. And if you were out of work, if you lost that picture deal, if you had some great sorrow pressing down on you, The Black Orchis was an excellent place to sit, wander, brood and dream about the facts of life and death in Hollywood.

The Black Orchis changed you, transformed you. People returned to it as to a fix. It refreshed them to be someone else, a secret self, a dream self here in this city of dreams.

The Black Orchis—where Mabel Eastlake was discovered by Otto Kranzler. The Black Orchis—where Hilda Hatter took Mabel Eastlake in her arms one thrilling dangerous night and tangoed with her on the black glass of the dance floor, as Flame—lover of one, rival of the other—watched from his overhead office window. The Black Orchis—where Fancy Barlow decided one night that she would have Abe West. If she could not have him of his own volition, she would have him by paying to be his trick.

On that particular night, Jimmy told Abe to go upstairs to the Suite of Silk. He told Abe that a specialty number was waiting for him. "A woman," Jimmy said. "She's arranged it to her exact specifications. You're not to speak. Don't say a word. She'll tell you what she wants and how she wants it."

Of all the fantasy rooms at The Black Orchis, the Suite of Silk was the most voluptuous and therefore the most expensive. Lit only by candles, it was given over to great swathes of flowing fabric draped from ceiling to floor. You walked on silk, you saw it in a thousand subtle gradations of color, glowing in the candlelight.

The bed, of course, was enormous, with a canopy of silk spilling down around it. The sheets and pillows were black and had the sheen of a lake at midnight, a lake you wanted to drown in.

Fancy Barlow was already on this bed when Abe entered the room. She had had herself tied. Her wrists were bound with black ribbon to the back posts of the bed. Her legs were tucked back under her, her ankles similarly bound. The huge black pillows had been plumped up behind her according to command, and against them her scented and lightly oiled body moved slowly, slowly, back and forth, as though some fine watery current were passing over her and she was flowing with it, a creature in a soft black sea. Her legs were spread. A black silk mask covered her eyes.

Recognizing her, Abe stopped. Did she know it was he?

Fancy said, "I told Jimmy to send me his best. The chef's recommendation. Undress now." And when he had, she summoned him. "Come close to me, let me feel you on my belly. Rub your cock on my belly." And when he had, titillated by her blindness, she whispered, "Now on my breasts. Rub yourself on my breasts." Abe was being paid to do as he was told. He said not a word.

"Run your tongue over my body—slowly," Fancy said. "Lick me everywhere, like a big hungry animal." Abe did as she requested. "Blow gently on my forehead, cool me down," she panted, fired and wet. After that she was quiet, and left the rest up to him.

Neither of them ever mentioned this encounter. Fancy's mask, preventing their eyes from meeting and recognizing the intimate reality of one another, kept their memories of it quite separate.

And then Abe West slowly disappeared . . . evaporated by degrees, as people in Hollywood so often do. What happened to him? Where did he go? It was the time Mabel Eastlake arrived. And Abe could never compete with Miss Eastlake. No one could. Fate and fame struck Mabel Eastlake and elevated her to stardom. Abe West was overthrown, jettisoned, and cast away as so much detritus in the dazzling ferocity of Mabel Eastlake's wake.

But rumors hung about, spread, and grew, as they always do in Hollywood. Abe West became more whispered about once he had disappeared than he ever had been when he was around. One night, near Glendale, Jimmy Flame was set upon by masked thugs, his face slashed, a rib or two broken. Hadn't it been Abe West, leaving his signature in Jimmy's faithless flesh? In fact, didn't

Abe West have a record by the time he arrived in Holly-wood, and wasn't that why he'd gone to The Black Orchis in the first place? To hide? And that strange case in Oklahoma, the son who murdered his mother and her pimp-lover . . . who'd then escaped with the help of his wife and ended up on the wanted list in four states. Assault, robbery, another murder . . . "Sure," they said, "that must have been him."

Fancy Barlow, always anxious to fan more interest in herself, took the part of Abe's jilted girlfriend and claimed he always abused her. "I knew that guy as intimately as any-one could . . . or wanted to," she said. "He's dangerous and unpredictable and God help us all if he shows up again. He was always after revenge, he was always thinking about vio-lence. And I've always had this crazy fear . . . this really cra-zy fear that he'd come back to get me . . . and that I'd have to be the one to kill him when he did."

But what, then, of the servants in Glass House, back in Miss Eastlake's hey-day, when a whole brigade of them were employed and overseen by Cygnet? On more than one occasion they had come to him, startled out of their wits, claiming to have seen a strange-looking man in Glass House. Cygnet, of course, laughed at them. They spoke of a violent curse, a haunting, a restless spirit, embroidering their stories until it was Miss Eastlake herself, they said, who had hidden away this other lover, perhaps a demon spirit, or perhaps her own brother.

Mabel Eastlake, the glamorous star, said nothing about Abe West and acted as if she'd never heard of him. The fewer associations made between her and The Black Orchis the better.

13.

Alex flitted in and out of consciousness to the sound of Cygnet's dry, emotionless voice. He heard the story of Mabel Eastlake being told as if his own inner voice were telling it. With his eyes closed and the stunning, relentless weight of the makeup lights upon them, he was no longer quite the same Alex Klein. But who was he? There was a secret, anarchic, guilty delight in casting off the rites of personality, the continuities that made him Alex, that bound him to one identity. But there was, now, a vague fear as well, not fully present to his flickering consciousness. Did he dare give himself over to some entirely new identity? Did he dare to become this creature Sackville was creating? And if he did, what would happen to the old Alex?

Cygnet continued his metamorphic work throughout the afternoon. That Alex—as an object to be worked on—excited Cygnet was increasingly apparent. As the afternoon progressed, a laserlike intensity appeared in Mr. Sackville's grey eyes and once Alex even saw him pat his forehead dry with a folded linen handkerchief.

Strange old queer, Alex thought. Or was he? Cygnet's dainty feminine side was offset by an indefinable masculinity, nothing more than a scent perhaps, but one that defined him as a man. A sexless man, to be sure, one who had long ago turned off the tap of sensuality and sat now in the dry powder of his own unused gender; a fussy celibate priest in the temple of Mabel Eastlake.

But it was also apparent that not all was well between the priest and the goddess he served. To preserve his dignity at the most humiliating moment of his life—when he was thrown out of motion pictures forever, cursed by the high vocal timbre of his voice and by his affected, High Style silent movie method of acting—Cygnet gave up his beloved Glass House to Mabel Eastlake. But he made himself believe there was no actual exchange of ownership. To this end he had concocted the fantasy that he still directed Glass House and that he continued to own everything in it, including its new owner.

Mabel Eastlake, so terrified of preserving the image she had so painfully acquired, was putty in his hands, just as she was in the hands of Jimmy Flame and Otto Kranzler and even Fancy Barlow and Hilda Hatter: horribly dependent, made generous by her fear of exposure, by her guilty, inescapable secret. No doubt she had moments of terrible clarity, when she knew she had no power, really, of her own. To be catapulted into fame and great fortune by others, that had been her ambition. It then became her prison sentence.

By the time she took Glass House from Cygnet, Mabel was well aware of the dangers that went along with acclaim at the box office. What she had thus far earned could be snatched away at any moment; a common enough fear in Hollywood, where the most ordinary of mortals could ascend into the heavens of stardom, appear briefly as new gods, and then awaken to find themselves back in the gutter, dreaming. Mabel Eastlake had been propelled by the strength of others. The protective network around her was made up of the most powerful people in Hollywood. And of course they wanted something in return, an emotion she couldn't always fabricate at will.

Only Jimmy had she loved; in the short time they

were together, her heart yielded, like a sprouting bulb, the full and final measure of one short season. And if great loves permanently alter the heart by ripening the soul then Mabel and Jimmy's was a great love; a love not comprehensible to everyone, perhaps, but no less a love for that.

Cygnet loved the image of Mabel Eastlake but resented from the beginning the person who served to project it. Yes, the image was beautiful. But Mabel Eastlake was rotten. And it was with pleasure that he slowly made the great star entrust her life to him. Without him, she had no valid image of her physical self, just as without Jimmy she had no valid image of her emotional self. She avoided mirrors, not daring to face the reflection that glanced back at her without the benefit of Cygnet's alterations, that flat, dead ghost trapped in the one-dimension of a mirror. For time spent not being Mabel Eastlake was meaningless once she had become Mabel Eastlake. It had no value. At the same time, *being* Mabel Eastlake, having to become her, was an arduous form of torture and produced an image just as hard to bear on account of all the humiliating self-abnegation that went into accepting it. She knew that her intensely dramatic beauty was a kind of forgery and she resented having to falsify herself to achieve it. Her only consolation was the money.

Although Mabel Eastlake loved Jimmy, she was wise enough to know that money in his hands quickly disappeared in transactions that never reappeared on the pages of "The Financial Times." When she left The Black Orchis, purchased by Kranzler and Paradise Studios, the reality of money, *her* money, became overwhelming. Again she turned elsewhere for help in managing it. Cygnet knew the value of money from hindsight, having lost most of his, and Miss Eastlake thought him the ideal person to begin those small, tentative negotiations that led eventually to the accrual of her massive fortune. "I want to have so much money, darling," she explained to Cygnet, "that I never have to think about it." So Cygnet thought about it for her. And later, when the various claims of the Eastlake estate were finally investigated and settled, it became clear just how much Cygnet regarded Miss Eastlake's money as his own.

It became apparent then, too, that Mr. Sackville was in collusion with Miss Barlow. Between them, and over the years, they had brutalized not only Miss Eastlake's soul but her pocketbook.

When Cygnet finished Alex's face, he would not let him look in a mirror. "Not yet, boy, not yet. Wait for the full effect." He was beside himself with exhilaration as he unstrapped Alex's wrist and neck.

Now that he could move his body again, Alex felt the strain of doing so. Movement was as strange and miraculous as it must be for a newly unswaddled baby. He could feel, too, the weight of the unseen visage, this new image, clamped like a tight mask over his face. What *did* he look like? Suddenly he was hot with fear. He saw that he had been given long crimson nails.

Cygnet had a costume waiting for him, and this time Alex was too dazed and exhausted to object when he was helped into what Cygnet called a "dinner suit." Designed by Patou for the famous rivalry scene between Mabel Eastlake and Constance Bennett in *Lady With a Past*, it was a creamy, flesh-colored silk with crepe-corded pockets, the jacket tight-fitting with thin, elongated shoulders. "Someone with breasts would be at a disadvantage wearing it," Cygnet said through pursed, unsatisfied lips as Alex modeled for him. "Since you don't have any, we must make a virtue of necessity."

Clothes designed for Mabel Eastlake always deaccentuated the bust, since she didn't have much of one, and directed attention to the hips, derriere, and of course the legs, all of which Kranzler had had insured by Lloyd's, just in case.

"Now Miss Eastlake, boy, would have worn a pale lavender chiffon blouse underneath, with a big billowing tie at the neck to disguise her lack of tit, but with you we'll go for a slightly more contemporary look . . . I think just to your clavicles showing and perhaps some piece of jewelry, high on the neck. And some bold earrings."

"Earrings?"

Cygnet left the studio and returned moments later with a pair that Alex recognized instantly. They'd been hidden in his room. His ears went blazing hot as Cygnet clipped them on.

"These belonged to Hilda Hatter," Cygnet said matter-of-factly, "but she won't be needing them anymore, so why don't you wear them? A man should always have a good pair of silver earrings for dress. I thought the diamond choker would look good too, but Miss Eastlake gave it to Cocaine. She felt if she wore it, it would give her an unfair edge. Now, boy, if we're to win this contest, you and I, you'll have to move with confidence and bravado, just as Miss Eastlake did in the scene where she wore this costume. Do you remember how confident she was when Connie Bennett first started flinging the mud of the past into her face, in front of all those guests? She flung it right back, and harder. Didn't believe in defeat, Mabel Eastlake, which was why women and men adored her. She never stopped until she got what she wanted."

"What happens if you win?" Alex asked. "What happens to me?"

"To you, boy?"

"Yeah, to me. How can I play in a game unless I know exactly what the stakes are?" He bluffed out more defiance than he felt, not wanting to give Sackville the pleasure of beholding his fear. "I don't have to do this. I can destroy all your work in a second." And he moved his now long, red nails towards his unseen face, threatening Cygnet's handiwork.

"I don't think you will," Cygnet said, moving quickly, "when you see what you actually look like." He twirled Alex around to a wall of mirrors and orchestrated a sudden chord of lighting that struck where Alex stood.

The image he saw flashed through him like lightning: electric, alarming, dislocating, repulsive, thrilling. "Jesus." He approached the image in the mirror. "Jesus." He put the reality of his transformed hands to the surface of the mirror. "No." The image, just as startled as he, stared back at him from the other side. "Mabel Eastlake," he murmured, and slowly put his fingers up to touch his marcelled, platinum blonde hair.

"Not quite," Cygnet said, "but reasonably close. Please try to walk with some style, boy, now that you're a woman. I know it's difficult, but please try. It's not enough that you physically resemble her. You must move as she did, with that same toughness of soul."

"And if I don't?" he said, trying to find the Alex submerged in this new image. Alex was there, but not entirely accessible. For a moment he wanted to cry out, fearing for the loss of himself. He stood, a stranger between two worlds, between two sexes, nowhere that he knew. "And if I don't?"

"You will, boy. If you know what's good for you, you will."

He told Alex to meet him in the foyer at midnight. Until then Alex was free.

But of course he was not, that was the whole point. If he were free, he would be on his way . . . where? The police department? Looking like this? Then New York? What *would* his life be like, after this, after these strange experiences, when he was back on the outside of Glass House? What part of his life there did he want to reclaim, *could* he reclaim?

The man in him felt absurd, angry and humiliated by the revelation of this new creature that he was. The woman in him felt triumphant and beautiful and proud. Alex could feel the battle going on within himself: furious war cries, soothing whispers, the laughter of ancient gods, the battle for balance and the expression of something older and deeper than male or female.

He spent the time until midnight walking slowly through Glass House, braving Miss Eastlake's cameras, daring them. If there was to be some kind of showdown he must be prepared for it, prepared for anything. It was the not knowing that made it unbearable, a nightmare of possibilities. But he must not show his anguish to the camera. The camera, he reminded himself, just as Otto Kranzler had reminded Mabel Eastlake, sees every flaw, every blemish. Miss Eastlake must see no cowardice, no cowering in himself. When they faced one another, Alex would see a murderess. Miss Eastlake would see herself.

As he paced through the quiet, expectant rooms, forcing leisure into his steps, like a star on a deserted soundless stage, he worked on conquering his fears. The fears inspired by the Mabel Eastlake he was to confront as well as by the Mabel Eastlake he had become. Great confidence was required. But it was like sitting in the hands of a god you couldn't see, not knowing if the god was going to crush or cuddle you.

Strange to say, if anything inspired his confidence it was the image of Mabel Eastlake, the image Alex saw reflected whenever he beheld himself in the polished surfaces of Glass House. He had long meditated on the image as he knew it in her films and now he did so again; an image of Mabel Eastlake complete unto itself, the image of a woman—a person—determined to win. In her films, Mabel Eastlake rarely pleaded and Alex had no intention of doing so either. He would not show humility; he would not give them the perverse pleasure of seeing him crawl. He would show them their equal.

They thought they held death in their hands. Wasn't it true that he could kill too, if he had to? He was young; they were old. Except for the Child, and Cocaine of course, he had to be stronger than anyone in Glass House. Age could command no reverence. He must repay violence with violence, if need be.

The pain and oddity of consciousness with the prospect of an absurd death before him gave Alex's vision a sweet, burning intensity. Seeing things in all their splendor was a kind of generous pain; even the frozen beauty of Glass House warmed now in his eyes.

But it was outside, with the warm fragrant balm of the night air and that enormous vista spread out before him that the splendid beauty of being alive made itself most palpable. How impossible to imagine the blankness of death, the confining prison wall surrounding life, when you could see all this!

And you saw it best from Mabel Eastlake's boudoir, whose glass windows commanded the upper half of the house, curving out like the prow of some great proud ship riding the tides of eternity. Alex saw someone quickly step back into the shadows of her room. This time he continued to stare, wanting to confront whatever was up there. Dark, mysterious world . . . the incoherence of its laws and plans. . .

He was beautiful. It was absurd and wonderful and terrible. He glanced at himself in a pool of water and met a shy, lovely stranger.

But reentering the house as midnight drew near, he suddenly remembered Fancy's dream of Mabel Eastlake appearing as Death. Death . . . moving in for a close-up. Alex walked to the foyer with as much dignity as he could muster. The way Mabel Eastlake would walk. The luxury of blind panic must now be resisted, put far behind him.

Cygnet had carefully arranged the lighting and an enormous bowlful of deep purple orchids that cast out a low, provocative scent. He had changed into a dark, slimly cut suit and knotted a mauve foulard around his pale neck. The tie matched his hands, tightly gloved in mauve glacé kid stitched with black. His thin black shoes were like dancing slippers.

Was Mabel Eastlake watching them from above on her monitors? What was she thinking? A solemn expectancy was building in the room, as though the ghosts of bygone guests were reassembling to stand with Alex and Cygnet, waiting for the miracle of her appearance.

And then she appeared.

Something stronger than intuition made Alex aware that he was to look up.

At the top of the stairs, hanging shyly back in the recess of her doorway, was Mabel Eastlake. There was a slight pause. Then she stepped into full view.

Alex's heart began to rave.

Mabel Eastlake was wearing the famous Erté-designed Snake Dress from *Doublecross*. The lamé of the suffocatingly tight gown had a hypnotic sheen offset by the soft glow from the white fox shoulder-piece rising behind her head like the hood of a cobra about to strike. And this time her face was almost fully visible behind a fine white lace veil.

For a few long seconds Alex stared at Mabel Eastlake and Mabel Eastlake stared at Alex.

"When a person truly sees my face, Mr. Klein, that person is no longer a stranger to Glass House," Mabel Eastlake slowly said. "I do not share my secrets with the common man."

"You have no face," Alex said.

"Haven't I?"

"You have the face he gives you," Alex said, pointing to Cygnet.

"Isn't that enough?" asked Mabel Eastlake. "The face of Mabel Eastlake. I am Mabel Eastlake."

"I don't believe you."

"You're a heretic then, not to believe your very own eyes. What further proof could you possibly need? And who am I, Mr. Klein, if I am not Mabel Eastlake?"

"You're not the Mabel Eastlake of the movies, I know that," Alex said. "That Mabel Eastlake was strong but she was human."

"And I am not?" asked Miss Eastlake.

"You're a murderer."

"Do you see that on my poor face, Mr. Klein?"

"I've never seen your face," Alex said. "Not close up. Not without the protection of a veil or a piece of glass or something you've used to hide behind."

"Are you certain you want to . . . see me?" asked Mabel Eastlake.

"Are you certain you would . . . show yourself?"

"Of course." She made a simple, dignified gesture. And the strangely youthful face appeared from behind its veil.

Standing above him was the screen image of Mabel Eastlake. Alex had the intensely strange sensation of having entered a movie, of having somehow crossed the mental barrier separating art from its audience. He was trapped in a movie with Mabel Eastlake. *As* Mabel Eastlake! But the other Mabel Eastlake was not the one with whom, in her movies, he had sympathized and even identified. This was a different Mabel Eastlake, a mad Mabel Eastlake, one whose image was a mere gloss over something else, something terrible.

Cygnet's steadily rising laughter disturbed the tension in the room.

Mabel Eastlake looked down at him. Her face never changed expression, making it peculiarly disturbing to behold. She moved, spoke, was obviously a human being, but one whose face showed no sign of human feeling, no sign of life. Flat and unreadable, turned in upon itself, upon nothing, without so much as a malicious smile or any other quirk that marks a face and gives it some readable and sympathetic humanity, her face had no soul. She had, somehow, unimaginably, erased it. Her face was a dead image of a dead life. She looked damned by her own will.

"Did you think I would be afraid to compare this face to his?" she cried down to Cygnet. And despite the absence of facial expression, the Voice expressed pure rage.

"There's no one here to compare them," Cygnet laughed. "*I* certainly can't referee because I made both of you."

"The Child!" said Mabel Eastlake. "He will know. He will tell you. Call the Child!" But it was she who did so, passing a hand over her mouth with the fluency of a magician separating cause from effect.

The Child appeared from darkness, conjured from back beyond the Vargas portrait. Leading Cocaine on a leash, his face was a dark, dreaming enigma. Seeing Alex—seeing Mabel Eastlake in Alex—he stopped short, his face sparked into wondering.

And knowing that the Child recognized him, that his presence broke through the illusion of the female image, Alex felt a small gloating triumph. He looked up to find Mabel Eastlake staring fixedly down at the two of them, a deep burning glow in her eyes.

"Take off the diamond choker!" she commanded the Child, pointing a long red fingernail.

Loath to take his eyes from Alex, the Child, stroking Cocaine, removed the stones from her neck.

"I'll wager the market value of the diamonds," Cygnet said.

"What are you betting on?" Alex asked tensely.

Mabel Eastlake gathered the cobra a little closer around her. "You, Mr. Klein," she said. "Your life."

Cocaine, leashless, took a few restless steps away from the Child. After the encounter in the library, Alex's breath was now strained every time he looked at the cat. It circled in a slow orbit around the Child's legs.

Unnerved, Alex faltered and stepped back as Cocaine took a small leap into motion and ran up the stairs to stand at the side of Mabel Eastlake.

Her voice rejoiced. "Cocaine is mine, as you can see. And as you will find, so is everything else."

"A pitifully vulgar delusion," Cygnet said. And when Miss Eastlake asked in obvious alarm what he meant, her dresser and makeup artist answered with calm, cold relish that it meant exactly that: legally, everything was his. Miss Eastlake stayed on in Glass House only through *his* generous grace.

"That can't be!" she shouted, panic fraying her voice.

"It can be," Cygnet said, "and it is."

"But where would you be without me?" Mabel Eastlake screamed. "I'm the one who made all this possible—you and I living here. I'm the one who planned it, who had the brains and the guts to think fast and grab a chance when it came."

"So you did, my poor girl, but that was then and this is now."

"I have the Child," Mabel Eastlake warned. "I could—"

"But if you did, dear Miss E, you'd be forced to face life without me, and without Glass House. How would you face the law courts? The reporters? The reopened investigation? For they would reopen it, you know, to accommodate certain new facts that would arise. The moment anyone opens my safe deposit box they see, right on top, a full confession. The presence of that document, I should think, would prevent you from doing anything to harm me."

"You put it in writing?" she shrieked. "You damned yourself?"

"For now, I am the only one who sees it," Cygnet said calmly. "A little scourge that has become almost a pleasure to me. And it's not only I who is damned by it, my dear. I take only half the credit."

"I've been on the stand before," said Mabel Eastlake fiercely, "and I can face it again."

"And what, my dear, will you do with *her* this time? How would the two of you live, with no one between you? How would you hold up the lie once my document had been read? They'd know your claim was fictitious and obtained from her under duress."

"Why are you being so perverse?" Mabel Eastlake demanded. "Why have you condemned yourself? I'm the one who lost everything—I'm the one who's suffered and paid. I'm the one who most deserves Glass House."

"That may be," Cygnet said. "But it's mine."

"No, *ours* darling," she said, persuasion in her voice. "We did it for one another. We own it in joint partnership, it's ours through blood. Together, working together, we got it from her."

Alex was suddenly aware of a silence in the room. Both Cygnet and Mabel Eastlake had stopped their bickering and were watching him. Alex felt a cold weight laid upon his neck. The Child's warm hands fastened the diamond choker behind him.

"Oh splendid, yes quite splendid," Cygnet said.

The sense of some kind of terrible outrage having been committed against Mabel Eastlake was now intensely palpable in the room. And in the high black gleam of one of the foyer walls, Alex again saw the reflection of someone standing in the Black and Blue Room, a presence revealed only by the mirrored surface of the walls. At first, with his imagination so prepped, he was certain that it was Abe West, and strangely welcomed it. But it was not Abe West, it was Fancy Barlow, and her reflection disappeared almost the moment it registered in Alex's consciousness.

"Diamonds are cold on a queer's neck, Mr. Klein," said Mabel Eastlake. "Wouldn't you prefer the hands of a man?" Again the moment of illusion, her hand in front of her mouth.

The Child's eyes shot upwards, held tense by her command. He slowly left Alex's side and walked stiffly up the stairs to where Mabel Eastlake stood.

"Carry me to my car," she said to him, drawing down her veil.

Alex watched, astonished, as the Child lifted Mabel Eastlake in her lamé and white furs and started down the stairs.

"When you can get a man to carry you, Mr. Klein, you know he's yours for life," Mabel Eastlake said. "Cygnet, open the door. I unlocked it before I came out. I assume you'll allow me the pleasure of a drive?"

Alex's vision was so breathlessly distorted by this time that he stood looking out the open front door, held wide by Cygnet, without realizing that it was freedom. He lost the chance almost the same moment he realized he'd had one.

Mabel Eastlake was carried past him and stopped only long enough to deliver, with a swift, sure aim, a ferocious slap that sent Alex reeling.

"I'll see all of you damned yet," she whispered as she was carried out.

Thinking now what to do—to push Mabel Eastlake

and the Child down the front stairs, to attack Cygnet, to injure one or all of them, Alex bolted for the door.

But Cygnet was faster, had probably anticipated such a move, and the door was closed and its electronic lock already humming when Alex reached it.

Alex turned to him, but Cygnet had snapped his face off, pulled down the blinds, refused to recognize him.

"What are you trying to do to me?" Alex cried.

"I'd go to my room if I were you, boy," Cygnet said. "Cocaine has the run of the house tonight, and she may just want her diamond collar back."

He left Alex standing in the foyer and disappeared, gulped up by the silence of Glass House, leaving not so much as a ripple behind him.

14.

Miss Eastlake's monitors were never turned off so that the intake of images from all over Glass House poured into her boudoir like an incessant stream of disregarded prayer. The cameras throughout Glass House continued to record. Alex Klein could be seen in Monitor 3, crouched in agony and banging the door with his hands . . . now with his arms stretched flat against its shining black surface. A blonde Alex, a transformed Alex, an Alex who looked like Mabel Eastlake.

The cameras did not comment, they merely watched.

Alex as Mabel Eastlake wiped his face and watched with fierce and fearful concentration as the white panther slowly padded down the great staircase.

"I'm not afraid of you, you sonofabitch!" His voice, picked up by Miss Eastlake's microphones, could be heard clearly in her boudoir. "It's your turn, *darling*."

Cocaine, her fierce, blue, unknowable eyes fixed on the diamonds around Alex's neck, came very close. She opened her mouth, showed her teeth, took a threatening stance.

Alex, with a shoo of his hands, took a quick, bold step towards the cat, hoping to frighten it. Cocaine backed away.

In Monitor 6 (lower foyer) Alex could be seen slowly forcing the panther into the Black and Blue Room, where the action continued on Monitors 7 and 8. Cocaine, as though hypnotized by the force of the diamonds she stared at, backed slowly through the bar and into the next room, there scanned by camera hook-ups to Monitors 9 and 10.

By sheer force of will, Alex pushed Cocaine back to the inner garden, scatted her in and slammed the door. He stood trying to catch a breath that would not easily come.

Now he ran from the glass wall of the inner garden back to the foyer, kicked off his shoes, and started up the stairs, reappearing in Monitor 2 (its camera directly outside Mabel Eastlake's room, looking down her staircase). He tried the door, pushing violently on it, kicking it; stood for a moment considering; and then ran back to the Black and Blue Room.

There, in Monitor 8, he could be viewed pulling a large crystal bowl from behind the bar and filling it with various liquors. This he carried into the next room, cautiously opening the door to the inner garden and setting the bowl inside. Cocaine's snout registered in Monitor 10, where it could be seen approaching the bowl with lowered and cautious uncertainty. Cocaine sniffed the bowl, and then began to lap up the potent cocktail.

Alex's progress through Glass House was charted and displayed in Mabel Eastlake's monitors. Through rooms, down corridors, and finally in his own room—clearly visible—tearing Mabel Eastlake's beautiful clothes from his body. He looked deeply into a mirror—as though to memorize the image he saw there—and then turned on the taps and began hectically to scrub his face, erase the image of a moment earlier. Not all of it would disappear. His hair remained weirdly blonde and the shape of his face had been altered in such a way that soap and water would not change it. It would have to reform itself over time to what it had been. He pulled off the earrings that had belonged to Hilda Hatter. He worked frantically to undo the clasp from the diamond choker but couldn't master it.

He pulled on a pair of jeans, an old shirt, ran from his room. Then he was seen in the kitchen, pulling a handful of silver hypodermic syringes from their special refrigerator. With these he made his way back to the door of the inner garden. There he stood watching with clinical dispassion as Cocaine tried to climb up the lowest of the steplike branches of the banyan tree and slipped.

When the cat began to weave drunkenly through the garden, Alex entered.

The silver syringe . . . the needle sliding so smoothly into the panther's flank. The animal was barely able to lift its head. It gave Alex pleasure to rob it of its wild potency, to anesthetize at least one part of the nightmare.

"There, darling," he said grimly, watching his own hands, his crimson-painted nails, his thumb pushing the plunger. "Doesn't that feel good?"

He could have sworn that the cat smiled a drugged, drunken smile before collapsing entirely. Alex prodded it with the toe of his Nike.

Dealing with the others, Cygnet or Fancy, meant losing time.

Gauging the tree, Alex began to climb. The diamonds hung around his neck like a heavy collar—but the clasp was too complicated to deal with now. Up he went, the thick branches of the tree easily carrying his weight. The massacred face of Mabel Eastlake's statue, its glamorously dramatic pose ruptured into madness, stared fixedly at its own living reflection in Alex.

At the top he could look down and see the inner garden laid out below him. Beneath the tropical overgrowth the faint outlines of its past classical formality could be discerned. The white panther lay passive on the soil in the moonlight. The scene had the strangely familiar look of a primitive painting. What other eyes were watching from the green depths of foliage, from behind razor-sharp palm branches, waiting to spring, to pounce?

Alex took hold of Mabel Eastlake's balcony, pulled himself up to it, and climbed over the railing. There was a sudden flurry of wings, a chorus of sharp screaming cries, as roosting birds swooped terrified from their perches. Alex stood on the balcony, claiming it, stood where Mabel Eastlake stood as she surveyed *her* inner garden, robbing the Child by exerting her jealous presence over the very place she had supposedly given him.

A sense of inexorable fate, a sense of his own power thus far, came over him as he faced the door leading into Mabel Eastlake's bedroom. He touched the simple handle. The door was not locked.

Every inch of his exposed arm, as he slowly pushed the door open, was bitten by freezing cold air. Forbidden territory. Uncharted land. Alex gave the door a final push and stood for one last moment in the doorway between the humid inner garden and Mabel Eastlake's freezing black boudoir.

Slowly . . . slowly he entered, his body assailed by the perversity of the cold. The diamonds around his neck seemed to swell and grow heavier with it.

A place beyond darkness, with a sense of vast, hollow emptiness where he'd expected the warmth of luxury. The cold created a barrier, pushed him back, warned him off. The hairs on his arms and at the back of his neck stiffened with it.

The coldness of a refrigerated vault, he thought, preserving Mabel Eastlake's flesh, just as the cold in the wardrobe chamber preserved her clothing. The eternal coldness and silence of a tomb.

Alex allowed his eyes to adjust, rubbing his arms to keep warm. As his vision gradually extended itself, he saw that he was in a cavernous and nearly empty room. The dark, sudden yawn of space awed him, shrank him. At last I have entered the true consciousness of Mabel Eastlake, he thought. The cold, heartless brain of Glass House. It was a huge black introspection, a terrifying emotional void.

A long curving wall of draperies glowed at the edges with the insistent pressure of moonlight. Inching his way over, Alex found the cord and pulled it. As the view from this room was gradually exposed, inch by inch, his heart beat faster.

At last he was able to look out and see what Mabel Eastlake, alone in this room, alone in the world, saw. And seeing it for himself, Alex understood instantly how Cygnet, Fancy or anyone else would covet it for their own. What did anything inside matter? The unearthly sense of power and the strange timelessness that went with the vista were overwhelming. Whatever there was to see, Mabel Eastlake saw it. Viewing the estate, the city below, the sea, the sky, sun and moon, above everything, remote but all-seeing, the eye of Glass House had nothing to obstruct it. It scrutinized the world with the infinite haughtiness and grandeur of a god.

But Alex wanted the comfort of seeing *inside* the room, and searched everywhere for a light switch. Moonlight sifted in and powdered the outlines of various objects in the darkness. But without light, how could he find his way out, how could he find the telephone?

Definition was difficult to judge. What he thought to be open space was, at one point, a wall, and he rammed his shoulder against a cold, hard, solid surface.

The famous black bed, draped with black silk, enormous, floating in the darkness of the mirrored walls around it. How powerful it looked, how demanding, voluptuous, terrifying.

On an impulse, an attempt to map out his route of escape, Alex ran to check the door that opened onto the front staircase. It could not be opened. Mabel Eastlake must control it.

Trapped in a maze. Not knowing where, specifically, he must look to find the precious telephone, Alex could feel panic seeping into his veins.

And then, as he began to search the room with his eyes, scouring it for the phone, looking in every direction, he glanced up and stifled a cry.

On one wall, softly brushed by the moonlight, disembodied faces looked down at him. Mabel Eastlake, eyeless, looked down on him, several Mabel Eastlakes. A wall of masks. He cautiously touched one but drew his finger quickly back, afraid it might stick to the cold, semipliable material. It was like touching the repulsively disinterested face of a corpse.

For a moment he could not move and just stood there, summoning all his reserves. Having come this far he must go further. Yet it was like stumbling into a world beyond any he had known, a secret, terrifying world where identity was not what it seemed and where the appearance of things, the image seen, had nothing to do with its internal reality. A world guarding itself against discovery. Guarding itself against itself.

The eyeless faces of Mabel Eastlake stared out on their black eternity.

Alex forced himself to press on, taking the short, tiny steps of one newly blinded by the careening impact of a vision. Across the room, a steamy gray and cheerless light rose from the monitoring control board. Now he was able to look down and observe the rooms of Glass House. Silent. Still. Empty. He looked at each room in turn, his senses disjointed by the oddity of seeing them instead of being seen in them. The set of Glass House.

The last monitor caught and held his gaze. For there, as the camera slowly scanned through the darkness in the projection room, it picked up, bit by bit, the image of a seated figure.

The figure of a man, or what Alex assumed to be a man. He no longer trusted his eyes. A man seen from behind. Not Cygnet, and not Fancy Barlow. A man watching Mabel Eastlake's movie *Desperate Woman*. Alex could see and hear Mabel Eastlake on the screen: image within an image.

"I've pulled this trigger before," Mabel Eastlake was saying, standing tense and drawn with a small gun pointed at Charles Boyer. "And I can pull it again. Don't back me into a corner. Don't make me do it."

Alex checked the other monitors, looking for Cygnet, for Fancy, unable to locate either of them. There were three blank monitors: Fancy's suite, he supposed, and probably Cygnet's. The third?

And then, assembling itself, crystallizing, precipitating itself out from the jumble of possibilities, the identity of the unknown man in the projection room fixed itself in his mind. Abe West. Terror punched him in the stomach and he nearly doubled over from the internal blow. Abe West had revealed himself at last. He was in Glass House to kill, to slaughter, biding his time in this timeless place, hidden away and outwitting Mabel Eastlake's cameras like a cunning animal. Abe West was not a ghost. Whoever he was, he was very real.

Alex's eyes swept the room, the control board, trying to will the telephone into vision. The room felt hostile and completely impervious to his desires. Laughing at him. Then he saw it, a strange-looking device, and grabbed it, feeling its reality in his hands. But where was the dialing mechanism? What was this receiver connected to? He shouted into it, furious with its deadness, wanting to slap life into it, make it the life-saving object found in a dream.

Panic was useless, but frustration and fear goaded it on. Why should Abe West harm him? Must not Fancy know that Abe West was here? Or had she helped him get in? But Fancy was herself afraid of Abe West, wasn't she? The man of death and mystery. If Abe West had gotten in, there must be some way that he, Alex, could get out.

Clenching and unclenching his fists, Alex tried to force a method of escape to shape itself in his thoughts so that he could take hold of it, act on it.

It was with half an eye that he first became aware of the reel of film. The film. Intuitively, instinctively, aware of its power, its legend, he knew it to be the film whose images precipitated the murders of '39. Jimmy Flame's footage from The Black Orchis. THE SECRETS OF MABEL EASTLAKE. Seen by all assembled in Glass House on that fatal, star-crossed night. Stolen by Hilda Hatter and used to blackmail Mabel Eastlake. Stolen back from Hilda Hatter, who paid with her life for having stolen it. Alex's fingertips buzzed as he reached for it, took it, held it, like a shield, to his chest. It might be his magic way out of Glass House.

He ran back to the monitors. The figure in the projection room was gone.

Quickly he looked for a switch to activate the cameras hooked up to the blank monitors. The image must be in one of those. The control panels were hopelessly complicated to his technically inexperienced eye. One lever he pressed blacked out the entire system. With hands that had to be forced to move, stiff and swollen with the cold, Alex managed to reactivate the system.

It was then that he remembered Fancy telling him of the passage between the projection room and Mabel Eastlake's bedroom. Was Abe West—was the Man, the image, whoever, whatever it was—in the passageway now, moving slowly up the stairs, contemplating the pleasures of murder?

Then how could Alex get back out? The front door was locked, and the lost image, that ghostly figure now

missing from the monitor, might be lurking in the passageway that led down to the projection room.

Suddenly he heard gunshots in the projection room
and grabbed the monitor with both hands, staring down
into it, the images burning his eyes with the awful intensity
of things seen in a crystal ball, a strange fusion of past
knowledge, present fear and future foreboding trapped in
glass.

In the projection room he saw that it was Mabel
Eastlake who had fired the shots. There she stood, Mabel
Eastlake, her beautiful body in a clinging Vionnet gown,
pointing the gun she had just fired, one hand moving slowly to touch her face, to test the reality of the being who had
just committed murder.

In Monitor 3, Alex could see the front foyer door
opening. The Child and Mabel Eastlake had returned.
Mabel Eastlake looked oddly, sinisterly doll-like in the
Child's arms. Alex watched, breathless, as the Child kicked
the door closed behind him and carried Mabel Eastlake
towards the stairs. They were coming up here.

Mabel Eastlake as she had been, the screen image of
Mabel Eastlake, torrid murderess of Charles Boyer. *Desperate Woman.*

Mabel Eastlake as she was now, passive in the strong
arms of the Child, feigning weakness to attract his touch.

It had to be timed, but time, past, present, future,
was pounding in Alex's brain, jumbling the images, teas-
ing, stretching, distorting his perception of himself now, in
the present moment. *I am in danger*, he thought. He had to
leave, leave now, leave before Mabel Eastlake reached her
room and before the man, Abe West, the lost image in the
projection room, found him. And what if instead of Alex,
Abe West should find Mabel Eastlake and the Child?
Would he murder them in Alex's place?

Murder the Child?

But his own desire for survival in this potential slaughterhouse won out. He ran to pull the curtains, leaving the door to the balcony enough ajar to be located in the darkness. The soaring spread of outside view disappeared. With the curtains closed, the interior of Glass House reclaimed him entirely.

Back to the monitors. The Child was slowly carrying Mabel Eastlake, veiled, up the great black curving staircase.

Moments before they reached the landing, Alex, with the film under his arm, ran to the balcony door, stepped out and closed it behind him. He crouched outside, peering down into the inner garden, checking beyond its glass walls to see if anyone was in the gallery beyond. When he was back down he could plan his next move. Tormenting to think that perhaps there truly was no way out; that escape was simply a trick of his mind, something he had to believe in to remain sane.

Through a crack in the balcony door he could hear movement inside Mabel Eastlake's boudoir. They were in there now, Mabel Eastlake and the Child. Alex heard Mabel Eastlake's low, intense voice, at once passionate and ridiculous.

"You cannot love him. He is nothing to you. He is dangerous, Child. It's not you that he wants, no. He wants to harm me, see me gone. Yes, he wants to hurt me. You would never allow that to happen, would you? No, no my own darling, my own guardian angel, my own love. You will protect me from him, won't you, because you are my own, mine, and you will stay here with me always because I need you."

A strangling web of words. Mabel Eastlake imprisoning the Child with a voice he could not even hear. In her mouth the grace of love—freely chosen, freely bestowed—turned black, her words an abomination of the very emotions she professed. An actress. A liar. A murderess.

Alex tossed the film into the garden and quickly began to climb back down the tree after it. He felt naked, vulnerable, an easy target for anyone who might see him. At the bottom he retrieved the film and turned to make for the door.

But there stood the Child, watching him. Neither of them moved. The Child went to crouch beside the drugged cat. He stroked it. When he looked up at Alex his face was troubled, alarmed, angry. He picked up one of Cocaine's paws and let it fall. Suddenly fearful, he put his ear to the cat's heart. His face became stony, terrible, unreadable.

"I had to," Alex said, watching him, trying to move away. "I didn't want to but I had to."

The Child slowly raised his head to Mabel Eastlake's balcony. Was she up there? Alex did not dare turn around to look. His body froze as the Child approached him. This time he will kill me, he thought, watching the Child's hand as it reached out to touch the diamonds on his neck.

"Please," he said.

The Child's hand engulfed his throat, pressing the stones into it.

"I love you."

The Child's hand moved down to Alex's shoulder, down his arm. He stared as if his eyes were ears and hearing something for the first time.

Fear made his touch sweet and painful, something uncertain, unknown. "We can leave here together."

The Child took his hand and rushed him from the inner garden. Alex had not know that the Child was so aware of the scanning cameras. In each room they entered the Child paused, holding back, waiting for the camera to move past, away from them and what their images would tell Mabel Eastlake. He led Alex on, furtively, to the next room, knowing that their two images together must not be seen by her cameras. It was the first time in his life he had disobeyed their presumed authority.

In Alex's room the Child wanted love, instantly, urgently, as some kind of guarantee, as a promise. Alex held back, out of focus, unsure of his own identity. He had been pulled too deeply into the mysteries of Glass House, was himself now one of them, a distorted reflection he could not recognize, an image whose inner reality was hopelessly confused. Was it Alex Klein who kept thinking of violence, of having to use it against the Child, against all of them? Was it A. Liddell or Mabel Eastlake whispering in his ear, "Don't think what you need to do in order to survive, just do it"?

The Child pushed him to the bed, pressed him to the bed, pressed him down on it.

"You've got to help me."

The Child's mouth was on his neck, on his ear, his body pressed heavily on Alex's.

"No," Alex said, trying to push him away, afraid at the same time that he would lose the Child to Mabel Eastlake if he didn't respond now and in kind. "You've got to get us away from here."

The Child stared at him, eyes half-closed, breath heavy.

"You know the code. You must. You know how to activate it to open the front door and the gates, don't you?"

The Child stared at Alex's mouth, stared at the words formed by Alex's lips, stared at what they suggested.

"Together," Alex said, "we'll leave here together."

Now the Child looked frightened, bewildered. This was his home.

Alex got him back by stroking him, kissing him, feeling an instant erotic response from the Child's body as he did so. "Look, we'll go away. We'll leave them. I have the film. You know that code, don't you?"

The Child nodded.

"Write it down for me." Alex said. "Write it down and tell me how to use it. I've seen her room. Tell me what to do."

But the Child refused, indicating that he would do it himself.

"No, look, you might have to hold her back ... *I* have to know how to do it myself." Alex had no intention of leaving it up to the Child, whose allegiance to the will of Mabel Eastlake was so powerful.

The Child rolled over onto his back, his face tormented.

"Look, write it down for me. Write down the instructions as clearly as you can. Do that for me and I'll take you away from here. I'll take you away from Mabel Eastlake. You don't know her, Child, you don't know who she is or what she's done to you." And with a kind of dazzling wonderment that couldn't be considered now, Alex realized that he really did want to take this man away ... to "save" him.

And the Child seemed to understand this, this sudden passionate allegiance, this promise of togetherness, and what it might mean, for his desire returned in an intense, overpowering wave.

But Alex pulled away. "No. Write down the code first."

The Child took the pen and paper. Alex, biting his lips, looked on over his shoulder. The code appeared.

"Draw me a diagram," he said, holding the Child's face excitedly in his hands. "Show me exactly where the control is and what I do to activate it."

The Child sketched out a plan of Mabel Eastlake's bedroom, marking it clearly so that Alex could understand, could visualize the necessary steps. In his mind he entered that cold room one last time, found the control, punched in the code. He saw the front door of Glass House swing open. Saw himself standing outside, the film under his arm, running down the staircase of pink marble. Saw the giant front gates slowly swinging wide and himself stepping through them to the glory of freedom. He saw the film in his hand, saw the story of Mabel Eastlake as it would appear in bookstores . . . the dark, terrible, true story. He saw himself free, free, outside, able to move, unimpeded by fear, by walls, by lost images, unwatched by Mabel Eastlake's murderous eye, a man once again.

When the Child had finished and Alex was certain he understood what to do, the Child again turned to him. This time it was for reassurance, with a look of wavering resolve in the face of fear, a look of uncertainty as to where this plan would lead them.

That face! Alex looked closely, seeing with a charge of emotion its strength and its confusion and its awakening to the possibility of love. He took it in his hands and kissed it. "We can't be afraid now," he said. "We have to promise that we'll stay with one another until we're outside."

A low, rumbling groan of passion rose from the Child's throat. He took Alex in his arms and brought him down to the bed.

In the midst of their frantic lovemaking the Child's head jerked up with the sudden alertness of an animal sensing an intruder.

Alex was instantly awash with fear. "What?"

As he looked at Alex, the Child's eyes became evasive, indecipherable, blue runestones, unconnected to the moment. Alex was losing him.

"So that's where you are," said the voice of Mabel Eastlake. "With the servants. What a cozy little den of perversity."

Alex bolted up. "Get the fuck out of here!" he screamed. The camera was still covered. How could Mabel

Eastlake see them? "Leave us alone!" Grabbing a small,
heavy clock from the dresser, he jumped up on a chair and
struck the lens of the camera, shattering it, pounding it
with fury.

"Leave *you* alone?" Mabel Eastlake exclaimed with
an incredulous tone. "Leave you *alone?* The moment I do
you steal things from me. Just like Fancy. A thief. Now my
film is missing and I see that you have it."

But how did she see?

The second camera in Alex's room was much more
carefully concealed.

"You are a fool, little Mr. Liddell, if you think you
can outwit me. Mabel Eastlake outwitted every single fan
who went to see her. I didn't need that pathetic letter of
yours to tell me why you'd come to Glass House."

"What letter?"

"The one you stupidly thought my Child would
smuggle out for you, of course. I didn't ask for it. He *gave* it
to me."

Alex said nothing, stung into fear. Another escape
route cut off.

"A little game we've been playing for some time, Mr.
Liddell. I let her believe that the filth she writes using my
name actually gets mailed. She knows quite well, of course,
that it never does and that only I will see it."

"What about the letter I received?" Alex said, wanting to trip her up, confuse her, frighten her.

"Ah yes," 'Forget Mabel Eastlake, let her die with her
secrets.' The one letter of hers I did allow to be mailed." A
pause. "You should have heeded that advice, little Mr.
Liddell. The old fool insisted on warning you away from
here, and I saw no harm in letting her try. But of course I
knew the truth about you from our very first meeting."

"Truth," Alex said bitterly. "What truth?"

"That you think yourself cunning. So it was only natural that by cunning you would try to find a way out of Glass House once you'd found your way in. I hope you know by now that there is no way out."

Alex said nothing.

"Yes, cunning, and I knew you were a thief, too," Mabel Eastlake said. "Just like Fancy, just like Cygnet, just like Hilda. Perverted and cunning, wanting to profit from the secrets of others. From my secret."

"What secret?" Alex said. "I know you killed Hilda Hatter."

To which Miss Eastlake only responded with deep, soft laughter.

"I know you killed Boyd Powers and Otto Kranzler too."

"Did I? And what, pray, do you intend to do with what you know?" she asked.

"Murderer!" Alex shouted, holding up the film. "I'll get this out and show the world."

"Ah, the voice of justice," mocked the voice of Mabel Eastlake.

"And if I don't, Cygnet's confession will get you in the end."

"But in the meantime, little Mr. Liddell, I'm afraid Cygnet will have to get *you*. He's on his way down this very moment to retrieve my film. Cygnet may have chosen to confess, but I suffer from no similar compulsion. That film is Mabel Eastlake's confession and it will not leave Glass House again. Nor, little Mr. Liddell, will you."

"I'm not afraid of you."

"You aren't?" she teased. "You should be. The third murder is always easier than the second, and the fourth is mere child's play."

"You're insane."

"Am I? They always did say that of Mabel Eastlake, you know. Those were the very first words she heard when she came to that night and found the gun in her hand and Kranzler's body on the floor. 'Look what you've done, Mabel! Look what you've done!' That's what she heard Cygnet shouting at her, mercilessly. Poor Miss Eastlake had no recollection of murder, but she believed what she was told. She accepted the guilt. Oh how Miss Eastlake accepted the guilt. Weak people always do. And she's lived with it all these years. Guilt has made her quite generous."

"Spare me your generosity," Alex said.

"I have, thus far. But now it's time for all little witnesses to go to sleep in a profound and endless slumber. So fortunate to have run into you that night, darling. And I'm so glad you kept your part of the deal and told no one where you were going."

"Hilda Hatter was with you in the car that night," Alex said. "You thought I knew and would go to the police."

"Witnesses are unfair," said Mabel Eastlake. "They see only an act, a motion. They don't see circumstances. They don't understand necessity. They don't comprehend motivation."

The Child was sitting on the edge of the bed, his face a drained, numbed, powerful absence.

"What's your motivation for killing him?" Alex cried. "What's your motivation for taking control of his will? How can you do that to your own blood?" He stopped his ears against Mabel Eastlake's laughter.

"No, darling, not my blood at all. *Her* blood."

"Fancy's?"

"Yes. The last thing of hers that I want to have. And I can have him whenever I want, as you know. Don't you think I've trained him well, as a man should be trained?"

Nothing could be heard but the Child flinched as if in pain and rose confusedly from the bed.

"You can't! You can't do that, it's too—"

"Too what, little Mr. Liddell? I can make him come to me now. I can look at him and tell him, finally, to kill you. And he will kill you. Wearing the same diamonds, even, that Hilda was wearing. They stand up to a great deal of pressure, but quality jewelry always does."

Alex turned to the Child, shaking him. "Don't go to her," he pleaded, directing the Child to look at him, to see his words. "Don't go. Don't do what she'll tell you to do."

"You think the perversity of your ridiculous love can win out over me?" shouted the enraged voice of Mabel Eastlake. "I have taken everything I ever wanted. Everything! I took her house, I took *her*, Mabel Eastlake, and her hideous Mary P. I took them and I made them mine, converted their lives to mine. And everything I've taken has been just payment. Jimmy tried to kill me in that car. He didn't want me to catch Hilda. He *wanted* Hilda to have the film, to show it and ruin Mabel. Expose her for what she was. I paid with my face, Mr. Klein, trying to keep her secret. And that gives me the right to demand payment in return."

"You've been amply rewarded over the years, Fancy." Cygnet Sackville stood in the doorway of Alex's room, holding a silver hypodermic. "I gave you the illusion, after all, that Glass House was partly yours."

"Glass House wouldn't be yours if I hadn't planned it!" shouted the infuriated unseen voice. "I'm the one who got your prissy hands to murder for it. I'm the one who put the bludgeon into your lily-white hand and told you to bring it down as hard as you could on the skulls of Boyd and Hilda. You would never have done it without me. And as it was, you missed Hilda entirely. She got away because of your incompetence. *I* was the one who had the presence of mind to chase her to get the film back."

"But you'd already shot Kranzler," Cygnet replied. "You were already in far over your head. You *lost* your head, Fancy, in the passion of the moment. I'm the one who stayed behind to persuade Miss Eastlake that she was the murderess. It was I who broke her down and made her submissive to our terms."

"And it was *I* who became Mabel Eastlake!" raged the Voice.

"Impossible, my dear, without me," Cygnet said. "I am the sole guardian of the Eastlake face. I own it. I own whoever has it."

"But the film, darling, is mine. *I* own that."

"No, Fancy girl, THE SECRETS OF MABEL EASTLAKE also belongs to me. I shall take possession of Miss Eastlake's past. I shall watch it once again and then I shall destroy it." He smiled terribly as he moved towards Alex.

Holding the film tight against his chest, Alex tried desperately to get the Child's attention.

"You should have stayed away, boy," Cygnet said as he slowly shifted the syringe in his hand, grasping it like a knife.

"Christ, how can you—" Alex found his answer in Sackville's eyes. There was no mercy in them, only a terrifying nullity of emotion.

"Child!" he cried.

But by this time Alex himself could almost hear the whistle, that high-pitched inhuman frequency summoning the Child to his goddess of annihilation.

He cried out again, watching the Child's agony.

For the Child, resisting the call, lay bent double with his hands over his ears and his contorted face blinded by tears. He pounded the floor with his hands, slapped it, fought it, got up to hurl things, smash things, fell down again. But then . . . slowly . . . he rose with a terrifying look of utter submission in his eyes.

"Don't! Don't!" Alex shouted, trying to claim him back.

"Did you doubt my power, little Mr. Liddell?" laughed the voice of Mabel Eastlake. Only now Alex heard it as Fancy Barlow's voice, for it was Fancy Barlow speaking. The presumed Fancy Barlow, whom he had met outside the day he arrived at Glass House . . . that Fancy Barlow was the true Mabel Eastlake.

The Mabel Eastlake they had framed for their guilt, framed for the murders committed by Fancy Barlow and Cygnet Sackville. Where *was* the real Mabel Eastlake? Was Mabel Eastlake the figure he had seen in the projection room? Impossible! That had been a man—Abe West.

The Child, summoned, unable to resist, ran crookedly from Alex's room.

Alex faced Cygnet. "Don't," he threatened. "Don't. I'll kill you if I have to." And then, filled with a sudden, wild, self-protective instinct, he rushed the old man, holding the film out for protection, swinging it like a club, and knocked the syringe from his hands.

Sackville lunged at him in a fury and Alex dropped the film, then struck out blindly, hefting his knee into Sackville's groin. Cygnet doubled over with a gasping shriek.

Head pounding, Alex tore from the room and up to the front door, banging it with his fists, kicking it, screaming, enraged, knowing it was locked. He ran through the Black and Blue Room, into the next. There, through the glass wall of the inner garden, he saw the Child standing on Mabel Eastlake's balcony. Seeing Alex, the Child leapt to the tree and began to scramble down its branches. Alex cried out. He heard the splinter of glass behind him . . . the Child had smashed the giant glass wall of the inner garden.

Through the doors leading to the terrace, blinded by sheer terror, down the stairs towards the pool, down the cypress-lined avenue towards the gazebo. He knew his escape was not there. He knew there was no escape. But his body refused to believe it. In the distance the high stone walls rose up to surround and imprison him, to laugh at his fear.

Over his shoulder he saw a streaking blur of white. The bloodied Child, broken free of the glass, running towards him. The Child, transformed into Mabel Eastlake's beast of prey. Her animal of death.

Reaching it, having no breath but gulping it somehow, Alex flung himself against the wall of the estate, insisting on his freedom, his escape, clawing despite the hard reality of stone, tearing at the ivy with awful cries coming from his throat, his soul.

He felt the weight of the Child's body on him, felt himself grabbed and pulled away, and he screamed, turning to fight, scratching the Child's face and eyes with his crimson Mabel Eastlake fingernails. Panting, moaning, his clothes torn, battling for his life, terrified to look into the Child's face and see the emotional anonymity that made him Alex's murderer, the radiant face of love transformed into the violent face of death.

A strangled, distorted sound came from the Child as he grasped Alex's throat, pressing the stones into his neck. And looking up, his head snapped back, his vision blurred, Alex saw that the Child, killing him, was crying.

And then another image appeared and he assumed he was hallucinating the symbol of his death. For wasn't it death now? Vision was leaving him. His head was red and light and ready to go. Death, appearing now to claim him.

A figure dressed in a white satin tuxedo stepped out from the gazebo, raised a small pistol, and fired.

A bullet tore through the Child's shoulder. He let out a high, inhuman scream and was hurled to the ground by the impact.

15.

Getting out was all that mattered now. Finally he knew what he must do to gain his freedom from this nightmarish web of illusion and death. Glass House had to be faced one last time. This time it had to be conquered. He had to get back into Mabel Eastlake's room, activate the code. He knew the code, and the code meant escape . . . or death.

Death! The Child!

But he blinded himself, would not allow himself even to think of all that lay behind him. He had run from the Child, run wildly, crazily, without daring to look into the gazebo, afraid of what he would see there. Hadn't the bullet been meant for him instead?

The choices were suddenly so clear. He could wait here, outside the glass doors, a passive instrument of fate. Or he could at least attempt to decide his own fate, his own survival. The power of action.

Standing on the terrace, gasping for breath, Alex faced the door in the great curving wall of glass, suppressing the flurry of possibilities, regrouped, rearmed, waiting for him inside. Unknown images. Again he conjured up the code, making sure he did remember it. Then he entered.

Never had Glass House felt so distorted, so hostile and protective of its violent secrets. For violence had been done to it: in front of him he could see the shattered glass wall of the inner garden. Jagged shards lay scattered over the black floor, the brittle tears of Glass House. Alex picked up the longest and sharpest shard he could find. An absurd weapon, but with something dangerous in his hand he felt less vulnerable.

Trust no one and nothing, he thought, darting into the Black and Blue Room and from there, through the hidden door, into the library. In the library he carefully searched through the webs of shadow . . . looking for he hardly knew what. What image? Nothing stirred. Where was Cygnet now? Where was Mabel Eastlake? Where was Fancy Barlow? And the stranger in the gazebo, where was he—or she? Was it Abe West. Or was it some other figure from the murderous past of Glass House?

Access to Mabel Eastlake's room was what he needed. The room from which Glass House was manipulated, controlled, directed. Who was this usurper, Fancy Barlow? This Fancy Barlow who was Mabel Eastlake? This Fancy Barlow who had been impersonating Mabel Eastlake for so many years that she had become her?

The foyer was empty, black, expectant. The Vargas portrait of Mabel Eastlake had been slashed. Cygnet's bowl of purple orchids lay shattered on the floor, the dark beauty of the flowers mutilated in what looked like a fit of wet, brutal glee.

Cocaine, was she dead? He, Alex, had perhaps killed the animal. And Cygnet? Perhaps he had killed the old man as well. The Child, dead or severely wounded, sprawled somewhere near the gazebo. He, Alex, would have tried to kill the Child had not the stranger's bullet done it for him.

The realization of his own capacity for violence, this potential for death, was a thick, heavy slur on his consciousness. Knowing it to be there added a disorienting and oppressive element to his already overwrought nervous state and created an almost unbearable moral distortion of his vision, altering the peripheries of the life that had until now contained him. The burden of accepting this ancient blood-guilt sat heavy as stone on Alex's shoulders. He was becoming aware, however dimly, that because of it he would never be the same, the old Alex.

Watching the scan of the camera, he waited until he was outside its range before darting across the foyer. To enter via the front door of Miss Eastlake's room was impossible: The cameras made him far too vulnerable, and the door itself was probably locked. It was only through the passageway from the projection room that he could enter her room without having his progress monitored.

The silence of the house was immense, throbbing in his ears and heart as he stealthily followed his chosen route. Slipping into the projection room, he closed the door behind him as quickly as he could, so that a monitor would not register a light change and thereby draw Miss Eastlake's eye.

The long suppressed film was playing. A spreading gray triangle of light from the projector, the small screen splashed with the outtakes he had seen once before. Filmed moments of life, situations the images contained on the film had once experienced as reality on the other side of the camera.

There was Mabel Eastlake breaking down on the set of *Desperate Woman*. Mabel Eastlake in smoked glasses standing with Flame, both of them furious with the persistence and perversity of a camera that would not stop observing them. Mabel Eastlake, frozen, as Fancy Barlow took the dog from her arms and hurled it into the pool. Mabel Eastlake, the beautiful, brutalized and brutalizing image, exposing the past torments of her life.

Now came the strange nightclub footage from The

Black Orchis, and the camera moved in to focus on the face Alex knew to be Abe West's. Why was it that the face haunted him so, standing just on the threshold of recognition but never crossing it? That conceited, smiling, flirtatious, enigmatic image, what was it telling him that he didn't already know?

THE SECRETS OF MABEL EASTLAKE appeared on the screen. This is where the footage had stopped the last time. Now, at last, Alex was to see the film that so many people had died—or murdered—for.

On the screen was Mabel Eastlake. Drugged, perhaps—at least smiling somewhat artificially. A less cosmetically perfect Mabel Eastlake than the later star of feature films. Almost coarse, almost laughable. This was Jimmy Flame's Mabel, the Mabel of The Black Orchis, wearing a semitransparent chemise.

On a bed lay Otto Kranzler, huge, naked, repulsive, masturbating as he viewed his future star, the one he would buy from Flame, the one who allowed herself to be bought and sold like a slave, never knowing that she could own herself.

Mabel Eastlake, soon to become aesthetically perfect and a dream icon to millions of Americans, was doing a slow, involved strip. Her back was to the camera—the Eastlake back, how beautiful it was! Strong and tapering to her waist, and then the firm, abrupt punctuation of the buttocks and the straight flow of leg. Yes, the body was beautiful, even in the degradation of its sordid environment.

The chemise dropped to the floor.

Mabel Eastlake, back to the camera, naked except for garters, nylons, and a pair of charmeuse satin panties. Mabel Eastlake, looking flirtatiously over her shoulder at Kranzler, the man so hated, so powerful. Smiling an early version of what would become the Eastlake Killer Smile.

Daring Kranzler, luring him on; the artifice of forced sexuality, the motions instead of the emotions.

And when Mabel Eastlake turned then, slowly, to face the camera, Alex's eyes were full of tears. Finally he knew why Abe West's face had been haunting him so.

Finally he knew Mabel Eastlake's last and most incredible secret.

One of Mabel Eastlake's hands dug down into her panties, while the other grasped her opposite shoulder, hiding nonexistent breasts. Mabel Eastlake—"the woman even women can adore"—slowly removed the last of her garments and uncupped her protective hand, finally confessing before the relentless vigilance of the camera. The size of the genitals bore witness to an astonishing virility.

Abe West had disappeared. He had come back as Mabel Eastlake. It was the face of Abe West that lay buried in the face of Mabel Eastlake.

Mabel Eastlake had been a man.

Was a man.

The film ran out and the screen was suddenly, blindingly, bared.

And below its blank white stare, like a sacrifice upon an altar, lay the body of Cygnet Sackville. His arms were outspread and his glassy eyes gleamed with joy. The cause of this cold rapture, one of his deadly but pleasurable potions, could be inferred from a silver gleam at his heart. Mr. Sackville looked now as if he had welcomed the plunge of that syringe, and the dark, endless silence that it brought him.

Alex, fighting a spasm of terror, staggered further back into the projection room. He heard his groans from somewhere outside himself. He could not fail now. Finding the door in the storage area behind the projector, he steeled himself. He then began to climb, one final time, the shadowy stairs to Mabel Eastlake's waiting black boudoir.

The passage was steep, dark, the walls on either side

narrow, close. Alex clenched the glass shard tightly in his hand, and then stood before the door, thinking, she'll be able to hear my heart. My heart will give me away. But he could not allow himself to think. Now was the time to act. Opening the door he stepped again into Mabel Eastlake's domain.

The same biting cold assailed his senses. The draperies had been opened and a soft, grainy light fell over the contours of the room, chasing the darkness into corners, under tables, inside the canopied bed.

The masks of Mabel Eastlake—those perfect works of art, sculpted by Cygnet Sackville—guarded the place from the wall.

The computer control was to one side of the monitors. Alex went through the Child's instructions. Every detail must be remembered perfectly. He moved quickly as a shadow to the controls.

But an image flashed by on one of the monitors, distracting his concentration. Whose was it? In what room? Terror pulsed through his veins as he turned his panicked attention back to the control. Press in seven letters, turn one switch, press in three symbols. He was fighting back so much fear of his own failure that his hands would not work, were thick and clumsy. He stopped, put down the glass shard and tried to breathe deeply, grasping the control board with both hands. "Do it!" he commanded himself. "For Christ's sake, Alex, do it, do it, do it!"

Before he could, however, the glass had been swept from the control board, flung across the room, and the Eastlake voice said close behind him: "At last, darling—alone . . . face to face."

Alex whirled around with a startled cry.

The weirdly youthful form of Mabel Eastlake, its veiled face radiant and fixed, stood watching him from a distance of only two yards. In her hand he recognized the needle-tipped stopper from the bottle of *Forbidden!* in

Fancy's room. Fancy, who was the real Mabel, who was a man. The perfect, emotionless face stared with the concentrated intensity of madness, the gloved hands played with the stopper.

"What have you done to her?" Alex demanded.

"To whom, darling?"

"Mabel Eastlake."

"Darling, I am Mabel Eastlake. This is my home. My perfect home, as perfect as I. And if you don't believe me, ask Cyggie. He'll tell you who Glass House belongs to now."

"You're not Mabel Eastlake. You're Fancy Barlow."

"I?" The veiled figure laughed. "Fancy Barlow?" The voice turned vicious. "Fancy Barlow is nothing more than a ridiculous housekeeper. An old pet you keep on because you can't bring yourself to kill it. Poor Miss Barlow, once so very beautiful. She lost her face in an unfortunate accident many years ago. Did you know? And do you know what it's like for a beautiful woman to lose her beauty? To become . . . a monster?"

"You were a monster even when you had your face."

"Miss Barlow couldn't bear the awful shame of it. She'd lost her face in the service of Mabel Eastlake."

"You didn't murder Kranzler and Boyd Powers and Hilda to help protect Miss Eastlake. You did it for yourself. For your own rotten greed. You profited from her weakness."

"You mean *his* weakness." She paused. "Miss Barlow returned to Glass House to be protected from prying eyes. The world loves to pry, little Mr. Liddell, as you know best. Loves to judge without knowing all the details."

"The details are simple. You murdered Kranzler and had Sackville kill Boyd Powers. And you wanted Hilda Hatter dead that night too."

"Hilda knew our secret, darling. And anyone who knew our secret could ruin us all."

"You told Sackville to stay here and convince Mabel Eastlake she'd murdered Kranzler and Powers."

"She had murdered them often enough in her thoughts. We simply murdered them in deed."

"And when Hilda grabbed the film and ran, it was you who chased her in the Duesenberg. Fancy Barlow, dressed like Mabel Eastlake, in Mabel Eastlake's white satin tuxedo."

"No, darling, a copy of it. But I got the real thing when I returned to Glass House as Mabel Eastlake."

"It was you in the Duesenberg."

"Yes, but Jimmy didn't know that until he finally got into the car with me. He was very surprised! The fool thought he was going to get her away from us. Jimmy to the rescue!"

"And it was Fancy Barlow's face that was ruined," Alex said. "Yours. And it was you, Fancy Barlow, on the witness stand, telling them that Jimmy was the murderer."

"After all those years of having to be her, finally I *was* her. And I've been her ever since. My very just reward for a very unjust fate." The veiled figure laughed and moved slowly, with a certain stiff dignity, towards the wall of glass. "Do you see this view? When you see it, don't you understand ambition? Great ambition? It makes you feel small, this view, unless you own it. Unless it is yours. And I wanted it from the moment I first saw it, the very first time Miss Barlow and I came to Glass House. *He* wanted it too. It was *his* at first. But I got it in the end. In the end I got everything I ever wanted. Including, little Mr. Liddell, the Child."

"He doesn't love you. You're grotesque."

"He loves my image, darling. I wouldn't want a man to love me for my soul."

"You made him into a dog—an animal—with your silver whistle and your trick masks."

Fancy Barlow grasped the small whistle hanging like a tiny charm around her neck. "It doesn't matter how, darling, so long as I have him, so long as he is mine."

"You don't have him!" Alex cried, fighting a deep sudden rush of emotion. "He's dead!"

"And so, darling, are you." The figure rushed towards Alex with the crystal stopper raised high to strike.

The rest happened with the assault of a dream.

A wave of black, furious, uncontrollable rage pumped through him. He grabbed and easily stopped the raised hand. She was old but surprisingly strong and, of course, she was taller than he. They fought in the moonlit darkness of the room, violent partners in a violent dance. The stopper fell from Fancy Barlow's hand. And Alex, with a look of raging, vengeful, hate-filled triumph, ripped away her veil. For one moment the pale face of Mabel Eastlake shone forth—beautiful and ghastly.

"I'll show you who you are," he said, reaching for the face. He could feel it in his hand, feel the life-like pliancy of the rubber. She gasped and tried to squirm away. With a triumphant gesture Alex tore off the mask and, holding her face, or what remained of it, in his hands, hardly looking at it himself, thrust it before the nearest mirror.

A soul–piercing scream filled the room, filled his ears, filled Glass House.

He had expected to see something awful. But even so, catching sight of the image in the glass, he was horrified by what he saw. Flinging his hands away from the hideous object they held, he leapt away in horror.

Looking at him, startled, shy, abashed as some nocturnal creature caught in a sudden, inquisitive beam of light, Fancy Barlow half-lowered her face. The pitiful semblance of a face, monstrous in its disfigurement, grotesque and appalling. The face of Fancy Barlow, destroyed as time alone could never have destroyed it, not without the savage collaboration of flying glass, burning metal, and the merciless afterthoughts of medical science. Seeing that face, Alex had to fight back the dark wave of repugnance that instantly rose to unnerve, to overpower him.

Giving way to a sudden, frantic impulse, she made a desperate lunge for the mask Alex still held. But then, sensing Alex's sudden paralysis, she recovered herself, and stopped. She realized, now, the power of her devastated face. *This* image, then, was her triumph. She slowly raised it, as if it were the most beautiful object in the world, worthy of endless and minute adoration. She stared intensely at Alex, and when she spoke her voice was low and gloating.

"So, little Mr. Liddell, you now see for yourself just how beautiful I am. You now understand the power of a face." Opening what had been her mouth, her eyes fixed on Alex, she crouched over and felt for the glass stopper until she had it and could clench it in her hand. Then she moved toward him.

But a figure appeared in the monitor of the projection room, and catching sight of it—hoping for salvation—Alex ran to see who it was.

"Abe West!" he cried, wanting to frighten her. "Abe West's come back!"

With a shrill cry, Fancy Barlow ran to the door leading to the projection room and disappeared.

Dazed, Alex stared into the monitor. There again he saw the image of a man. Now he knew it was Abe West. He knew it was Mabel Eastlake. Dressed in the white satin tuxedo from *Desperate Woman*, Mabel Eastlake stood in front of Cygnet's body, in the full light emanating from the projector, staring up into the surveillance camera. The camera moved away from her, or him, to scan the rest of the room.

"She's coming down there!" Alex shouted, to warn Mabel Eastlake of Fancy's imminent appearance.

But by then it was too late. Miss Barlow's silhouette appeared on the monitor. In the empty glare of the light from the projector, the two faced one another with a terrible, mutually understood finality.

"I didn't kill them," Mabel Eastlake said. "All these years, Fancy, my soul could have felt free." She—or Abe West—raised the gun.

With a scream, Fancy Barlow made a sudden rush, clenching the stopper.

Her body was knocked backwards by the impact of the blast, her blood impressing the screen in a way her image never had.

The survivor looked up into the camera, looked at Alex, looked with a face melting with violent emotion. "My double, darling, is dead." Mabel Eastlake threw down the gun. "Mabel Eastlake is dead."

And Alex Klein, A. Liddle, romance writer, seeker of truth, pilgrim of love, felt his whole being explode. The rigid barriers that confined the fullest expression of his heart, that held it in check by repressing the tenderness of desire, crumpled in the fire that now roared through him. He cried out. His eyes filled with tears. The ordeal was not over. The mystery for him would remain forever unsolved, for the mystery was love itself: and love, realizing itself, recognizing itself in the Child, had finally come to Alex only to be destroyed. Too late, his heart sobbed; your love is dead. And that was the ordeal yet to be faced and lived with. The absence of the one person who had dealt the decisive, shattering blow to his glass coffin, and slapped awake the sleeping, waiting heart within.

His body moved, following an overwhelming call, something beyond words. He ran, wanting to submerge his passion in the miraculous waters of love. There was no Alex, only a consuming need to see, to hold, to cry out the truth of this new wonder and pain.

Out from Glass House, tortured by its own mysteries, out into the unimpeded freedom of space, where there were no walls, no checks, nothing to impinge upon the enormous cry and capacity of his awakened heart.

"Child!" he cried, running, hardly able to see, "Child! Child!"

Down the stairs, past the pool, down to the lowest wildest level of garden, and towards the gazebo, crazed to hold his body, to mourn and wail his loss. "Child!" He wanted his voice to awaken the waiting darkness, to register his outrage with the blind, unhearing misery of a fate that would not allow for love.

Then he saw him, saw a figure slowly raise itself and pitifully crawl towards him. Joy blended with suffering as Alex fell upon the blood-soaked Child, took him in his arms, held him tight, rocked him, sobbing, unable to express in any other way the fullness of his heart.

It was the Child, the one of rare speech, who proclaimed their future. His eyes, as he looked deep into Alex's, silently spoke Alex's name. His hand drew Alex close to the tongue struggling in his mouth. His one word, simple as it was, required considerable effort, for he had never before spoken it aloud. "Love," he said.

16.

"My double, darling, is dead," she had said. "Mabel Eastlake is dead."

But of course she wasn't and Mabel Eastlake regained possession of herself and Glass House at the same time as the police took it over, later that night. Nothing in the house could be touched until a full investigation had been completed. Usually indifferent to the feelings of great stars, the police on this case were unusually deferential to the wishes of Miss Eastlake. The D.A. was a Mabel Eastlake fan.

Using Alex as spokesman, Mabel Eastlake, a silent figure behind her veils, admitted to the murder of Fancy Barlow, her one time double and stand-in. She had done it, she said, in self-defense. But it was Miss Barlow, not Miss Eastlake, who had killed Cygnet Sackville. And it was Cygnet Sackville who had carefully planned Hilda Hatter's murder.

Neither Alex nor Miss Eastlake acknowledged the existence of any film. It quietly disappeared when Mabel Eastlake went into seclusion in her great black boudoir. As far as the police were concerned, satisfied as they were with the preliminary details of the case, the past played no part in this homicidal episode. The case belonged entirely to the present.

The police had not yet been in her room. Mabel Eastlake vowed that she would vacate it only when she absolutely had to. When, in other words, she allowed herself to be handled, to be taken to police headquarters, where she would issue a full statement and allow herself to be formally charged with murder.

In the meantime, before he had carefully weighed the enormous potential consequences of doing so, Alex notified the detective of Cygnet Sackville's confession in the safe deposit box. Almost instantly he regretted his action. He did not know what information Cygnet had given, after all, and neither did Miss Eastlake. There was suddenly, because of this, an added, shared tension between them. What details had Cygnet chosen to put down on paper?

It was apparent to Alex, even though no word on the subject was ever spoken, that Mabel Eastlake was still terrified, after all these years, of the effect her secret might have on the world.

"I'll become a monkey in their eyes, I know," she said to Alex at one vulnerable moment, when the two of them were briefly left alone together while the police pursued their business downstairs without them.

For Glass House had been invaded. The time of the house had changed. The cameras, still scanning, now picked up incessant images of uniformed men carrying out their duties with the brisk impersonal officiousness of modern everyday life. Life was suddenly like speeded-up film, fast and full of motion. The cadence of ordinary speech sounded cheap and meaningless when compared to the kind of dialogue that Glass House had known. Mabel Eastlake had always been fast, but this kind of demand—harsh, instant answers to questions that allowed for no wit or style—frankly rattled her. She had existed out of time for so long that she felt the full, startling impact of modern time, modern life, in the space of a day.

The invasion was unnerving to Alex as well. The images now visible on the monitors did not look right, looked reduced and ordinary like the images of television; forgettable the moment they were seen, images that clashed harshly with the distinctive lines and style of Glass House. And Alex felt unusually protective of Miss Eastlake at this crucial point in the fabulous old star's life. There was no one but Alex to help see her through it.

"For there's no one left," Miss Eastlake said to him, wringing a small handkerchief. "Glass House must start out fresh." She gave a strange little laugh. "We'll mop up the old blood together, darling, just as we mopped the floors together." There was a show of bravado in her otherwise shaky voice, as though the shock of suddenly being Cinderella with the glass slipper was a dubious honor at best. "See to it, darling, that blood is never shed here again."

She watched with great emotion, staring into the monitors with a shocked, shamed and sorrowful face, as the bodies of Cygnet Sackville and Fancy Barlow, her oldest friends and cruelest adversaries, were put into giant black plastic bags and removed from the projection room. Miss Eastlake claimed not to know where the body of Hilda Hatter was to be found. (What remained of the columnist was finally located in the same deep freeze where Alex had once imagined seeing a frozen face, an odd coincidence he never spoke of.) Miss Eastlake believed, and investigation finally concluded on less than wholly convincing evidence, that Miss Barlow had forcibly abducted Miss Hatter from her home. Mr. Sackville had had the pleasure of actually cutting out her tongue. But the actual cause of death? So little of the body actually remained, and what was left had been so neatly carved up in preparation for disposal, that it was impossible to tell. Alex never raised the possibility with the police that the Child may in any way have been involved and Cocaine was never suspected.

Why was he, Alex Klein, here in Miss Eastlake's home? Miss Eastlake quickly explained for the tongue-tied

Alex. "Mr. Klein here is a close personal friend of my grandson. They were visiting me at my invitation."

At any rate, Mabel Eastlake ordered that the three corpses be buried in Forest Lawn at her expense. Having the onus of guilt lifted from her shoulders, realizing at last that she had not committed the murders in '39, made Miss Eastlake unusually generous with the burial costs.

But the profound psychic shock of having murdered now, and her former stand-in at that, was undeniable. "It's like having an organ cut off from your body," she said to Alex, "and not being given anything to replace it."

Alex and she shared the other horror, just as great, of having seen the real face of Fancy Barlow, the true image under the false. The recollection of it, so majestically rotten, was not easily dispelled.

It troubled Miss Eastlake greatly to think she might have lived out her days believing herself to be the murderer of Kranzler and Boyd Powers. "And I would have, darling, were it not for you," she said to Alex. "You brought the truth into this house, you brought the truth to me. It's their cunning over the years that hurts me the most. Taking advantage of me when my eyes were closed. Never believe anything people tell you to believe, Alex darling, unless you've actually seen the truth of it with your own two peepers! To think that I just gave myself up to them, to the guilt that's always there waiting. You must never do that."

There was a sensation downstairs when the panther was found in the inner garden. "Jeez, what's this?" one of the policemen exclaimed. Alex, who thought he had killed her, watched with a racing heart as Cocaine groggily lifted her head.

"She's alive." He ran to tell the Child. "She's still alive!"

And all around him now, as he carried out these necessary duties, Alex was aware of Glass House, a presence with folded arms, waiting for him, watching him. Not an enemy, as he'd supposed, but an ally and a friend. He'd known it in some instinctive way from the very beginning. Even before the haunting actually began, he knew that this place, Glass House, would be a part of him for life.

It had to be, for love had come into it, to him in it, like an epiphany to a disbeliever. He hadn't been able to weep for Fancy, Hilda or Cygnet. But when he ran outside after the last gunshot, when he found himself flying down the stairs towards the gazebo and then saw the Child dragging his body slowly towards the house, saw him alive, Alex's heart had exploded with the painful awe of love. The sap of its mystery now filled him, lifted him, exulted him. The Child felt it, too. They'd been through it and lived. Some black enchantment had been lifted from their spirits.

The Child was treated for his gunshot wound up in Mabel Eastlake's boudoir. He refused to leave, refused to enter a hospital, as afraid as a mute and trembling animal in the hands of strangers.

So it was Alex who took charge, and said that he would bring the Child to a hospital after accompanying Miss Eastlake to police headquarters.

Clear and tenderly blue, the early morning light spread through the enormous black room, exploring it, softening it, transforming it. The Child lay sleeping on the silk-draped bed, his arm wrapped and his head bandaged. At the giant wall of glass, her back to Alex, stood Mabel Eastlake. She was wearing the Snake Dress, and its white fox collar hid her face from view.

She stood staring out, participating again in the view that was hers.

This is the real Mabel Eastlake, Alex thought—the genuine, the original, the one who knocked her competitors flat. This is the one whose films had inspired and amused a nation trapped in the Depression. The one whose image was potent and lasting; ever more so now that Alex knew the secret that lay behind it.

He felt it was a sacrilege to disturb the deep reverie of the old star, but he had to. "Miss Eastlake?" he said softly.

The hood of fur quivered but Miss Eastlake did not respond.

"It's getting to be time now," Alex said. "The police want the gun."

"They may have it when I vacate this room."

"You do have it then?"

"Of course, darling. On my persona."

"The reporters are stacking up by the front gates," Alex said. In the monitor they could be seen, the people of the press, amassing like a virus about to invade an organism.

"The police may let them in when everything's ready. When *I'm* ready," said the old star. "You will go down first, with the Child, to tell them that I will not answer any of their ridiculous questions. You, darling, may say anything you wish, but I intend to preserve whatever small dignity is left to me in my very undignified position."

"Are you ready now?"

"Are *you* ready, darling?" Mabel Eastlake asked, still refusing to turn around. "Do you realize what an ordeal this will be?"

"I've been through so much already that this hardly counts," Alex said.

With this, and with what sounded like a small sob, Mabel Eastlake turned to face him. She was wearing an enormous pair of dark glasses. These she removed so that Alex could see her tears. Miss Eastlake hesitantly held out her arms.

Alex rushed to her. For an intense moment they embraced, fused tight by shared emotions.

"I'm sorry, darling," Mabel Eastlake said, "so very sorry for what you've been through here. I tried to warn you from the beginning. But once you were here, nothing could be stopped. Fate took over."

"Miss Eastlake, *I'm* so sorry. For all *you've* gone through over the years."

"*Centuries*, darling." She raised her hands together. "Oh, I *wish* we could go to The Black Orchis tonight to celebrate! Go to dance and drink and pretend we're really free! The police won't mind if we have one last glass of truly excellent champagne will they?" And not caring one way or another she produced a fine vintage and poured out two glasses.

Alex stared at her, wanting to fix her image, as they toasted and drank with unsteady hands.

"Heavens," she laughed, "I'm so nervous and breathless after all this."

Alex was assaulted by a vision of the *real* Mabel Eastlake, an image even now of incomparable substance and magnificent presence. And he was the only one in the world who knew. . .

"I want to make things up to you," Miss Eastlake said, approaching Alex with the diamond choker. "I want you to have these. Sell them wisely if you wish, and they'll fetch a very pretty price. Don't show them to the police, do you hear me?"

Alex eyed the deadly stones with apprehension.

"They *are* mine, darling," Mabel Eastlake said softly. "The last piece of ransom that Hilda was going to get from us. And I wish, Alex, for you to wear them when you leave Glass House today. Our secret. Promise me you will."

"Wear them how?"

"Under your shirt. If you turn the collar up, no one will see. But *you'll* know. That's the best way to wear wealth, you know." Her gloved fingers unbuttoned his shirt and Alex raised his head to receive the gift.

The familiar weight, the primitive delight of wearing stones. Encouraging his appreciation Mabel Eastlake brought him to a mirror and showed him how he looked from all angles. His neck shot out fiery sparks in every direction. And, stranger than that, he looked and saw himself as a blond, a fascinating sight completely unlike the image he had had of himself.

Miss Eastlake stood quietly appraising the effect, nodded, and the diamonds disappeared under his turned up shirt collar. "Promise you'll keep them?"

"Of course I promise."

"It's a pact between us, like blood-brotherhood. Isn't there something in the Bible about what greater sacrifice can one man make to another than his diamonds?"

And since generosity embarrassed her, she turned to walk back to the windows, drawn there by a comfort that had no words. The morning light wriggled hypnotically up the lamé of her gown, settling with a delicate radiance on the soft white fur. "I never really thought I'd be standing here again seeing this," she said. One of her gloved hands rested on the glass. A moment of silence. "Do you know where the film is?" she asked quietly.

"Yes, I know."

"Will you tell them?"

"The film will. You can't disguise what's there in front of you."

Mabel Eastlake let out a deep, soft laugh. "The magic of motion pictures," he said. "The glory of the human image. The great art of this century." Suddenly nervous, he went to gaze down on the sleeping Child, victim of his gun and Alex's lacerating nails.

The Child's face was barely visible through the gauze wrappings. Very tenderly Mabel Eastlake bent over and kissed his grandson gently on the mouth. "Do you think he'll ever understand why I had to do it?" he asked

Alex.

"He's lived a strange life."

"But he won't know *how* strange, darling, until you tell him." Another pause. "You know that I did it for you, don't you? It was the only way to stop her hold—she wanted him to kill you . . . and it's possible that he would have."

Remembering the horror of that struggle, Alex had to turn away.

"So strange, darling, to see you made up like me last night," Mabel Eastlake said, searching his face for a moment. "You did remind me a little of myself when I was young. But you, darling, you have the luxury of not having to protect yourself from the damning eyes of the world"

"Wouldn't it be better if you told them?" Alex asked. "Won't you have to?"

"No, I couldn't. For once I wouldn't know what to say! Don't you understand how they'd laugh? How I'd change in their eyes into some sort of freakish joke? I couldn't face it back then, and I certainly can't face it now. I'm too old to squander what little respect is left me." She made him understand with her look and tone of voice. "I won't tell them. I won't say anything. Won't tell them about the film. But . . . *you* can . . . if you wish. My fate, darling, is really in *your* hands"

"No, I—" He didn't want this responsibility, it was too great. His temptation to tell, to reveal all, weakened considerably when he realized the full extent of Miss Eastlake's anguish.

Mabel Eastlake stood staring, staring out the window. "I dreamed of Jimmy last night," she said. "He finally came for me. Took my hand . . . and I walked away with him. We didn't say a word, but it was so peaceful and . . . lovely."

The Child stirred on the bed. In one of the monitors Alex could see the police open the front gates to allow the news crews through. He glanced uneasily at Mabel

Eastlake. "They're coming." He followed their progress up the drive, watched them pour into the foyer. "They're here. It's time."

"Time?" Mabel Eastlake turned to face him, a distant, amused look on his face. "Well, they say there's no cheating *that*."

But somehow, with a sudden, inspired grace, he managed to do so.

Alex had been watching a figure of tragedy, standing human and vulnerable in a white lamé gown. Now, before his startled eyes, there took place a weird and thrilling transformation.

For a few brief seconds Mabel Eastlake materialized before him. The true image. A young, beautiful, free Mabel Eastlake.

Was it acting ability? Will power? Madness?

Mabel Eastlake's face, its expression steadily intensifying, almost seemed to change physically, as though transformed by the beneficent power of a god. Those old violet eyes drove home their magic, their power. The chemicals ignited. And as beautiful and mysterious as she had ever been in her films, the image of Mabel Eastlake, for a few chilling moments, flickered and burned again before him.

"I'll go down now," Alex said dazedly. "Will you be all right?"

"Take the Child with you," she said. The illusion vanished. "Go first and give me just a few moments alone to compose myself . . . I haven't made an appearance in so long."

"Is there—"

The smile was oddly serene, much different from the pearly glare of an Eastlake Killer Smile. "No, darling, nothing. Except. . ."

Alex waited.

"Whatever happens, take care of him. Take good

care of him."

Alex took the Child by the hand. They looked back at Mabel Eastlake. But the old star had returned to her spot by the glass wall and was gazing off through her enormous dark glasses into the depths of the view.

The reporters swarmed in, buzzing, flashbulbs flaring, photographing everything there was to be seen in the foyer.

With the dazed and nervous Child beside him, Alex stepped out of Mabel Eastlake's bedroom and stood at the top of the great curving staircase. The cameras began clicking immediately, and he was aware then that he was playing a part, giving them an image. He straightened his back.

The staircase that had once nearly been his death. This time he would be in full command of it. There were several photographs of him taken at the top, blond, one hand touching his neck, the other either clutching or reassuring the Child.

Police kept reporters from rushing up the stairs, but the noise and lights rose to deafen the ear and eye. Questions were hurled with violent insistence. Mabel Eastlake's name was heard over and over again, inserted into a thousand different questions. Alex did not miss a beat in his descent.

The Child froze for a moment and clung tightly to Alex. "It's all right," Alex said. "Stay close and it'll be all right."

As they slowly came down, the question of one reporter rose higher and louder than the others. "Where is she now? Where is Mabel Eastlake now?"

Alex halted, shocked by his sudden knowledge. He looked into the Child's eyes. The question was answered for them by the sound of Miss Eastlake's pistol, fired once in the room above.

17.   *Cygnet's Confession*

No detective, I believe, could reconstruct with absolute accuracy the crimes of Glass House and how they have been committed. Mine is a house that has attracted oddness from the beginning; a place, it has always seemed to me, that demanded sacrifice; a polished marble floor for the violent ballet of fate.

There are certain ancient spots on this earth that are magnetic, that call irresistibly to kindred individuals. Once together, those magneticized souls create a world. Glass House stands on such a spot, here in Beverly Hills, close to Hollywood. The world that it helped to create has not been a particularly happy one. Yet, as a secret criminal, I have not been entirely unhappy. I could say that many pleasures have been mine.

On the night of December 28, 1939, Fancy Barlow and I killed two men between us. We have deliberately made Mabel Eastlake believe herself to be guilty of our sins. She, consequently, has suffered torments of conscience while we—Miss Barlow and I—discuss over herbal tea the plans for our next victim.

For by the time this document is found and read, barring some miracle of bad luck or planning, Hilda Hatter will be added to the list of those who have tampered with Glass House and must pay the price.

As I write this, Miss Barlow and I anticipate with a

certain relish our return to the theatre of murder. We are so much wiser now, so much more orderly and methodical in our ways. And certainly we are better actors off camera than on. We'll get Miss Hatter in the end.

But not all is well between Miss Barlow and myself. There are certain warning signs before any partnership disintegrates, both parties retreating into separate instead of shared secrecies, for instance. And Miss Barlow and I came together because of the secret of Mabel Eastlake, and then the deeper secret of knowing ourselves to have killed to protect it. Quite a bond is formed this way, as you can imagine. Yet now Miss Barlow is withdrawing from me, and I from her. Perhaps the magnetic poles of our sexes are reversing with age. Perhaps it is time for our showdown with one another. I've always anticipated that we would, in the end, destroy one another. I therefore want my version of our shared truth to be known.

I have given you the facts. We murdered Boyd Powers and Otto Kranzler and we expect to murder Hilda Hatter. But you will no doubt want to know our motives as well. The psychology of an act is so important today. Man cannot rest without knowing why.

Why have we murdered? Because we are murderers.

A murderer can burn hot in the fuel of the moment, acting without premeditation but with all the internalized motives necessary for combustion. Motives merely make the act understandable in retrospect, and are offered as an excuse. I have never excused myself, nor do I intend to do so here. I offer no defense and remain forever unreformed. What Miss Barlow and I did was irrational, if one considers murder irrational. We released the dark internal god of chaos. But through a subsequent series of events we were able to restructure that chaos into a new version of life. Only a fool, after all, believes that luck is reserved solely for the pure in heart, mind and deed. It has aided many a murderer as well.

But motives, *why?* One knows the question will be asked. There must be some *psychological flaw* to explain our actions. We've hung our guilt on Mabel Eastlake for so many years now, however, that those great sins of the past have been practically erased from our memories. What good is it, after all, to retain them? Yet memory remains, subverted by now to a kind of forbidden myth that lingers in odd, unused corners of the mind.

I remember and can reconstruct, quite architectonically, the structure of events that night the way *I* saw them. But I cannot give you the endless nuance of psychological detail behind everyone's action. Their actions must speak for themselves.

On the night of December 28, 1939, after the premiere of Mabel Eastlake's last picture for Paradise Studios (*Desperate Woman* was the titile), the following individuals were gathered in the projection room of Glass House: Hilda Hatter, Boyd Powers, Otto Kranzler, Jimmy Flame and myself. Upstairs, in her boudoir, collapsed from overwork caused by Kranzler, copious drugs administered by myself, and severe mental stress arising from every other aspect of her life as she was living it at the time, lay Mabel Eastlake, watched over by Fancy Barlow.

Jimmy Flame had a reel of film which he was about to show to those gathered in the projection room. Certain of us were privy to a secret of Miss Eastlake's, which I do not wish to reveal. Suffice it to say that this secret, if uncovered, would have ended Miss Eastlake's career immediately and shaken the very fabric of Hollywood. It involved a hoax of such magnitude and daring that the repercussions of its discovery would have been felt by every dedicated moviegoer in the world.

Of those present in the projection room, only Hilda Hatter and Boyd Powers did *not* know what this secret was.

It had been kept from them for various reasons. To those of us who comprised the conspiracy of silence around Mabel Eastlake, Boyd and Hilda were dangerous in their separate ways. Potential informants, fellow blackmailers, as unscrupulous as we. Boyd and Hilda stood to gain a great deal once they were let in on the secret, while we who already knew could easily lose everything if they found out.

The lives of those of us who knew Mabel Eastlake's secret were strangely and intricately entwined. Over the years, our successful protection of it had assumed a terrible significance; it became a secret mass over which we alone presided, but resenting the very service we had to give. What had begun as little more than a game had become, by '39, the very stuff of our lives. Glass House was our secret kingdom—designed by me, I should like to add—and here in Glass House, and in the studios, on the vast sound stages, in front of the lights and cameras of Hollywood, we perpetrated the image of Mabel Eastlake. She was our *raison d'être*, our goddess, our art—everything we wanted to be and were not—and believe me, she was the best.

Mabel Eastlake had become a successful fantasy image to America. Her image had infiltrated American consciousness. There is great wealth to be found in acceptable, desired images. So is it any wonder that we did not want to escape from the extraordinary image we had created? The image whose fatal flaw we hid from her huge, adoring public?

Flame, who first created Mabel Eastlake when she worked under a different name at The Black Orchis, now wanted to take her away from us, expose that gorgeous hoax to Hilda, vengeful and trigger-happy with a typewriter, and perennially–broke Boyd Powers. The Eastlake edifice that we had worked so hard to build, Jimmy wanted to pull down and ruin.

The fool wanted Mabel Eastlake exposed. He wanted her career to end. He wanted her back, I suppose, in his needle-scarred arms. He wanted to take her away from Glass House, and that reel of film was his most powerful weapon, for on the film the hoax in question was revealed.

There is a connecting passage between the projection room and Miss Eastlake's *chambre à coucheur*. When I first became aware of what Jimmy was up to that night and began to imagine the consequences—as surely he realized them himself—I quickly made for the connecting passage.

Once upstairs, I told Miss Barlow what was taking place. She is a cold woman, calculating, heartless and unemotional, the only kind of woman I am attracted to. She had, in fact, many qualities that Kranzler used in creating the Eastlake image: a certain hardness, a refusal to give up or give in, a mind that broke taboos with pleasure. "Born to try everything once," Fancy had confessed at one time. And now it was plain to us that we would stop at nothing to keep what we had, and take some very dangerous risks on the chance that we'd have even more.

I either asked Fancy where Mabel kept her gun, or Fancy simply went over to the drawer and pulled it out. In any event, there she was, feeling it in her hand, nervously rubbing it, caressing it with her fingers, gaining strength and ideas from its latent power.

She was wearing a copy of the white satin tuxedo that Mabel had worn (so much better) to the premiere of *Desperate Woman*. But was she wearing it when I entered, or did I suggest that she don it? I don't know.

Suddenly there were loud knocks on the front door to the room and we heard Kranzler's voice, muffled, tormented, the voice of an abandoned lover. "Mabel, let me in. *Ich muss sofort hinein.* We must talk, my love."

The door was not locked, and so I slipped back out the door leading to the projection room. Miss Eastlake's chamber is inordinately large, and Fancy quickly dimmed the lights to almost nothing.

The mighty Kranzler had no time for Prussian formality now. Discovering the door unlocked, he quickly entered. It was a different Kranzler who entered, no longer the Kranzler Hollywood knew. This Kranzler was terrified, perspiring, desperate. Altogether a delight to behold. This Kranzler knew that the game for him was up, and that his career was over the moment Hilda saw that footage. *Sehr geehrter Herr Kranzler* had acquired great respectability in Hollywood by that time, thanks to his lucky partnership with Mabel Eastlake. Now he was about to lose her, the Eve of his creation, a rib from his own beefy side. He was about to lose his career. In short, he was mad, backed into a corner by Flame, that hated worm in the core of his apple.

I knew that Fancy Barlow, holding a loaded pistol, in a room which contained Otto Kranzler and Mabel Eastlake, was a dangerous woman. She would have done anything to be the star that Mabel was. She forever hoped to be recognized by Kranzler as the more talented. But she never was. Kranzler used her as a goad, nothing more, to get Mabel to work harder, fanning the rivalry between them.

The lights were very low, the room was very large, Fancy was dressed in the costume Kranzler had seen Mabel wearing at the premiere . . . Fancy kept her distance and Kranzler was half-blind with panic. I heard their voices. Kranzler insisted that she leave with him. He predicted an Armageddon for everyone unless they—he and Mabel—left for Germany that night. "We will return together. You will go with me. We will not part."

Fancy's replies were low, indistinct, pitched as Mabel's would have been—taunting, half-menacing, mocking.

What actually led up to the gunshots? I believe he was stalking her in crazy earnest, finally lunged and grabbed to pull her close. "You!" he said, seeing now that it was not his Mabel, that still another trick had been perpetrated on him—on charmed mighty Kranzler—so that fate suddenly seemed terrible and hilarious and he laughed. Then he struck Fancy hard across the face and moved towards Mabel on the bed. "Never has it been you, Miss Barlow, that I have wanted. *Du bist gar nichts bei mir.* Only Mabel Eastlake do I desire."

Fancy got up and ran to the side of Mabel's bed just as Kranzler was leaning Othellolike over Mabel's body, his powerful hands stretched wide over his star's neck, the fat spatulate thumbs ready to press. Was Fancy protecting Mabel? Or repaying Kranzler for the final truth of what she was in his eyes—nothing. She pulled the trigger.

And she let out strange, off-pitch, half-sounds, not exactly screams or gasps, each time she shot him. I ran back into the room after the first. And Fancy, even after I had entered and we had looked into one another's eyes, shot him again, and still again. I saw her standing there, covered with blood, and I knew that we had started something that now had to be finished. We both knew this. The chain began to link us closer. We were in league and would protect one another; everyone else must be considered an enemy.

"They have to be stopped," Fancy said. Her eyes glittered, burned from within; she had crossed some boundary, some magical line, moved with a dark new freedom.

Did I look for and take the object in my hand? Or was it pressed into my palm by Fancy?

"Hilda and Boyd. We're ruined if they leave this house."

Was this what I thought, or what Fancy said out loud?

It was a black onyx phallus, a joke gift from Hilda that sat on Mabel's bedside table. I took it and made my way to the projection room.

It was dark there. Flame had already run out and was even now banging on the front door of Mabel's room. Fancy had wisely locked it. She would have to deal with him. I had Boyd and Hilda to take care of.

Boyd was sitting nearest me when I entered, in the back, giggling occasionally—he was very drunk—shaking his head and whispering, "My God, my *wife*." Hilda paid no attention to him. She had finished pulling the reel of film from the projector and was starting for the door.

It should have been Hilda first, that would have given me more pleasure. But Boyd was nearer. I brought the onyx phallus down with all my force. And I could feel his skull split, like a ripe melon, under my blow.

He let out a small, confused whimper and slumped forward.

And I stood there in the darkness, stunned, a murderer.

There was another gunshot above, and I didn't then know whose it was or what had happened. I know now that it was Jimmy, firing to get into Mabel's room. I could do nothing. I was flattened against the wall, immobilized by the immensity of what I had done. Hilda now had the film. She had run out, leapt into her Stutz and sped off with her prize.

There was a sound in the passageway and Fancy appeared. Jimmy was firing again from above, unaware of what had happened. He, who had provoked it all!

"Hilda's taken the film and run," I panted.

"Then I'm going after her," Fancy said. "Do something about Flame!" She handed me the gun and ran into the foyer.

There, as she was running for the door, Jimmy saw her. I believe he thought it was Mabel, trying for some reason to escape from him. But Fancy isn't sure that Jimmy didn't know it was she.

As it turned out, luck was on our side. Jimmy, whether or not he knew it was Fancy in the Duesenberg, ran after it and managed to jump on the running board as Fancy started down the drive after Hilda. What were consequences at this point? Something had been set into motion that we were powerless and unwilling to stop.

But luck has its dark side, too, and Miss Barlow was its victim. Jimmy managed to get into the Duesenberg and force it off the road. In doing so he caused his own death and the destruction of Fancy's face.

I was not yet aware of this new twist, and was alone in Glass House with our victims and the sleeping Miss Eastlake. How odd, even to me, the place felt then. A whole new atmosphere of blood and violence hung in the quiet, fatal air, infecting my masterpiece, my Glass House. The place seemed to have suddenly grown up and come to dark maturity.

I went back to Mabel's room, cleaned the fingerprints from the gun and replaced the phallus. And I looked down through all that silence, all those layers and layers of it, surrounding Mabel Eastlake. I wanted to feel pity for that haunted, beautiful image, that rare object of my creation. But instead I felt a kind of hatred. I wanted that beauty humiliated and dethroned. I enjoyed viciously shaking her out of her slumber. I slapped her and screamed for her to look at what she had done in her drugged and dissociated state. I dragged her by the hair, she shrieking and incoherent, down the stairs to the projection room, and pointed to the bloody mess that was Boyd Powers. I kicked her back upstairs and held her face down to stare into Kranzler's gaping wounds.

"You did that! You did that! Look at what you've done!"

And poor Mabel believed me, and has continued to do so ever since, believing and serving her guilt although she can remember nothing of that night except what Fancy and I have told her. Oh yes, we've been cruel—very cruel—but she has fought back in her own way, over the years. By this time she half-sees herself as a romantic heroine waiting for the return of her dead lover.

Miss Barlow is solely responsible for the final configuration of events. It was left up to her to decide the public version of the story.

Identified as Mabel Eastlake, Fancy was brought unconscious from the wreck of the Duesenberg to the hospital. When the police came to Glass House, I feigned complete and utter ignorance, acting, miming shock as I directed them to the two bodies. Mabel was under my strict tutelage, frightened into absolute submission because she thought I was protecting her. She had killed, even if she didn't remember the act, and now she didn't want to be discovered. If panic had forced her to blurt out a confession, the first instinct of remorse, events would not have occurred as they did.

It was terrible then, a kind of waiting void, not knowing what Fancy's story would be. Obviously the two of us had to collaborate on the details, get our stories to match. But also I knew that I should have a story ready in case Fancy died or, under questioning, put the blame on me. I must be prepared for anything. In the meantime, the story for Mabel and myself was that we had been in our respective rooms at the time of the murders. The real Mabel identified herself, for the first time, as Fancy Barlow, and said the child Mary P had been with her. The child was in such shock that her story counted for nothing.

From the police I learned only that Mabel Eastlake (Fancy) was still alive and that Jimmy Flame was dead.

At last, and admittedly under less than ideal circumstances, Fancy Barlow attained her ambition of becoming Mabel Eastlake. For so she identified herself when roused to consciousness.

"Do you know who you are?" they asked.

"Yes," she said, "I am Mabel Eastlake."

When I was allowed to see her, or rather view the bandaged face that had once been her, she told me the story of what had happened. Just as she had told it to the police. I memorized it instantly.

She told me that Flame had murdered Kranzler and Boyd Powers and then had tried to murder her. So that was the public story to follow. And I told her in return, whispering in her gauzed ear, what our private version was to be: Mabel Eastlake was the killer. We were protecting her. And in return for our protection, she would do anything we wanted. She would even turn her identity over to us.

Small wonder that Hilda remained silent throughout the investigation and inquest. To be in any way associated with Glass House on that night would have been an unwise professional investment. Miss Hatter was not known to have been present, and because she had the film, we of course were her prey. Her blackmail demands began only after we had returned to the altered circumstances of our new lives.

But with senility Miss Hatter has become even greedier than she was.

I said our lives had been altered. Now Mabel Eastlake, going under Fancy Barlow's name, worked for us. Fancy, as was only right, became the symbolic ruler, the Mabel Eastlake, of Glass House.

But of course I am cleverer than she, and most of the money that runs this estate has been successfully diverted to my accounts.

"Trust nothing and nobody in Lotus Land," as Mabel says in *Doublecross*, my least favorite of her pictures. "There are scorpions in the palm trees."

Believing on our evidence alone that she was the murderer, Mabel Eastlake would have agreed to anything. The alternative was, as we made her believe, imprisonment or the Chair.

It is known that the press coverage of the event was phenomenal. And Mabel Eastlake (Fancy) put on an award-winning performance. By some she was thought to be a heroine. But the association with Flame injured her reputation in the eyes of others. Everyone knew, without saying so, that the damage to her face—irreparable at that time, and botched further by severe infections and an inept physician—had ended her film career and the life she had known. It was all over for Mabel Eastlake.

But queer, the power of a face, of an image, even a ruined face and a false image. Fancy obtained a new kind of power she had never known when she was merely beautiful. And she has used that power in her conquest of Mabel Eastlake, in whose former image she now presides. Over the years I have perfected the beautiful, youthful Mabel-images that mask the outrage of her ruined face.

The D.A. at that time, for political reasons, wanted the case solved quickly and conveniently. There was no reason to disbelieve Mabel Eastlake (Fancy) when she pinned the blame on Jimmy. There could not have been a better scapegoat. Jimmy had a long record and was known to have underworld dealings. There were many who wanted him out of the way. His death helped account for more than a few crimes unsolved until then. Sensational press comes easily to Babylon, and another reason to wrap it up as quickly as possible was simple protection of Hollywood itself, and the glowing image it tried to promote for itself in those days.

After such terrible and traumatic events, it seemed only right and fitting that Mabel Eastlake (Fancy) would want to lock the gates of Glass House and have nothing more to do with the outside world. It suited all of us, really. The gates have remained locked since that time, and we within them.

I have never claimed to be a common man, and my

life has not been an ordinary one. I admit to being a murderer. I do not believe in the accepted forms of common justice, for anything common is not to my taste. I hated the relentless and false emotional glare of California long before I had Glass House built, however. Glass House has been my black sun, my delicious Hades, a smooth, quiet darkness where my spirit feels contained and in its proper place. I suppose I can say that I murdered because I wanted to stay here. I cannot imagine existence without it. Glass House has been my companion, steady and true and certain as death. How could I think to leave?

Does it matter, then, in the end, if I say that I am unrepentant? That I have even enjoyed deceiving Mabel Eastlake and, through her, the world? The usual purpose of confession is absolution, but one can only be absolved through contrition. I am not contrite, and have never pretended to be.

Life in Hollywood taught me from the beginning that pity, especially self-pity, is valueless. It is dime-store jewelry. I recognize my guilt, but I do not feel guilty. I seek no further salvation, for I have achieved my earthly paradise in Glass House. And it pleases me to think that when my image is no more, Glass House will remain, and others may find the truth of themselves in contemplation of its dark reflections.

18.

In the back? I want to sit in front with you."

But the Child, gallantly insistent, opened the rear door of the Duesenberg.

Alex slid in, the door was closed, and he settled back for the ride to Forest Lawn. The Child's head was a faint shadow through the tinted glass. On impulse, wanting to savor fully the new reality of him, Alex lowered the glass barrier.

The Child's eyes instantly met his in the rear-view mirror, love–hot and love–hungry. He turned around and smiled shyly, handing back the remote gate control and, with it, Alex's tape of Gershwin's Concerto in F.

"I wish you could hear this, " Alex said, starting the music.

The Child indicated that he almost could.

It was a kind of ritual by now, regular but certainly not unpleasant. The trip had been made several times over the past year and a half. At first it had been a superstitious, compulsive duty. Alex *needed* to go stand in the airy silence of the cemetery and look at Mabel Eastlake's name on the black Art Deco monument. He and the Child had decided on its design and material. Strange, the power of that name, cut now in black marble.

Usually there were small floral tributes left on Miss Eastlake's grave by her fans. The other graves—Fancy

Barlow's, Cygnet Sackville's, Hilda Hatters's, and Mary P's—remained unmemorialized until Alex began to bring flowers for them as well. Why not? The gardens of Glass House never stopped blooming. It was a marvel, the abundance of what they had, what the Child had created and tended with such care.

Mary P's grave always received an especially choice bouquet. The Child had no memory of his mother, and it was Alex's burden to live with Mary P's strange history implanted more vividly in his own mind than in her son's. He experienced a similarly odd sensation—recognizing someone otherwise forgotten by the world—when after long and tedious research he believed that he had tracked down Mary P's mother. One hot, too-bright afternoon he and the Child stood in another graveyard, looking down at a name that meant nothing, really, and yet was responsible for the tall blond man standing beside Alex. The Child was reverent but unemotional. It was Alex who felt the occasion's solemnity. The long strange line of his lover's ancestry impressed him deeply. He felt himself to be a part of it as though something of Mabel Eastlake lived on in him, too.

The newspapers, of course, never got the facts right, and Alex saw no reason to give them, or the police, information that would distort and sensationalize what could only, by its very nature, be distorted and sensationalized. The resolve, once he had acquired it, remained strong within him. He consistently refused to divulge what he knew, turning down the lucrative offers that came his way.

People had the skeleton, the externals of the story. He had the insider's information. But instead of writing the Eastlake biography as he had once planned, he became fiercely protective of the Eastlake legend. He knew it was a legend, but he felt no obligation to release it to the misinterpretive winds of history. There was a secret pleasure, greater pleasure, in withholding certain facts. A quiet sense of power came from knowing more than Mabel Eastlake's public ever would. And Miss Eastlake, he was certain, would have approved.

Now that Glass House was theirs, even though the loose ends of the estate and especially Cygnet's brilliantly complicated claim on it would not be settled for years, time had taken on a new dimension for Alex. He returned to New York only once, the first and only time in his life that he was a media celebrity. His blond image, standing on Mabel Eastlake's staircase, the Child beside him, had been picked up by a major news service and widely published. Even Frank, awed and romantically tantalized by the publicity, had called to suggest a midnight drink at the Plaza. "Sorry," Alex said, "but I'm flying back to Beverly Hills tonight."

Frank was New York incredulous. "You're going *back* there?"

Alex laughed at his wonder. "I'm going to live there now. But please, if you're ever in California, come to Glass House for that drink."

For finally its silence became him, and in its silence he was oddly content. Around him, in all directions, the view belittled at least a few human pretensions. Consistently startled by its beauty, Alex was also warned by its magnitude. In the evenings, just before sunset, he liked to leash Cocaine and walk out with the Child to the highest terrace. There they would stand, immersed and attentive, until the impatient tug of the cat on her leash reminded them of mortal duties.

In sharing Miss Eastlake's view, Alex shared, in some curious way, the very soul of her secret.

The autopsy report of the deceased star was made public, but one crucial physical detail regarding the body was withheld thanks to Alex's swift and forceful intervention. The diamond choker fetched a startling price, and Alex did not hesitate in using the money on Miss Eastlake's posthumous behalf. She would have understood the intrigue and approved of the measures he had to take.

Mabel Eastlake's body was then cremated. Alex and the Child scattered the ashes from the terrace one windy twilight. That human vessel of pain, power and intrigue, that most beautiful and pathetic of images, was rendered imageless at last.

Or was it?

Once, turning a corner into the foyer, he saw her standing in its open front door, clear as the daylight that streamed through her, smiling from the white depths of the Snake Dress.

Sometimes when he and the Child were making love—which they did wildly, in every room, reclaiming nature by marking out their future territory together—a warm flow of vibration, like a feeling of laughter or pleasure stirred loose from deep within the body, would suddenly capture, spread, and dissolve around them.

It was difficult at first to adjust to this sense of otherness, of lives being lived just outside the realm of the five senses. It was like being in the lobby of a movie theatre, with an unseen movie playing inside. But there would come a time when he'd stop being surprised, when he could look up, see a slender male figure, more often two, standing together at the glass wall of Mabel Eastlake's boudoir, and turn away, leaving them to their own unknowable reflections.

The Child, more accustomed to Glass House than Alex was, his senses more finely attuned from long residence, accepted these quiet occurrences as he would the fact that a flower is stored within a seed or bulb. In its proper season the sun always teases awake the full revelation of beauty.

Beauty, here amidst the grotesque manipulations of

Hollywood! Alex, the movie lover, pondered this as the Duesenberg wound its way down the drive. Hollywood. Artists and thieves; glamour and corruption. A strange fusion of power and personality that left a few masterpieces along a road strewn with corpses. Old Hollywood, its temples abandoned or destroyed, but its black and white images captured on and still haunting all the film devoted to them. Images living on outside of time.

In Mabel Eastlake's day, celluloid and high explosives were made from the same ingredients. Perhaps, then, there was some chemical transformation taking place even now on the reel of film buried beneath her monument in Forest Lawn. Images breaking down and dissolving into a blur of eternity not theirs to see until some final, violent rupture of the grave.

Alex caught the Child's eye and punched in the code.

Ahead of them, the giant Deco gates slowly began to swing open.